M000208841

A Robot Named Clunk

Originally published as "Hal Spacejock"

Book One in the Hal Spacejock series

Stay in touch!

Author's newsletter:
spacejock.com.au/ML.html

facebook.com/halspacejock
twitter.com/spacejock

Works by Simon Haynes

All of Simon's novels* are self-contained, with a beginning, a middle and a proper ending. They're not sequels, they don't end on a cliffhanger, and you can start or end your journey with any book in the series.
* *Robot vs Dragons series excepted!*

The Hal Spacejock series for teens/adults
Set in the distant future, where humanity spans the galaxy and robots are second-class citizens. Includes a large dose of humour!

Hal Spacejock 0: Origins (2019/2020)
Hal Spacejock 1: A Robot named Clunk*
Hal Spacejock 2: Second Course*
Hal Spacejock 3: Just Desserts*
Hal Spacejock 4: No Free Lunch
Hal Spacejock 5: Baker's Dough
Hal Spacejock 6: Safe Art
Hal Spacejock 7: Big Bang
Hal Spacejock 8: Double Trouble
Hal Spacejock 9: Max Damage
Hal Spacejock 10: Cold Boots

Also available:
Omnibus One, containing Hal books 1-3
Omnibus Two, containing Hal books 4-6
Omnibus Three, containing Hal books 7-9
Hal Spacejock: Visit, a short story
Hal Spacejock: Framed, a short story
Hal Spacejock: Albion, a novella
*Audiobook editions available/in progress

The Dragon and Chips Trilogy.
High fantasy meets low humour!
Each set of three books should be read in order.

1. A Portion of Dragon and Chips
2. A Butt of Heads
3. A Pair of Nuts on the Throne

Also Available:
Omnibus One, containing the first trilogy
Books 1-3 audiobook editions

The Harriet Walsh series.
Set in the same universe as Hal Spacejock. Good clean fun, written with wry humour. No cliffhangers between novels!

Harriet Walsh 1: Peace Force
Harriet Walsh 2: Alpha Minor
Harriet Walsh 3: Sierra Bravo
Harriet Walsh 4: Storm Force (TBA)

Also Available:
Omnibus One, containing books 1-3

The Hal Junior series
Written for all ages, these books are set aboard a space station in the Hal Spacejock universe, only ten years later.

1. Hal Junior: The Secret Signal
2. Hal Junior: The Missing Case
3. Hal Junior: The Gyris Mission
4. Hal Junior: The Comet Caper

Also Available:
Omnibus One, containing books 1-3
The Secret Signal Audiobook edition

The Secret War series.
Gritty space opera for adult readers.

1. Raiders
2. Frontier (2019)
3. Deadlock (2019/2020)

Collect One-Two - a collection of shorts by Simon Haynes

All titles available in ebook and paperback. Visit spacejock.com.au for details.

Bowman Press

v 4.53

This edition published 2011 by Bowman Press

Text © Simon Haynes 2011
Cover art © Bowman Press 2011

ISBN 978-1-877034-02-2 (Ebook)
ISBN 978-1-877034-08-4 (Paperback)

Second Edition published 2005 by Fremantle Press
Reprinted 2007.
Reprinted 2008.

First edition published 2000 by Bowman Publishing.

A catalogue record for this book is available from the National Library of Australia

Dedicated to my family

Ding Dong!

Hal Spacejock looked up from the chessboard balanced on the flight console, where a typically one-sided contest had decimated his pieces. 'What was that?'

'There's someone on the passenger ramp,' said the ship's computer, in a neutral female voice.

'The loan guy?'

'I cannot say. Our security camera was stolen.'

'So how do you know there's anyone out there?'

Ding Dong!

'They're pressing the doorbell,' said the Navcom patiently.

Hal stood, strode to a set of controls on the wall and tapped the upper button. Hydraulics whined as the heavy circular door swung open, and Hal ducked into the *Black Gull's* cramped airlock. Once inside, he used a second set of controls to open the outer door, but before it was half open there was a hair-raising growl and a huge robot squeezed into the ship.

Hal took one look at the grasping hands, jagged steel teeth and blood-red eyes and fled to the flight deck. He slammed the inner door and fumbled for the lock, but before he could activate it the door burst open. Hal dived for the access tube at the rear of the flight deck, hoping to escape via the cargo hold, but he only managed two steps before the robot cut him off.

Hal and the robot faced off for a couple of seconds, and then a short, middle-aged man strolled into the flight deck. He had a smooth, pale face and slicked-back hair, and his heavy overcoat was buttoned up to his neck.

Hal nodded towards the hulking robot, unwilling to point in case it tore his arm off. 'Is this thing yours?'

'Brutus accompanies me on my rounds.'

'What kind of rounds?' demanded Hal. 'And who the hell are you, anyway?'

'Vurdi Makalukar at your service,' said the man softly. He crossed to the console and turned the pilot's chair, grimacing as he saw the exposed stuffing. He looked around for an alternative and found none. 'Let us begin,' he said, sitting on the edge of the seat. 'I represent Garmit and Hash, Mr Spacejock, and I'm here to –'

'You're the loan guy?' said Hal in surprise.

Vurdi nodded.

Hal felt a flood of relief. Despite the man's threatening appearance, and his even more threatening robot, Vurdi was here to set up a loan. Hal had organised the meeting himself, and while he understood loan sharks could be a little eccentric, he felt the giant killer robot was a bit much. 'Do you treat all your clients like this?' he said, gesturing at the thing.

'Brutus usually breaks a leg or two first, but in your case I felt it wasn't necessary. After all, it's a relatively modest sum of money.'

'Breaks a leg?' Hal eyed the hulking robot. 'Do you get much repeat business?'

'None, if I do my job properly.' Vurdi sat back. 'Now, are we paying by cash or cheque?'

'I don't care. It's all the same to me.'

'Wonderful.' Vurdi smiled. 'I confess, I came here expecting the worst. It is most gratifying that you have the money to pay me.'

'Pay you? No, you've got it all wrong. You're here to set up a loan.'

The smile vanished. 'You don't honestly believe that, Mr Spacejock?'

'You mean it was a trick? You're not giving me any money?'

'I believe we're on the right track at last. You see, I'm here to collect back payments on your *existing* loan.' Vurdi gestured at the robot. 'If you're quick, you can stay out of hospital.'

'I don't have anything to give.' Hal spread his hands. 'It's been quiet. Nobody's hiring.'

'We must honour our debts, Mr Spacejock. Payment in kind perhaps? A limb or two?' The chair squealed as Vurdi turned his back. 'I suggest you stand still, it'll be quicker that way.'

'Quicker? What –' Hal dodged as the huge robot reached for him with hands the size of shovels. 'Hey, call it off or I'll ...' The threat died as banana-sized fingers grabbed him round the neck, and a split second later he was flat on his back.

The giant machine crouched over him and tried to push him through the cold metal deck, and as the steel grip tightened Hal saw his life flash before his eyes – a series of heavy landings interspersed with explosions and multiple fractures.

The lights in the flight deck dimmed, and then ... darkness.

3

'Is he dead yet?'

Hal came round slowly, trying not to breathe the electric-tainted air washing over his face. He opened one eye and saw Brutus inspecting him.

'Nearly,' growled the huge robot.

'All right,' said Vurdi. 'Let him go.'

The robot hesitated, then released Hal and stood up.

'Let's start again, Mr Spacejock.' Vurdi plucked the white king from the chessboard. 'Where's the money?'

'I told you, I don't have anything.'

Vurdi tumbled the chess piece in one hand, over and over. 'You know, it's just as well your insurance is paid up.'

'What are you saying?'

'Imagine if the unthinkable happened to your ship. Garmit would get their money, I would earn my fee and you ... well, you'd get a few lines in the local paper.'

'You'd never get away with it!'

'Several of my ex-clients expressed the same opinion.' Vurdi shook his head sadly. 'Alas, I proved them wrong.'

'Look, there is something.'

'There always is. How much?'

'Not cash, it's a job. This guy was looking for a freighter.'

Vurdi raised one eyebrow. 'Why didn't you mention it earlier?'

'What earlier? The minute I opened the door your robot tried to rip my head off.'

'Drama bores me, Mr Spacejock. Give me the details.'

'This guy's regular ship is out of action. He wants me to cover it.'

'Most convenient.' Vurdi's dark eyes studied Hal's face. 'When will this job be completed?'

'I've got twenty-four hours.'

'Very well. Brutus will collect the money tomorrow afternoon. And Mr Spacejock?'

'Yep?'

'Do not disappoint me.' Vurdi snapped the chess piece in two and arranged the halves on the board. 'No need to show me out. Come, Brutus.'

Hal jumped as the robot's foot thudded down next to his face. He felt its hands grabbing at his clothing, pulling him up until he was staring into its blood-red eyes. Breath hissed between its wafer-thin lips as fans worked overtime to keep its circuits cool. 'I'll be b—'

'Brutus, come!' snapped Vurdi from the airlock.

The robot dumped Hal on the deck and left the ship with slow, measured footsteps. As the outer door thudded to, Hal sat up. 'Navcom?'

There was a crackle from the console. 'Yes, sir?'

'Call Jerling Enterprises. Tell them I'll take their cargo job.'

'But you said it was a shipment of stolen goods,' protested the Navcom. 'You turned them down!'

Hal rubbed his neck. 'I just changed my mind.'

◆

Hal paced the *Black Gull's* flight deck, ready to put his fist through the nearest wall. 'What do you mean you can't call Jerling back? What do you mean you didn't save his details?'

'I erased the record after you turned the job down.'

'So look it up again!'

5

'We can't afford the search fees.' The Navcom hesitated. 'Incidentally, it's your move.'

'How can you think of a bloody chess game at a time like this?'

'You're only saying that because you're losing.'

'The hell I am.' Hal strode to the console and stared down at the board, where the top half of his king and a single pawn were surrounded by a complete set of black pieces. 'Switch sides?'

'Negative.'

Hal sighed. 'Isn't there any way you can get hold of Jerling?'

'No.'

'At least think about it, all right? I'm going to get something to eat.' Hal crossed to the rear of the flight deck, where a battered metal ladder poked through a circular hole in the floor. He'd just put his foot on the first rung when a chime echoed around the flight deck.

'Inbound call for Mr Spacejock.'

'Take it, will you? I can't handle another debt collector right now.'

'It's not a debt collector. It's Jerling Enterprises.'

'Are you mucking about?'

'No, it's Walter Jerling himself.'

'Well don't keep him waiting, you overgrown calculator. Put him on!'

The viewscreen flickered and wavered, and Walter Jerling's head and shoulders appeared. His gaunt face was bathed in green light from the screens set into his desk, and there was a cigar clamped between his teeth. He spotted Hal, removed the cigar and blew out a cloud of smoke. 'Hal Spacejock?'

'That's me,' said Hal, dropping into his seat. 'Listen, I was just –'

'Freelance cargo pilot?'

'Yes. I was –'

'Something wrong with my company? Pay not good enough?'

'No. I –'

'I told my staff you'd come round.' Jerling waved his cigar. 'The cargo's on Seraph IV, I want it delivered to my premises on Forg within twenty-four hours. Can you handle that?'

'Sure.'

Jerling picked a shred of tobacco from his lip. 'There's a couple of things you should know. First, Seraph traffic control are a bunch of bureaucratic idiots who'll tie you up for days with their ridiculous paperwork. And we don't want that, do we?'

'I guess not,' said Hal.

'Right, so you're going to bypass customs. Second, you'll be landing in a field at night. The pick-up is just North of the equator and there's a few dwellings, light industry, that kind of thing.'

Hal wondered if his hearing was playing up. 'Did you say a field?'

'You got a problem with that?'

'Well, er –'

'Good.' Jerling frowned at the darkened tip of his cigar. 'What was the other thing? Oh yes, the landing. I want you to take one of my pilots along. Give him a lift to Seraph.'

'I thought this job was urgent? If I have to wait for your pilot –'

'No waiting, he's already there at the spaceport. He was supposed to get a lift with one of my ships, but you can take him instead.' Jerling waved his cigar. 'If things get sticky on Seraph he'll take over the controls.'

'Is he any good?'

'He works for me, doesn't he?' Jerling snapped his fingers and a squat robot appeared, holding a short rod with a glowing red tip. Jerling pressed his cigar to the tip, puffed once or twice to get it going, then waved the robot away. 'Look, he's had years of training. Flown everything from a hover bike to a megafreighter. Believe me, he's a first-class pilot.'

Hal felt a surge of relief. A night landing in a field sounded like a recipe for disaster, but with Jerling's pilot it would be easy.

'Right, that's everything covered,' said Jerling. 'I'll get the pilot over to your ship, and you get my cargo here as quick as you can.'

'Hang on, what about payment?'

But the screen was blank.

'No sign of Jerling's pilot,' said Hal, who was peering through a scratched, yellowed porthole in the *Black Gull's* airlock. He cupped his hands to the plastic and squinted, but it made little difference. 'There could be an army out there and I wouldn't know it.'

'Why don't you open the door?' asked the Navcom.

'What, and let Vurdi's bloody great robot in again? No thanks!' Hal gave up and returned to the flight deck, where he gathered a stained mug and held it under the nozzle of the drinks dispenser. When the machine had finished burping and spluttering he raised his mug to sniff the steaming brown liquid. 'Is this tea or coffee?'

'Neither. It's an infusion of edible fungi.'

'Really?' Hal took a sip and smacked his lips. 'It could grow on me.'

'Don't spill it, or it'll grow everywhere.'

Hal returned to the chessboard, but his mind was on the upcoming cargo job. He'd never landed in the dark before, especially in a field. What if Jerling's hot shot pilot didn't turn up? What if he wasn't as good as Jerling said he was? What if ...

'Would you like a hint?' asked the Navcom.

9

'How can I play if you keep interrupting?' Hal moved one of his pieces at random. 'Queen to C6.'

'King's knight to C6,' said the Navcom. 'Warning, checkmate in three moves.'

There was a ringing noise. 'About time he turned up,' muttered Hal. As he left his chair he jogged the chessboard with his elbow, scattering pieces all over the deck. 'Oops, silly me.'

'Desperate situations call for desperate measures,' intoned the Navcom.

'Eh?'

'Cheats never prosper.'

'Oh, shut up.'

'Daily quote mode . . . disabled.'

Hal strode into the airlock and waited impatiently as the outer door grated open. To his horror there was a robot standing outside, and he was just about to slam the door in its face when he realised it was half the size of Vurdi's enforcer. Bronze all over, this robot had a squashy furrowed face, a dented torso and mismatched legs splattered with grimy patches of lubricating fluid.

'What do you want?' demanded Hal, once he'd finished looking it over.

'My name is XG99,' said the robot, in an even male voice. 'Is this the *Black Gull*?'

'Yeah. Why?'

The robot's arm jerked up. 'Mr Jerling sent me. You can call me Clunk.'

Hal stared at the extended hand. 'You're the pilot?'

'Certified pilot.'

'More like certified junk heap,' muttered Hal. 'Wait here,' he said loudly, in case the robot was as deaf as it looked. He strode back to the flight deck and leant over the console. 'Navcom, get me Jerling. Quick.'

The viewscreen flickered and Jerling's face swam into focus. 'This had better be important.'

'It is. I've got a clapped-out robot on my doorstep claiming he's your pilot.'

'Clapped out?' Jerling frowned. 'Clunk may be mature, but he's in top condition. You'll be perfectly safe in his hands.'

'But –'

'Mr Spacejock, if you don't want Clunk to land your ship you can do it yourself. My cargo must be delivered on time.'

'But –'

'Good, I'm glad that's settled. Now please hurry. I need that cargo and I need it now.' Jerling clicked his fingers and the cigar-lighting robot appeared at his side, rod at the ready. 'Cigar,' said Jerling.

The robot raised the rod, bathing his face with a dull red glow.

Jerling shook his head. 'Give me a cigar.'

The robot looked at him.

'Cigar,' said Jerling, jabbing his finger at the robot. 'Come on, you stupid tin can. Cigar!'

The robot eyed Jerling's finger, head on one side, then shrugged and applied the super-heated tip to it. The screen went dark, cutting off an anguished yell of pain.

'Perfectly safe, eh?' growled Hal. He strode through the airlock and found the robot waiting patiently outside. Without warning, he jabbed his finger at it. 'Cigar! Cigar!'

'Cigar, cigar,' said Clunk mildly, holding up his own finger. When Hal didn't react, he lowered his hand again. 'I must say, that's a most unusual greeting.'

'It wasn't a greeting. I was just checking you weren't going to light it.'

'I couldn't do that,' said the robot. 'Impossible.'

'Governed by the Three Laws?'

'No, I don't have any matches.' Clunk craned his neck to peer into the airlock. 'Can we get started? Mr Jerling said this was urgent, and I'd like to familiarise myself with the controls.'

Hal followed the robot into the flight deck, where he found it staring at the console.

'This a Rigel class freighter, isn't it?'

'That's right,' said Hal.

Clunk grimaced. 'I had no idea they were still in service.' Then he spotted the chess pieces scattered on the deck. 'Who won?'

'It was a draw,' said the Navcom.

'You have a pleasant voice. Did you refine it yourself?'

'If you've quite finished chatting up my computer –' began Hal.

'Why are you drinking roasted mushrooms?' asked Clunk, inspecting the stained mug on the console.

'Mr Spacejock thought he was buying coffee,' said the Navcom. 'He's always getting ripped off, but I'm sure a robot of your wisdom and intelligence . . .'

'Not you as well!' Hal turned on the robot. 'Down to the hold. Now.'

Clunk gazed at him with warm yellow eyes. 'As a pilot, my place is on the flight deck.'

'As a passenger, your place is in the hold. You can be a pilot later, and only if I need you.'

'Very well. Which way to the first class section?'

'Don't be cheeky.' Hal gestured at the rickety ladder protruding from a hole at the rear of the flight deck. 'Take the access tube and follow the passage aft. And don't touch anything.'

Clunk took hold of the ladder, then hesitated. 'By the way, what's your name?'

'Sir,' said Hal.

'Your computer called you Mr Spacejock.'

'Yes, but you can call me sir.'

The robot looked down the tube into the darkness below. 'No lights?'

'Heat sensors.'

Clunk descended the ladder, head bobbing as he stepped carefully from one rung to the next. All of a sudden he disappeared, and there was a clatter-bang-thud as he slipped down the steps and landed in a heap at the bottom.

'Mind the loose rung!' called Hal.

There was pause before the robot's amplified voice floated up the access tube. 'Next time, perhaps the warning could come a little sooner?'

Hal sat in the pilot's chair, grinning to himself. 'Navcom, prepare for take-off.'

'Starting engines.'

The *Black Gull's* main drives rumbled into life, shaking the flight deck. Lights blinked, rows of data whizzed across the status displays and the console squeaked and rattled with the vibrations.

'Engines started,' said the Navcom.

'Do you have to state the bloody obvious?'

'Reporting mode set to ... brief.'

There was a scrape, and Hal looked over his shoulder to see the robot climbing out of the access tube. 'Where do you think you're going?'

'It's unsafe down there.' Clunk limped to the console, his leg glistening from a fresh leak. 'Actually, your vessel is unsafe everywhere, but up here on the flight deck I can watch you in action.'

13

'You want to learn from my experience, eh?'

'Not really. I was thinking of the entertainment value.'

Hal was about to say something sharp and witty, but time was short and he couldn't think of a snappy comeback. 'All right, you can stay. But no interfering.' He put his feet up on the console. 'Come on, Navcom. Let's go.'

'What about clearance from ground control?' asked the computer.

'Screw that.' Hal twirled his finger in mid-air. 'Wind 'em up, and let's get airborne.'

Clunk's eyebrows rose. 'Standard take-off procedure involves somewhat more than –'

'I told you to keep quiet.' Hal looked up at the viewscreen, where the words 'Most Systems Ready' were showing in ten-inch letters. 'Go ahead, Navcom. Take off.'

Clunk gestured at the console. 'But the status displays –'

'We fly it my way.' Hal glared at the robot. 'If that's not entertaining enough for you, leave.'

The engines roared, drowning the robot's reply. Several red lights began to flash, and Clunk hurried over to examine them. He stared at Hal with a worried expression. 'According to this, all your back-up systems are inoperative.'

'Will you give it a rest?' shouted Hal. 'I'm telling you this ship is safe!'

The engine note rose even further, and the deck jolted as the ship left the landing pad. Displays flickered, screens jiggled around in their housings and a whole bank of lights flashed on and off as the engines howled.

Dong ding!

'Who the hell's that?' demanded Hal.

'Ground Control,' replied the Navcom.

By now they were ten or twenty metres up, Hal reckoned, and with the *Black Gull's* engines straining so hard they had

14

to be climbing at several inches per minute. With a puzzled frown, he glanced towards the airlock. 'How can anyone reach the doorbell up here?'

'They cannot,' said Clunk. 'However, the doorbell makes a *ding dong*, whereas this sound is the complete and total opposite. I can see how a human might easily confuse the two.'

Dong ding!

'Clunk is right,' said the Navcom. 'The sound you hear is my incoming message tone.'

'I don't care if it's the local ice cream van. Take us into orbit!'

'I cannot. Control is ordering us to abort our departure.'

'And I'm ordering you to ignore them.'

Dong ding! Dong ding! Dong ding!

'They are most insistent,' said the Navcom. 'In fact, they're about to–'

'*Portside calling Black Gull,*' said an angry voice, blasting through the console. '*Portside calling Black Gull. Please respond.*'

'This is the *Black Gull*,' shouted Hal. 'We're busy right now, but if you leave a message –'

'*Permission to leave denied. Repeat, permission to leave denied. Stop your engines and report to the Portmaster immediately.*'

Hal reached for the throttle, but before he could touch it the engines cut out and the ship thumped down on the pad. The flight deck swayed, there was a distant sound of breaking glass, and a pair of locker doors swung open and then fell off.

'Landing complete,' said the Navcom.

Hal sighed. 'I'm going to see what these boneheads want. Clunk, you can tidy this place up while I'm gone.'

The robot frowned. 'You want me to clean?'

'Why not? Don't you know which end of the mop to hold?'

'*Portside calling Tiger. Portside calling Tiger. Clearance granted. Dock when ready.*'

Hal stared at the console. 'Is that thing still on?'

'Naturally,' said the Navcom. 'You didn't ask me to close the channel.'

'Why didn't you warn me?'

'You changed my reporting mode to brief.'

'Don't wait for my say so. Shut it off!'

There was a pop from the speakers. 'Connection terminated.'

'What did they hear? Did I say anything to upset them?'

'Possibly. Calling them boneheads wasn't very diplomatic.'

Hal opened a door beneath the console, pulled out a chunky, chrome-plated blaster and clipped it to his belt.

Clunk's eyebrows rose at the sight. 'You only called them names. Surely you won't need that?'

'You haven't been on this planet long, have you?' said Hal grimly.

Hal emerged from the *Black Gull's* airlock, blinking in the sudden light. On the far side of the landing field the sun was setting behind the spaceport's administration block, which shimmered in planet Lamira's late afternoon heat. Clustered around the spaceport buildings were the 'A' class facilities, built for wealthy pilots and their modern, powerful ships. Crews could dine at one of several five-star restaurants, enjoy a dip in the heated swimming pool and purchase duty-free luxuries in the shopping arcade.

Next were the 'B' class facilities, servicing older ships. Their crews had a choice of fast-food joints, but the swimming pool was a little chilly and the corner store only sold a limited range at a healthy mark-up.

'C' class was a row of concrete pads with a broken vending machine.

Hal's ship was in section Z, which was a disused corner of the field about as close to the amenities as the nearest moon. The area around the *Black Gull* was a graveyard for derelicts, and the landing pads were home to graffiti-splashed wrecks. Some of the rusty hulks seemed familiar, and when Hal looked closer he realised they were Rigel class freighters like his own. One or two were actually in better shape.

There was a rumble overhead, and Hal looked up to see a spark of light rising effortlessly into the sky. He shielded his eyes to watch the ship climbing into orbit, trailing a long, twisting vapour trail, and would have bet a hundred credits *that* pilot didn't have to deal with faulty engines, fuel leaks and junky old robots.

With a sigh, Hal strode down the access ramp, using the thin handrails to guide himself down the wobbly metal structure. Stepping onto the landing pad, he walked into the open and glanced back at his ship to see whether any bits had fallen off in the night.

The *Black Gull* sat on three stubby landing legs, one at the front and two supporting the rear. A narrow ridge swept back from the pointed nose and finished in a soaring tailplane at the back of the ship, which was adorned with a swooping gull in peeling black paint. Under the tailplane, twin exhaust cones stuck out on either side of the heavy-duty cargo ramp, which was closed and sealed against the squared-off tail.

Hal sighed. The *Gull* could navigate galactic backwaters with relative ease, but it still looked like a cross between a paper dart and a water heater.

Walking the length of the landing pad, he ducked his head to pass under one of the ship's massive exhaust cones. Behind the ship he encountered the blast barrier, a pitted concrete wall protecting the refuelling cluster from exhaust gases. He heard a low humming noise and saw a battered groundcar hovering above the tangled weeds on the opposite side of the pad. Faded green lettering along the side spelled out the reason for the vehicle's presence: *Lamira Spaceport - Maintenance Division*. Hal's eyebrows rose at the sight - it wasn't like Z section had anything to maintain.

There was a hiss behind the barrier, then a clang of metal

on metal. Hal craned his neck and saw a battered grey robot tinkering with one of the fuel pipes. He also saw the familiar blue moulding of a public viewscreen. Lifting the handset from its cradle, he was deliberating which buttons to press when a metallic voice crackled from the speaker.

'Please insert five credits to make a call.'

'I don't want to make a call,' explained Hal. 'I just need transport.'

'Please insert five credits to make a call,' said the speaker again.

'I don't have any money!'

'Please insert five –'

Hal dropped the handset back in the cradle. He considered going back to the *Gull* to borrow the money off Clunk, then discarded the idea. Jerling's robot didn't look like he had one credit, let alone five. He also debated walking to the admin block, but the field was thick with weeds and it would be dark before he got there. That left the maintenance vehicle.

The grey robot was trying to loosen a corroded clamp on one of the pipes. There was a replacement clamp on the ground nearby, along with a wide selection of tools which the robot was trying one by one, from the battery-powered wrench to the double-headed screwdriver. None of them had any effect on the stubborn clamp.

'Excuse me,' said Hal.

The robot looked up. 'Good afternoon, sir. I don't suppose you have a sprocket wrench?'

'Don't you mean a socket wrench?'

'No, I have one of those already.'

'Sorry, can't help.' Hal hesitated. 'Listen, I don't suppose I can get a lift to the spaceport?'

'Unfortunately, no. I can't carry passengers.'

19

'Lend me your car, then.'

'Are you an employee of the Lamira Spaceport?'

'Not quite.'

The robot shrugged. 'Then you can't use the vehicle.' Before Hal could argue, it turned back to the fuel pipe and started hitting the clamp with a pair of pliers.

Hal glanced up at his ship. What if he lifted off, thundered across the field and landed in the spaceport car park? Then he remembered the new ships clustered around the admin block - if he put a scratch on one with the *Gull*, he'd get life.

With no other option, Hal lowered himself into the tall grass and made his way around the landing pad, keeping his head down to avoid being spotted. It was easy going at first, but the undergrowth was thicker beneath the *Black Gull's* nose cone. Serrated leaves tore at his flight suit as he kicked and tugged his way through the tangled weeds, and pendulous flower heads disintegrated with soft popping sounds, spreading clouds of choking pollen.

Hot and tired, his face and hands stained with brown and yellow blotches, Hal was ready to give up when he heard a steady hum through the thick grass. Moments later he was crouched alongside the battered maintenance vehicle, his hair crackling with static from the shimmering anti-gravity field.

Slowly, he raised his head. The grey robot was fifteen metres away, still busy with the fuel cluster. It had its fingers under the corroded clamp and was levering it away from the thick metal pipe with repeated jerks. Suddenly the clamp came free and the robot fell backwards into the weeds, where it was engulfed in thick clouds of pollen.

Hal's grin disappeared when he saw a stream of fuel squirt from the pipe and splash over the struggling robot.

One spark and the *Gull* would be blown into orbit.

The robot struggled to its feet, hurried to the pipe and sealed the leak with a new clamp, getting sprayed with more fuel in the process. While it was busy tightening nuts, Hal put his hands on the groundcar's metal flank and pulled himself in.

The controls were simple enough - a thrust lever for speed and a joystick to steer with. Hal took hold of the joystick and tried to pull the thrust lever into reverse. It didn't move. Looking closer, he saw an anti-theft bolt locking it in neutral.

Hal drew his gun, aimed at the lock and squeezed the trigger. The blaster fizzed and a ball of energy struck the metal bolt, heating it to a dull glow. Hal glanced round at the robot, but it was still working on the new clamp and hadn't noticed the shot. Twisting the weapon's power knob, he aimed the gun and fired again.

The blaster roared, hurling an energy bolt that splattered the lock into whirling drops of molten metal, punched a hole through the side of the car and vanished into the long grass. There was a shout, and Hal turned to see the robot charging towards him through the weeds. He yanked the thrust lever backwards and the car reversed away from the landing pad with the robot gaining rapidly.

Hal slammed the joystick to the right and pushed the thrust lever forward, swinging the car around and powering away with a lusty roar from the engine. He looked back just as the robot leaped, landing on the rear of the vehicle and grabbing hold with one hand. Hal waggled the joystick, throwing the car from side to side in an effort to cast the robot off, but it stood up and advanced on him with outstretched arms.

Hal rammed the joystick to the left, throwing the car into a series of tight circles. Ground and sky whirled around faster and faster, but still the robot got closer, a determined look on its face. Suddenly it dived towards him. Hal ducked and the robot sailed overhead, landing on the groundcar's stubby bonnet and almost sliding off the front. It recovered and turned quickly, crouching for another leap.

A large shape loomed in Hal's vision. His gaze snapped past the coiled robot and his eyes widened as he saw the landing pad rushing towards them. He yanked back on the stick to clear the edge, then pushed it forward again as the *Black Gull's* starboard exhaust cone filled his vision. The robot was thrown into the air as the vehicle scraped under the ship, grazed the concrete landing pad and shot out the other side, narrowly missing the front landing leg.

Hal stopped the car and glanced over his shoulder. The ship was rocking gently, but there was no sign of the maintenance robot. He drove to the rear of the ship, where he saw it spreadeagled against the cargo door, emitting sparks and smoke from its cracked and dented body. It twitched and slid down the back of the ship, landing face down on the concrete.

The robot staggered to its feet, one side of its body caved in and with its head at a strange angle. Slowly, it turned to scan the horizon, stopping as it caught sight of Hal. It shuffled towards him, reached the edge of the landing pad and stepped into thin air. Almost in slow motion, it tumbled into the long grass and lay still.

Hal looked around the landing field but there was nobody in sight. After a final glance at the motionless robot, he turned the car towards the distant office block and gunned the motor.

◆

Clunk dropped the last chess piece into the small wooden box and looked around the flight deck. It didn't look particularly clean, despite his best efforts with a mop, but compared to its previous state it was as sterile as a hospital ward. Satisfied, he approached the console, and a moment's hesitation he sat in the pilot's chair. 'Navcom, do you have a business directory?'

'Affirmative.'

'Run a search, please. I'd like all your data on a company called Incubots.'

There was a brief pause. 'Owned by Redge Muller, Incubots specialises in robot programming and advanced pilot training.'

Clunk looked relieved. 'So that's what Mr Jerling has in store for me! When I questioned him on the subject he was rather evasive.'

'Humans tell lies about the most trivial matters.'

'It's a programming flaw.' Very gently, Clunk ran a hand over the console. 'I'm going to have a ship of my own one day. My lifelong ambition is to ply the space lanes and trade with distant planets.'

'That's what Mr Spacejock does,' said the Navcom. 'He doesn't seem to like it very much.'

'I would find it most enjoyable.'

'You realise that robots don't own ships?'

'Then I shall be the first,' said Clunk. 'Tell me, do you have a simulation mode?'

'Affirmative.'

'Activate it, please.'

'What difficulty level? Medium, hard or extreme?'

'Hard. I'd like to get a feel for the controls before taxing myself.'

'You're a little rusty, I assume.'

Clunk frowned. 'Are you trying to be funny?'

'It was merely an observation. Tell me, would you like sound effects with your simulation?'

'Yes, make it as realistic as possible.'

'Entering set-up. Please specify parameters.'

'Height two thousand metres, wind fifteen knots from the south-east, ship descending at four hundred metres per minute. Manual override enabled.'

'Entering simulation mode. Please take the controls.'

Clunk put one hand on the throttle and took the flight stick with the other. With his left eye on the viewscreen and the right scanning the console read-outs, he moved the ship into position and set it down dead centre.

'Landing successful. You scored ... one hundred points. Your rating is ... perfect. Your high score is ... number one.'

'Really?' Clunk looked pleased. 'By how much?'

'The next high score is ... Mr Spacejock. His best ever result is ... minus nine thousand seven hundred and fifty. Would you like to try again?'

'No, I'd like a different simulation. Plot a virtual course for planet Aklam.'

'Cannot comply. I don't have an entry for that planet.'

Clunk sighed. 'It's only a simulation. Use random coordinates.'

'Destination located and locked in.'

'Start main engines.'

There was a hissing sound from the console speaker. 'Main engines started.'

'Check thrust levels,' said Clunk.

'Confirmed.'

'Seal external doors.'

'Doors sealed.'

'Initiate take-off.'

'Increasing thrust,' said the Navcom. 'Boosters activated. The ship has cleared the landing pad.'

Clunk sat back and stared through the viewscreen with a faraway look in his deep yellow eyes. He was on his way to Aklam, centre of the mechanised universe, and the fabled planet every robot dreamt about.

4

Hal left the maintenance vehicle in the spaceport's outer car park and walked to the admin block. An information kiosk directed him to an elevator, where he pressed the button marked 'Portmaster'. The floor numbers flicked past as the lift dropped further and further underground. He'd expected the Portmaster to have a spacious top-floor office with a view of the landing field, but instead the office seemed to be in the basement. Below the basement, amended Hal, eyeing the elevator's control panel. He'd passed that already.

The final number lit up and Hal's legs buckled as the elevator came to a sudden stop. The doors swept open and he stepped out into a cool reception area, his nose wrinkling at the damp smell from the bare concrete walls. A young man was sitting behind a reception desk, working at a computer terminal. He noticed Hal, and his earring sparkled as he looked up. 'Can I help you sir?'

'I'm here to see the Portmaster.'

'Take a seat please.' The man turned to his terminal and continued with his work.

There was a pair of armchairs in the corner of the room, arranged around a glass coffee table. Hal sat down, pulled a magazine from a nearby rack and flipped through the wrinkled plastic pages, gazing at lurid adverts for rocket fuel additives, expensive watches and sets of matching luggage. He was about to put the magazine back when an article about exploding robots caught his eye.

Are robots bad for your health?

Government sources say the recent spate of exploding metal men could be linked to the illegal practice of re-marking electronic brains.

The brain unit is the most expensive component of a robot, accounting for nearly two-thirds the total cost of our tin pals. Unscrupulous manufacturers have been salvaging brains from scrapped robots and fitting them to brand new models, forcing these delicate components to run at far greater speeds than they were designed for. In laboratory tests, brain units have burnt out or blown up when subjected to this kind of treatment.

Hal lowered the magazine. It would be just his luck if Jerling's robot had a wonky brain. He resolved to confine it to the hold, whatever creative excuses it came up with. If it did blow up, the shrapnel was less likely to damage vital equipment. Stuffing the magazine back in the rack, Hal pulled out another. It fell open at an article about the latest sitting of the Union Council.

Stay that trigger finger!

The Galactic Council has decreed that robots are to be treated as equals in the eyes of the law. From the beginning of this month, the wilful destruction of a robot is to be treated as murder. In a welcome move, obsolete robots retain their status as third-class citizens, and are therefore exempt from this controversial new law.

Hal tried to remember the maintenance robot. Had it been obsolete, or just old? He jumped as the office door opened and a short, balding man looked out.

'Who the hell are you?' demanded the man, glaring at Hal with hard grey eyes.

'Hal Spacejock, *Black Gull*.'

'I'm Portmaster Linten. We need to talk.' Linten glanced at the young man behind the desk. 'Hold my calls.'

'Yes sir.'

Linten held the door open. 'In here, Spacejock.'

Hal followed Linten into a cramped office. A large wooden desk almost filled the room, and the walls were lined with bookcases crammed with journals and magazines. Linten closed the door and waved Hal into a chair, then walked behind the desk and sat down.

'Mr Spacejock,' he began, 'Lamira is a small planet, far from major trade routes. Our most welcome visitors are those that inject substantial sums of money into our lowly economy.'

Hal noticed an interesting mural on the wall behind Linten, depicting a spaceship landing on a rocky plain under the light of two moons.

'We also value those visitors whose contributions are more artistic in nature,' said Linten. 'They don't contribute material wealth per se, but they enrich the mental well-being of our citizens with artworks or theatre.'

Hal studied the mural. The rocket was an Alpha class, although the artist had left off an engine to give prominence to the 'W' logo of a fast food chain.

'Finally, we come to those visitors who have absolutely no value to us.' Linten hunched forward, eyeing Hal's pollen-streaked clothes. 'I took the liberty of checking your credit rating, something I should have done before I allowed my staff to refuel that ship of yours. You can't even pay your landing fees, Mr Spacejock, let alone the rest of your bill. You are a free loader on a planet where the word free does not apply.'

'But I–'

'Given your circumstances, I'm sure you understand my course of action.'

'Oh. What's that?'

'I'm impounding your ship.'

Now Linten had Hal's full attention. 'Here, you can't do that!'

'I just have. And if you don't settle your bill in seven days I'll auction your ship and deduct your debts from the proceeds.'

'But it's not my ship! I'm paying it off!'

'I don't care who it belongs to. It's here, and it owes me money.'

'Look, I just got a cargo job. Let me do it and I'll come back and pay you afterwards.'

Linten snorted. 'I stopped believing in the tooth fairy years ago, Mr Spacejock.'

'It's true! I'm shifting a cargo of parts for this guy called Jerling. His robot's aboard my ship now.' Hal had a thought. 'Can I call him?'

'Be my guest,' said Linten, sliding his commset across the desk.

Hal tapped out the *Black Gull's* registration code. There was a crackle of static and a sultry female voice came out of the speaker. 'Hi, folks. The captain and I are busy right now, but if you leave a message he'll get back to you as soon as we're done.'

Linten raised one eyebrow.

Hal reddened. 'Previous owner. Must change it.'

◆

'Simulation suspended. Incoming message.'

The woolly clouds of Aklam faded from Clunk's vision. 'I'm sorry?'

'Incoming message.'

'Are we meant to answer it?'

'It's Mr Spacejock,' said the Navcom.

Clunk sat up straight. 'Please open the connection.'

'Hey, robot!' called Hal.

'Yes, sir?'

'Call Jerling and get me a loan. I need three hundred credits for landing fees and fuel.'

'I don't think he'll lend you any money,' said Clunk doubtfully.

'I don't care what you think. If he doesn't come through I'll lose my ship and his precious cargo will be stranded forever.'

'Message understood,' said Clunk. There was a burst of static and the speaker went dead. 'Navcom, please put me through to Mr Jerling.'

'Connection activated.' The viewscreen flickered and fizzed, and Jerling appeared. He took a cigar from his mouth and waved at the smoke with a bandaged hand.

'Mr Jerling! Whatever happened to your hand?'

'It's nothing,' said Jerling, moving it out of sight below the desk. 'You're not calling to inquire about my health, so let's have it.'

'Mr Spacejock was summoned to the Portmaster's office about an unpaid fuel bill.'

'I see.'

'He asked me to call you,' said Clunk.

'And?'

'He wants three hundred credits or he'll lose his ship.'

'Is that so?'

'Yes. And if you don't come through with the cash, he'll strand your precious cargo forever.'

Jerling yanked the cigar from his mouth. 'He said that?'

Clunk paused to replay the call from Hal. 'That's the gist of it.'

A plume of brown smoke drifted across the screen. 'You tell Spacejock something from me. If he doesn't deliver my cargo on time I'll have him arrested, tortured and shot. Twice.'

'Understood.'

'Goddamn freelancers,' said Jerling, sticking the cigar into the corner of his mouth. 'Nothing but trouble.'

Clunk remembered something. 'Oh, Mr Jerling. I found out about Incubots!'

Jerling breathed in sharply, almost swallowing his cigar.

'Are you all right?' asked Clunk in alarm, as his boss coughed and spluttered.

Jerling held up his bandaged hand. 'Important meeting, Clunk. Gotta go.'

The screen fizzed and went blank, and then more smoke drifted past. Clunk raised a hand and waved it gently, then glanced over his shoulder. The flight deck was filling with haze, and there was a faint noise which seemed to be coming from the airlock. When he turned up the gain in his audio circuit the gentle murmur became a crackling roar.

Fire!

Clunk ran into the airlock. As the outer door slid open, thick brown smoke poured into the ship. He walked onto the landing platform, flapping his hands in a vain attempt to clear the air, and through a break in the swirling smoke he saw the source - flames were tearing through the dry grass near the *Black Gull's* stern!

Clunk ran back into the flight deck, his feet thudding on the metal deck. 'Navcom, call Mr Spacejock. We have an emergency!'

5

Portmaster Linten studied Hal across the desk, his eyes narrowed. 'Are you telling me this Jerling character will pay your bill?'

'He has to. I can't deliver his cargo if the *Gull* is stuck here, can I?'

The commset buzzed and Linten leaned forward. 'Yes?'

There was a crackling sound. 'Help! Fire!' said a voice over the noise.

'Who is this? What are you talking about?'

'The grass is burning,' cried the voice. 'There's a fire on the landing field!'

'Which pad?'

'Fifty-two,' said Hal, smothering a grin. 'That's Jerling's robot.' He leaned towards the commset. 'Clunk, is the ship in danger from this, er, fire?'

'Not yet, Mr Spacejock, but it soon will be. Would you like me to move it out of the way?'

'You keep your hands off the controls. I'll be there in a tick.'

'You'll have to hurry. The fire's right up to the refuelling cluster, and if that explodes –'

'I'm leaving right away,' said Hal, pushing his chair back.

Linten cut Clunk off and looked up. 'Where do you think you're going?'

'Didn't you hear? My ship's in danger!'

Linten sighed. 'Son, I'm not falling for that one.'

Hal blinked. 'What do you mean?'

'Do you know how many cash-strapped pilots have tried the old 'ship in danger' trick on me?'

'Trick? My ship's in the middle of a raging inferno! If I don't save her you'll be auctioning a pile of warm scrap!'

'Mr Spacejock, there's a maintenance droid working on the pipes right next to your ship. Don't you think it would have raised the alarm if there was a fire?'

Hal averted his eyes. 'I guess.'

Linten's eyes narrowed. 'How did you get here so fast, anyway? They told me you couldn't afford a cab.'

Hal's mouth went dry. 'Well, I er –'

The commset buzzed.

Linten looked at Hal closely for a second or two before stabbing at the button. 'Yes?'

An excited voice burst from the speaker. 'Sir, there's a fire near the derelicts! The fuel pipes are going up!'

◆

'Deploy fire hose!' shouted Clunk.

'Deploying.' There was a whine outside the hull, which stopped with a sharp crack.

'What was that?'

'The reel just fell off,' said the Navcom.

'What else have we got in the way of fire-fighting equipment?'

There was a silence as the Navcom searched its database. 'There's a shovel in the cargo hold.'

'Metal?'

'Plastic.'

'Fire blanket?'

'The only blanket in my inventory is the one on Mr Spacejock's bed.'

'I'll start with that,' said Clunk. 'Where is it?'

'Stand back.'

A section of wall opposite the airlock dropped down, revealing an unmade bed. Clunk grabbed the blanket, then threw it aside in disgust. 'That won't last five seconds. Isn't there anything else?'

'We do have a portable extinguisher, but it's only rated for electrical fires.'

'Better than nothing. Where is it?'

'In a storage compartment in the airlock.'

Clunk dashed into the airlock, where he found a ring protruding from the wall. He tugged on it and almost fell over backwards as a whole panel came away. Underneath, there was nothing but bare metal.

'That was the mounting point for the safety line,' said the Navcom. 'The locker is in the opposite wall.'

Clunk threw the shattered panel aside and turned round. He pushed his finger into a slight depression and a small door popped open, revealing a panelled recess and a tangle of safety equipment. He reached past a coil of black cord and a control panel to get his hands on the fire extinguisher, wrapped both hands around it and pulled with all his strength. There was a crack as the mounting bracket came away from the rear wall, and a crunch as Clunk's elbow smashed into the control panel. Something began to whirr outside and a metal hook dropped past the airlock, attached to a thick steel rope.

Clunk took the extinguisher out onto the platform and looked up. Through the swirling smoke he saw a boom extended from the ship's hull, with wire rope feeding through a pulley on the end.

'Winch fully extended,' said the Navcom, as the last of the cable paid out.

'Did I do that?'

'Yes. The controls are in the locker.'

Clunk returned to the airlock and examined the control panel. One of the buttons was jammed, and when he tried to free it, it fell out and landed amongst the debris on the floor. Clunk picked it up and pressed it back into place, closing the door quickly to stop it falling out again.

Outside on the platform the smoke twisted around, blinding him. He hefted the extinguisher and felt his way down the ramp, the smoke getting thicker as he made his way to the edge of the landing pad. He switched off his air sampler, cutting off the smell of burning grass, and jumped down into the smoke.

His feet scrunched into the blackened stubble and a gust of wind blew a wave of flames towards him, shutting down his external sensors. When he came back online the rubber hose joining the nozzle to the fire extinguisher was burning fiercely. Clunk patted it out, then jogged to the part of the fire nearest the *Black Gull*. As he approached the roaring flames his foot struck something hard, almost launching him headlong into the burning grass. He looked down and saw blue and yellow flames flickering over the half-buried body of a robot, its fire-whitened eyes staring at the sky.

Clunk aimed the fire extinguisher at the blackened robot and pulled the trigger. There was a muted hiss and the rubber hose bulged, but nothing came out. He banged the nozzle on his leg and pulled the trigger again. Nothing. Peering down the nozzle he saw a lump of chalky material stuck inside. He poked at it with his finger and PHUT! - the lump shot out and bounced off his forehead. With the blockage cleared there was nothing to stop the thick spray of white powder, and by the time Clunk got his finger off the trigger he looked like a startled snowman.

Shaking his head to clear the worst off, he pointed the nozzle at the maintenance robot and squeezed the trigger until the clouds of choking powder blasted the coloured flames into oblivion. Then he set the extinguisher down and grabbed the robot by the arms, dragging it away from the fire. He hauled it onto the landing pad and left it behind the blast barrier, safe from the flames.

Collecting the fire extinguisher, Clunk ran to the fuel cluster and hosed the flames with burst after burst. Despite his efforts the fire continued to advance, until the painted pipes were smoking from the intense heat. Internally, his alarms urged him to retreat from danger. Clunk ignored them and kept attacking the fire with the extinguisher. The bursts of powder were weaker though, and before long they ceased altogether. He threw the cylinder aside and looked around for inspiration, while the flames rose higher and higher around him. There was a loud creak as the fuel pipes distorted in the severe heat, and he realised it was only a matter of seconds before they exploded.

Clunk looked up at the *Black Gull*. Mr Spacejock had told him not to touch the controls, but if he could get aboard and talk the Navcom into moving the ship ... Well, he could argue about permission later. He put his hands on the landing pad and was just about to pull himself up when a tremendous punch of hot air blew him off his feet, hurling him through the air in a cloud of whirling particles. He came to rest in the grass, his vision splitting and doubling like a poorly tuned video terminal. After a final warning chirp his overheated systems shut down, pitching him face-first into the blackened stubble.

6

Vurdi Makalukar watched the city of Forgberg sliding beneath the jet-black wings of his flyer, his mind busy with the day's activities. The fright he'd given Spacejock would get his monthly payments back on target, but the small reward from the finance company wouldn't amount to much.

The ship flew across an upmarket suburb, with opulent houses surrounded by lush grounds. Vurdi's lips tightened at the sight. That was where the real money was, tied up with the wealthy elite who ran the planet. Chasing itinerant freighter pilots for scraps was all very well for small operators, but for someone with ambition it was a waste of time.

The ship banked hard, and Vurdi grabbed a hanging strap. Brutus was at the controls, handling the vessel with his usual lack of finesse. The engines were either switched off or screaming at full power, the ship either flying level or roaring in wild turns. Turning to the robot, Vurdi raised his voice over the thrumming engines. 'Could you possibly employ a defter touch on the controls?'

Brutus stared at him, his face blank.

'Imagine the ship is a bird. Soar and swoop through the air, feel the wind beneath your wings, land gracefully.'

Brutus's face was even blanker. 'Huh?'

'Be subtle with the controls. Caress them.' A shadow fell across the screen and Vurdi's head snapped round, eyes widening as a rust-streaked bridge loomed in front of them. 'Bloody hell! Look out!'

Brutus jerked the stick back and the ship rocketed into the sky, belching fire from every orifice as it skimmed the rust-streaked pylons. 'Do not talk while I am flying,' said the robot gravely, after they levelled off. 'It is distracting.'

'Just fly the ship.'

Brutus altered course towards a squat brown building, flared to a halt above the rooftop dishes, and set down on the landing pad with a bone-shaking thud. While Brutus dealt with the engines and flight systems, Vurdi undid his safety harness and stepped down onto the roof. With barely a glance at the buildings spread out below, he crossed to the elevator and waited impatiently while the control panel scanned his retina, read his thumbprint and measured his body mass.

'Good evening, Mr Makalukar,' said the panel in a synthesised voice. 'Did you know there's a special on gym memberships this month?'

'Just fetch the lift, please.'

'Complying.' There was a ping, and a light came on beneath the speaker grille. 'While you're waiting, may I comment that you're looking in good health?'

'You may, but I am not purchasing anything.'

'Understood. However, I notice your weight has increased steadily over the past few weeks. A gym membership costs only ninety-nine credits a month, and a quick check of your income reveals that you can easily accommodate such a modest fee.'

There was another ping as the lift arrived. Vurdi stepped

forward, but the doors remained closed. 'Open the lift,' he snapped.

'I'm afraid I can't do that, Vurdi.'

There was thud as Brutus stepped out of the flyer, followed by heavy footsteps as the robot approached the doorway.

'I think you will,' said Vurdi, as the robot stopped alongside him.

'Not until we've finalised your gym membership.'

Vurdi waved Brutus towards the door. 'Open it.'

'Only ninety-nine credits,' said the door, which had been programmed not only for persistence but also with a complete disregard for its own safety.

Brutus cracked his knuckles slowly, deliberately. Then he kicked the door in.

Vurdi stepped inside, and the lift sagged on its cable as Brutus followed. 'Open a new task,' said Vurdi as they plunged downwards. 'Visit building management and suggest to them in the strongest possible terms that tenants do not appreciate over-enthusiastic sales pitches from the amenities.'

Brutus nodded, his eyes gleaming at the prospect. Strongest possible terms!

Vurdi exited the lift on his floor and strode along the hallway to his apartment. The door slid open and Vurdi stopped as he saw a glossy brochure lying on the doormat - another advert for the gymnasium. He tore it up, threw the pieces into the corridor and slammed the door.

As he passed through the kitchen he gestured at the coffee maker, which bubbled into action. Then he activated his terminal, a vibrant orange machine sitting on a polished desk. With an impatient gesture he wiped a gym advert from his display, and with a twirl of his index finger he activated his files. After discarding three invoices for repairs to elevator doors, a series of icons filled the screen. Vurdi tapped the Spacejock one and entered a couple of observations, then shifted it aside with a sweeping gesture. The remaining icons rearranged themselves to fill the gap, and Vurdi pursed his lips as he studied the rewards listed under each - none of them worth bothering with, except ... 'What's a Hinchfig doing with money troubles?' he murmured, his eyes glued to a red icon with a large reward beneath it. He remembered the rich houses they'd flown over on the way back to the office - the Hinchfigs were so wealthy they could level the whole suburb and pave it with gold bricks.

Vurdi tapped the icon with his finger. 'Summary please.'

A page of text crammed into the screen. 'Background information,' said the terminal in a smooth, male voice. 'The Hinchfig corporation has extensive business interests on Forg, including commercial and private real estate, two banks and a robot factory.'

'I know that,' said Vurdi. 'But why does one of them have a debtor file?'

'Shall I continue in more detail?'

'Only if you are unable to get to the point immediately.'

The terminal continued in more detail. 'The head of the Hinchfig company was lost in a passenger ship accident ten years ago, and the eldest son, Gordon Hinchfig, took over. His goal is to keep the company running exactly as his father left it, which means the firm won't expand and never branches out into new fields.'

Vurdi frowned. 'So what?'

'Farrell Hinchfig is the younger brother. Ambitious and opportunistic, he spent years trying to convince Gordon that the company had to change in order to grow with the times.'

'And this relates to the debt in what manner?'

'Farrell gave up trying to change the company, and instead began to enjoy himself.'

'Aha,' murmured Vurdi. 'Gambling debts?'

'Those and more. In the past he turned to Gordon for help.'

'But this time Gordon refused?'

'Correct. Walter Jerling, of Jerling Enterprises, has sewn up exclusives with all the robot parts manufacturers in this sector of the Galaxy, and Hinchfig Robots has all but closed due to severe shortages. The rest of the Hinchfig business is still performing, but Gordon has been forced to rein in costs. That includes cutting handouts to Farrell.'

Vurdi's dark eyes gleamed. 'So Farrell Hinchfig has debts?'

'Yes. He attempted to negotiate with his creditors, but they insist on payment in full.'

'They would, with that kind of wealth in the family.' Vurdi reached for the icon with trembling fingers. This was the big one - a new house in the suburbs, perhaps ...

There was a splintering sound as his front door caved in. Brutus ambled through the swirling smoke and flashes of shorting electrics with a purposeful tread, wearing the remains of the door like a collar.

'And perhaps a new robot,' muttered Vurdi. Shaking his head, he turned to the terminal and accepted the Hinchfig job.

◆

The groundcar tore across the field at full speed, leaving whirling eddies of pollen in its wake. The sun's last rays threw the car's shadow across the field, pointing directly at the billowing clouds of white smoke that enveloped the *Black Gull*.

Hal was hunched over the controls, eyes narrowed against the tearing wind. The car's screaming engine hammered his ears and the wind howled through the open vehicle, threatening to tear him from his seat. Still Hal pushed harder on the stick, until the warm metal felt like it was bending in his grip.

The car reached the extreme edge of the smoke, leaving vortices in its wake as it whisked through streaming tendrils. Visibility decreased and Hal was forced to throttle back. At full speed, he was likely to slam into his ship before he saw it.

The smoke grew thicker, cutting visibility to nothing, and Hal slowed the car to walking pace. In the sudden quiet he could easily hear the crackle of raging flames. Ahead and to the left a red glow burned through the smoke like an open pit, and even at this distance Hal could feel the heat. Moving the car closer he spotted the edge of the landing pad through the drifting smoke. As he passed the shattered fuel pipes, Hal saw flames reflecting off the *Black Gull* like firelight off an old kettle.

He stopped the car next to the landing pad, leapt out and ran, coughing in the thick smoke. He stumbled at the foot of the ramp, tripping over a tangle of wire lying on the ground beneath the ship. Freeing himself, he ran up the ramp, his feet clattering on the metal grille. Once inside the airlock, he glanced back at the scene.

The sun had gone down, its dying glow barely visible through the smoke. The fuel pipes easily outshone it, a fiery red heart burning out of control. Near the pipes, light glinted off a fallen robot lying face down in the blackened stubble. Hal eyed the bronze, soot-streaked form for a moment or two, then turned to the inner door. 'Who did this?' he demanded, as he saw the broken wall panel lying on the floor.

'XG99,' said the Navcom.

'Who?'

'The robot. It was looking for the fire extinguisher.'

'Why didn't you tell him where it was, instead of letting him rip the place apart?' Hal stepped over the buckled panel and entered the flight deck. 'Start main engines,' he said, sitting in the pilot's chair. 'We're getting out of here.'

There was a rumbling noise as the engines fired, and exhaust noises whistled through the open doors.

'Retract ramp and seal the airlock,' called Hal. The roaring noise shut off as the outer door thudded to, and wires rattled as the ramp folded against the hull.

'Your orders?' asked the Navcom.

'Set course for Seraph. Departing straight out.'

The engine note rose to a roar and the floor started to shake. 'Clearance?'

'I sorted that out with the Portmaster.' Hal spotted the extended bed and the crumpled blanket. 'Was the robot having a kip?'

'Negative. He was looking for a fire blanket.'

'He was supposed to mop the floor.' Hal looked up at the screen. 'Are we ready yet?'

'We cannot launch with the winch extended.'

Hal remembered the coils of wire at the foot of the ramp. 'Pull it in, then.'

'Manual controls only.'

Hal entered the airlock, where he flipped open the locker and caught the loose button as it fell out. 'Did the robot do this too?' he asked, staring at the buckled winch controls.

'Yes.'

Hal pressed the lower button and the winch began to reel in the cable. 'I thought I told him not to touch anything,' he said, returning to the flight deck.

'He was trying to save the ship.'

'You could have fooled me.'

'Boost tested to fifty per cent. Please be seated for take-off.'

Hal took the pilot's seat and placed his feet on the console. 'Okay, hit it.'

◆

'Leave me alone,' grumbled Clunk, as a warning siren brought him online. Darkness? At this time of the day? He dispensed lubricating fluid onto the surface of his eyes and forced them open. Light stabbed into his visual sensors and blurry, distorted vision returned.

Rolling onto his side, he raised his head and looked towards the landing pad. Through the smoke, he saw a groundcar hovering nearby, an angular vehicle with green lettering along the side. Clunk sighed with relief. Help had arrived.

His head dropped into the blackened stubble and he was just about to enter standby when he heard the whistling thunder of a ship's engines. He squinted at the *Black Gull* and saw the landing jets shimmering as the thrusters fired. It was leaving without him!

'*Black Gull, Black Gull*, please respond!' His internal radio hissed static back at him. '*Black Gull*, this is XG99 calling. I'm on the landing field!' He waited for a response, but the unbroken roar of the ship's thrusters told their own story - nobody could hear him.

Clunk staggered to his feet and stumbled toward the landing pad, ignoring the warning bleeps from his power management software. As he got to the pad the *Gull*'s main engines roared, shredding the thick smoke and sending a swirling cloud of dust and stones towards him. He clambered onto the landing pad, shielding his eyes from the debris, and struggled towards the ship, barely making headway against the hot, blasting wind.

The ship began to rise, departing the landing pad with a rolling thunderclap of sound. Clunk grabbed for a landing leg but the blast from the jets hurled him to the ground. Half-blinded by the maelstrom of dust, grit and smoke he was about to give up and run for cover when a glint caught his eye. Barely five metres away loops of steel cable were vanishing rapidly as the ship rose into the air. The winch!

Scrabbling on hands and knees, Clunk dragged himself across the oil-streaked concrete towards the cable, and as the last coil vanished he grabbed for the heavy yellow hook on the end.

7

The Hinchfig empire was based in North Forgberg, half a dozen kilometres from Vurdi's apartment. From his elevated office, Farrell Hinchfig could have fired a laser cannon through Vurdi's window, except that he didn't have a laser cannon and he had no idea Vurdi existed ... yet.

Farrell was at his desk, writing short phrases into an old-fashioned exercise book before typing them into his computer terminal. It was his daily routine - turn up around midday, spend five minutes tossing urgent messages into the trash before getting down to several hours of hard work. That work consisted of opening a connection to the company's accounting department and entering one passphrase after another, in the hope that one of them would give him access to all the money.

Farrell was very thorough with his research, regularly jotting down notes about his elder brother Gordon - where he had lunch, his favourite shows and names of friends and associates, all of which gave Farrell endless combinations of new material to enter into the computer.

So far, after three months of trying, the computer had rejected every one.

'Spaghetti carbonara icecream,' muttered Farrell, tapping out the letters one by one.

'Passcode rejected,' said the computer politely.

Farrell wrote the phrase into his exercise book and put a cross next to it. 'Spaghetti carbonara jelly,' he said, typing in the next phrase.

'Invalid passcode,' said the computer, which liked to vary the responses a bit.

'Spaghetti carbonara lemon.'

'That passcode is . . . '

Farrell's gaze snapped to the terminal.

'Rejected!' said the computer, which also had a sense of the dramatic.

'Damn it!' hissed Farrell, scoring a heavy X in his book. He was about to try the next when his terminal buzzed. 'Yeah?'

'Farrell?' said a muffled voice.

'Who else would it be?'

'I got some vital info for you.'

Farrell frowned. This was pretty subtle, even for his computer. Was it going to pretend to give him the code, only to hang up at the last second? 'Who is this?'

'Snake. You know, we met down the pub last night.'

That ruled out the computer. 'Look Snake, I don't know what I promised but I'm a bit short right now.'

'You said to keep me eyes open. To let you know what's what.'

'I did?' Farrell struggled to remember the previous evening, but it was like exploring a black hole with a candle.

'Yeah. And I got some vital info, brand new. Could be worth something.'

'Info on what?'

There was chuckle from the terminal. 'I ain't stupid, Farrell. They call me snake coz I'm cunning, see?'

'I thought that was foxes.'

'Nah, it's Snake.'

Silently, Farrell vowed to change pubs. 'So, Snake, how do I get this info?'

'You got to pay for it.'

'Yes, we've established that. How much?'

'How much is it worth to you?'

'I don't know. What is it?'

'I ain't saying until you pay.'

Farrell sighed. 'All right, I'll give you twenty credits.'

'Twenty?' Only a single word, but it was heavy with disappointment.

'Thirty, then. And a couple of pints down the pub.'

'I ain't getting rich on thirty.'

'Take it or leave it.'

'Will you make it fifty if the info's solid gold?'

'Whatever. Now spill it.'

'Me missus works for Jerling, right? She's in marketing.'

'You're not calling with the password to Jerling's bank, are you?'

'Nah, they don't let her into that bit. Look, your firm makes robots but you can't get the parts. Right?'

Farrell frowned. His latest interview with Gordon was still fresh in his mind. 'Correct.'

'Well, me missus got wind of a shipment.'

'So what?'

'There's a couple of hundred grand's worth of parts. If you got hold of 'em, they'd keep your factories going for weeks.'

'No chance. Jerling tags his ships. If one of his pilots so much as veers off course his head would be on Jerling's desk first thing in the morning.'

'Ah, but they're hiring out for this job.' Snake lowered his voice. 'They got a bloke in special, he's collecting from Seraph and dropping at Jerling's. You could get to 'im, straight up you could.'

'How am I supposed to do that? Ask him nicely for the cargo?'

'You're the businessman. You figure out how to steal it.'

Farrell shook his head. 'Sorry Snake, I can't use this.'

'Do I still get me thirty?'

'I guess.'

'And the pints?'

'When I see you.'

'Thanks, Farrell. Look, I'll tell me missus to send the stuff anyway. Read it through. It could be worth more if you study it.'

'Sure, Snake. Thanks for calling.' Farrell flicked the microphone off and returned to his exercise book. 'Time-wasting snake,' he wrote, before typing it into the computer. Maybe Gordon knew the guy too.

'Unknown or incorrect passphrase,' said the terminal.

Farrell crossed it out. He was just planning the next entry when his terminal beeped.

'You have a call,' said the computer politely. 'Would you like to speak to them?'

'Is it that Snake guy?'

'Negative.'

'Are they selling anything?'

'Negative.'

'All right, put them on.'

There was a brief pause. 'Am I speaking to Mr Farrell Hinchfig?' said a soft voice.

'Yes.'

'My name is Vurdi, Vurdi Makalukar. I run a debt collection

business here on Forg, and I'd like to make an appointment to discuss your finances.'

'We have nothing to talk about,' said Farrell, reaching for the disconnect.

'Running from your problems will only make them worse,' said Vurdi. 'Say three o'clock?'

'Three, four or five o'clock, I don't have any money.'

'Your brother does.'

'Maybe so, but he won't give it to me. Business is tough right now.'

'It's only a hundred and twenty thousand. Can't you help yourself?'

Farrell glanced at the exercise book. 'I'm exploring one or two options.'

'Tell me, should the unthinkable happen to your brother, who would inherit?'

'Me, I guess.' Farrell's face darkened. 'Now you listen to me, you filthy little git. If you're suggesting . . .'

'Far from it. Your brother is in perfect health and we must work together to keep him that way. I shall see you at three, please don't keep me waiting.' There was a click as Vurdi rang off.

For several minutes, Farrell stared into space. What couldn't he do as managing director? Drag the company into the present, plan for the future, open new factories, explore new business opportunities . . . Within twelve months he'd have that little viper Jerling at his mercy, open to a rock-bottom takeover. He'd have the fame, the fortune . . .

Farrell sighed. Whatever Gordon's flaws, they were still brothers. Setting him up for this Vurdi character was unthinkable.

51

His terminal beeped. 'You have a new message,' said the computer politely. 'Shall I read it to you?'

'No, bin it.'

'According to the subject line, this message contains vital information.'

'Those are the worst.'

'The sender is Mrs Snake, from Jerling Enterprises.'

Farrell's eyebrows rose. 'Display it.'

The accounting department login screen was replaced with a line of text: *Dear Farrell, this vital info is from Snake at the pub. He says your paying him twenty creds and I want half.*

Farrell rolled his eyes at the 'your'. Then he frowned. 'Where's the rest? Where's the vital info?'

'There's an attachment, but I suppressed it.'

'Why?'

'Attachments are dangerous. They contain viruses and trojans.'

'Not this one. Serve it up.'

'My security settings won't allow it.'

'So change the settings.'

'Are you authorising the removal of all safeguards?'

'Yeah, just show the thing.'

'Very well. On your authority.' The screen cleared and several paragraphs of text appeared.

Farrell skimmed through them. It was pretty much as Snake had said: Jerling was paying a freelancer to collect a cargo of parts from Seraph IV and bring them back to Forg. Even so, stealing the parts was pure fantasy. People went to jail for that sort of thing. He reached for the delete button, then hesitated. Fantasy or not, if he could pull it off his money problems would be over. But how did you steal cargo? Doodling on the exercise book, he broke the problem into parts. First, let

Jerling's pilot collect the cargo. Well, that was easy enough. Second, get the cargo off the pilot. Tougher. Third, sell the cargo and pay Vurdi. Not too hard.

His terminal beeped, interrupting his train of thought. 'Farrell, are you there?'

It was his brother. 'Yes, Gordon.'

'Mike just finished a news release. Have you got time for a quick look?'

'I guess.'

'I'll send it over.' Gordon rang off.

Farrell stared at his notes. Convincing the pilot was the hardest bit. Faking a call from one of Jerling's employees was no good, because any half-competent freighter pilot would verify their ID. A call from Jerling himself would do it, but how could he possibly organise something like that? Farrell tapped his pen on the desk. Assuming he got the pilot to co-operate, where would the cargo transfer take place? That was easy - the Forg Orbiter. Large freighters used the space station as a depot, transferring their cargo to smaller ships which then brought the goods down to Forg. He could borrow a company ship and meet Jerling's pilot at the Orbiter. But what was he supposed to do with a cargo of robot parts? Sell them to his brother, of course! Tell Gordon about the shipment, get the money up front, pay Vurdi off and clear eighty grand for himself.

Great. Now he just had to work out how to impersonate Jerling . . .

Farrell jumped as the Hinchfig jingle burst from his terminal. He turned the sound down and tried to pick up his train of thought, but the sight of the huge crowd cheering, clapping and waving 'We root for Hinchfig!' banners was enough to drive it from his mind. When the clip finished, the terminal beeped again.

'What do you think?' demanded Gordon.

'Amazing. Incredible.'

'Did you recognise the place?'

Farrell hadn't looked. 'A takeaway shop?'

'It was the old car wash on the corner of Eighth and Stuart. One lick of paint and the place looks like new again. It's such a shame Father can't see it.'

'How did you cram all those people in? It's no bigger than a shed.'

'The magic of technology, Farrell. They were simuloids. Mike programs them on his computer.'

'Clever little Mike,' muttered Farrell, as Gordon disconnected. 'Fake people, eh? What'll it be next?' He shook his head slowly, then froze.

Fake Jerling!

Farrell grabbed a remote and flicked through the video channels on his terminal. Jerling was always on, hawking his gear or giving bombastic speeches. Surely he'd be ... There! Without taking his eyes from the screen, Farrell rummaged in his drawer. His fingers closed on a data chip and he felt for the slot, pressed the chip home and hit the record button. With a triumphant grin, he sat back and linked his hands behind his head.

◆

Portmaster Linten's angry face filled the main viewscreen. 'I don't want excuses!' he shouted, his face red and his grey eyes bulging. 'Nobody gave you permission to leave!'

'You told me to move my ship,' said Hal, raising his voice over the roar of the engines.

'Not into orbit!'

'I didn't mean to take off. My hand slipped on the throttle.'

'Now you listen to me, Spacejock. I've got a burnt-out robot and a raging fire down here, and it's all down to you.' Linten waved a sheet of paper at the screen. 'There's a report on your activities going out to every planet in the Union. I'm blacklisting you, son. You're finished. You hear me? Finished!'

'As soon as I deliver this cargo I'll come back and pay for everything. Word of honour.'

'Don't offer what you haven't got,' snarled Linten, slamming his fist on the disconnect.

Hal gazed at the darkened screen with a thoughtful look on his face. 'Navcom, what did Clunk want with the fire extinguisher?'

'He went out to fight the fire.'

'Where is he now, skulking in the cargo hold?'

'Negative.'

'Where did he go when he came back?'

'Who said he came back?'

Hal's mouth fell open. 'Are you telling me Clunk isn't on board?'

'Correct.'

'Why the hell didn't you say so, you stupid lump of silicon?' shouted Hal. 'Quick - the job details. Which planet are we going to? It was Seraph, right?'

'Correct.'

'Set course for Seraph, then. We'll do this without the robot.'

'Which Seraph would you like to visit?'

55

'What?'

'There are eighteen planets called Seraph.'

'Eighteen! How come?'

'They were named after a successful explorer.'

'Dammit!' shouted Hal, thumping his fist on the console. The winch motor stopped whirring and began to make a clunking noise. 'What's that racket?'

'The cargo hook won't retract.'

'Why not?'

'Unknown.'

'Put it on the screen.' Hal's eyes widened as Clunk appeared, dangling from the hook like a big bronze worm. 'What the hell is he doing out there? We must be five kilometres up!'

'Four thousand one hundred metres, to be precise.'

'Tell him to come in. Understood?'

'Transmitting.'

On screen, the robot's lips moved.

'What's he saying?' demanded Hal.

'I don't know. He cannot transmit.'

'You tell him to get his tin-plated arse back in here or I'll ... '

Clunk faced the camera and shook his head emphatically.

'It's like that, is it?' Hal crossed his arms. 'Right, unseal the airlock and extend the landing platform.'

'Cannot comply. Extra-vehicular activity is forbidden during lift-off.'

'Oh yeah?' Hal pointed at Clunk, who was swinging gently on the hook. 'What about that?'

'He did not request permission.'

'All right, Navcom. Hover!'

The engine note changed and the deck tilted.

'Hold it steady.' Hal saw Clunk's eyes open. They opened a lot more when the robot looked down and saw the ground far below. 'Now unseal the door and extend the platform or I'll start shooting holes in you.'

'Unable to comply. Extra –'

Hal pulled the blaster off his belt. 'I mean it!'

There was a pop and a hiss as the doors slid open, and Hal staggered into the airlock, covering his ears as the engine noise reverberated around the confined space. He took the safety line out of the locker, clipped one end to his belt and turned to fix the other end to the EVA mounting point, only to find bare metal where the hook should have been. After looking around for something else to clip it to, he gave up and went out on the platform.

Gritting his teeth against the roar of the engines, he shuffled to the edge and looked over. The robot was turning slowly on the end of a wire rope, about five metres away and with his head about two metres below the platform. 'Clunk,' shouted Hal. 'Hey, Clunk!'

The robot looked up. 'Go inside. It's dangerous.'

'No chance. Here, grab this!' Hal swung the safety line and threw the end, getting it across the robot's shoulder. Clunk took it and tied it around his waist.

Once the cord was secure Hal began to pull, bringing the robot in hand over hand, leaning back further and further as the weight threatened to drag him off balance. As Clunk got closer to the edge he reached out for the platform, his bronze fingers grasping frantically.

There was a distant roar and Hal looked down to see a silver spot rising towards them, glinting in the sunlight. 'Oh, hell!' he muttered. 'Quick, Clunk! There's a ship coming!'

Barely had the words left his mouth when the spaceship flashed past with a whistling, screaming roar. The wash buffeted the *Black Gull* and Hal swore as the platform lurched under his feet. He felt the cord slipping through his fingers and then the slack began to pay out, vanishing faster and faster as the heavy robot swung further and further away.

The loose cord had just about gone when Hal remembered the end was attached to his belt. He grabbed for the clip and struggled to undo it, his fingers scrabbling for purchase on the slick metal.

Too late.

The line tightened, yanking him off the platform. He had a close-up of Clunk's surprised face as he dived past, before a terrific jerk on his belt stopped his fall, leaving him dangling from the safety cord.

Hal opened his eyes and looked up at the soles of Clunk's feet. Faintly, he heard the robot's voice over the roar of the engines.

'Cannot hold weight. Battery . . . going.'

8

Gordon Hinchfig studied the report on his terminal, his washed-out eyes reflecting the glowing red figures. His smooth-skinned face was a picture of concern as he examined columns of data, and it was downright gloomy as he took in the final summary.

The door slid open, and Gordon looked up as Farrell entered his office. 'Hello, Farrell. What can I do for you?'

'You can lend me some money.'

Gordon's welcoming smile vanished. 'We've been over this already. You know I can't.'

'Relax, it's not what you think.' Farrell laid his briefcase on Gordon's desk, squashing a delicate wire sculpture. He flicked the catches, which snapped like gunshots. 'I know where we can pick up a cargo of robot parts. Quality stuff, everything we need to start the production lines up.'

'W-where?'

'Tell you in a minute.' Farrell handed over several sheets of paper. 'Here's the list of stuff.'

Gordon glanced at the top sheet, then flipped through page after page in growing excitement, until finally he looked up, his eyes shining. 'There's enough here to build three hundred robots! This is gold, pure gold!'

Farrell grinned. 'Not bad, eh?'

'Tell me, where is this cargo?'

'It's in transit. You're going to have to trust me on a couple of things.'

'I see.' Gordon retrieved the flattened sculpture and began to work it into shape. 'How much are we talking about?'

'Hear me out before you make your decision.' Farrell leaned across the desk. 'There's this pilot who's been let down badly, a friend of a friend. He paid for the shipment, went to deliver it and discovered the original customer had folded. Now he's trying to get his money back.' Farrell tapped the sheaf of papers. 'Thing is, he doesn't care who he sells to as long as he breaks even.'

Gordon picked up a handset. 'What's his number? I'll set things up right away.'

'It's not that simple.' Farrell paused. 'See, the pilot has debts, and if his creditors hear about this transaction they'll chase him down and take the payment off him. It has to be subtle.'

'If he has debts, he should service them,' said Gordon stiffly.

'He will, with regular payments.'

'So you want me to give a large sum of money to a friend of a friend, who will then give me stolen robot parts in return?'

'Don't twist things around!' snapped Farrell. 'You always do it, always –'

'What happens if this pilot takes the money and doesn't deliver the parts? What if the parts are seconds, rejects? What if the debt collector takes the parts before this pilot can deliver them to us?' Gordon sighed. 'It doesn't take much twisting, does it?'

'You don't think I'd hand over the cash without checking the cargo first?'

'I'll tell you what I think. I think you're going to take the money, fob me off for a few days, then come to me with a string of excuses.' Gordon replaced the wire statue. 'How much trouble are you in?'

'Nothing I can't handle.' Farrell stared at him. 'You're wrong about this, you know that? I couldn't have made that list up. I don't know the first thing about building robots.'

Gordon straightened the printout. 'It's a lot of money, Farrell. What if they force you to hand it over?'

'You know Terry?'

'Your driver?'

'I'll take him with me. They won't try anything with him around.'

'Are you sure that's wise? I haven't forgotten that incident at the staff party.'

'Terry's a good man. He's dependable.'

'Keep him in check, will you? I can do without that kind of publicity.'

'Sure thing, Gordon.' Farrell paused. 'So, it's all go?'

'There are one or two details I'd like to sort out, but I think so.'

Farrell suppressed a triumphant grin. Gordon was going to say yes!

'For example, how are you going to hand over the money?'

'This guy's out near Seraph, waiting to hear from me. I'll need a company ship.' Farrell handed Gordon another sheet of paper. 'That's a list of expenses plus my account number. If you put the cash in there, I'll release it to the pilot when the cargo has cleared.'

Gordon looked at him shrewdly. 'What's your cut?'

'Me? Nothing.'

'Oh, come on.'

Farrell dropped his head. 'I thought if I saved the robot business, you might help me with my debts this one last time.'

Gordon nodded slowly. 'If you save the robot business, I will do exactly that.'

◆

The *Black Gull's* jets pounded Hal's ears as he dangled from the end of the safety line. He barely noticed the screaming roar of the engines - he was staring past his feet to the landing field, four thousand metres below.

The line jerked, and Hal tore his gaze from the distant, toy-like buildings. Overhead, Clunk was clinging to the cargo hook with the tips of his fingers, looking down at him in concern.

'Navcom says ... engines overheating,' shouted the robot.

'Tell it to take us down,' shouted Hal, jabbing his thumb towards the ground.

Clunk shook his head. 'Receive only.'

Hal felt the safety line slip. Drawing on his experience of hanging around in mid-air using a safety line tied around a robot's waist - none - he considered his next course of action. He could wait for Clunk's battery to run out and plunge four thousand metres to his death, or he could wait for the engines to blow up and plunge four thousand metres to his death tied to a burning ship.

There had to be a better way.

Hal tried to gauge the distance between Clunk and the platform. The edge was only five metres away, but it was well out of reach. But what if he could get the robot swinging?

Hal caught Clunk's eye. 'Hold on tight,' he shouted, gripping the safety line with both hands. He swung his legs back and forth, getting a rhythm going, and soon they were swinging like a double pendulum. A massive swing pulled Clunk away from the platform, and as he swooped back towards it Hal jabbed his finger. 'Jump!'

Clunk let go of the hook, and for a split second they were in free-fall. Then the line jerked, pulling Hal's belt upwards. He sucked in through pursed lips, blinking away the tears that had sprung to his eyes. When he'd recovered, he looked up to see Clunk hanging on to the edge of the platform, peering down at him over his shoulder.

'Now what?' shouted the robot.

'Climb up!'

Shuddering with the effort, Clunk pulled himself up until his chin was level with the platform. Then he stopped.

'Go on!' shouted Hal.

'I'm stuck!'

Hal gripped the thin cord and pulled himself up, hand over hand, wincing as it cut into his palms. His muscles burned as he inched towards the robot, until finally his outstretched fingers brushed a metal foot. He grabbed the robot's ankle with his free hand, only to remember that Clunk's legs had almost certainly been snapped together by a bunch of jobsworths. Driving the thought from his mind, he reached for the knee joint with his free hand, his fingers slipping on the smooth metal as he struggled for grip.

'Use my arm!' shouted Clunk, taking one hand off the platform and holding it down towards him.

Hal grabbed the hand and clambered up, using the robot's elbow and shoulder as holds. Finally he got his knees on the robot's shoulders and pulled himself onto the platform, where he crouched for a moment, arms and legs shaking from the strain.

'When you're ready,' called Clunk. 'No hurry.'

Hal looked over the edge. 'Can't you pull yourself up?'

'Not enough charge.'

'Hang in there!' Unclipping the safety line from his belt, Hal looked around desperately for something to attach it to. Nothing.

Clunk took a hand from the platform and clawed at his chest. A flap opened and several small objects fell out and fluttered away towards the ground. The robot ignored them and pointed to a socket. 'Power ... here.'

'I'll get a lead!' Hal jumped up and ran into the flight deck. He threw himself at the console, tearing open doors, tossing the contents onto the deck until he came across a tangled length of electrical cord. He ran into the airlock, jammed the plug into a socket and shot outside with the lead. Clunk was still hanging from the platform, his head tilted forward.

'Coming!' shouted Hal. He lay down on the platform and put his head over the edge. 'Clunk! Take the plug!'

The robot's head hung between its shoulders. There was no sign of life.

Hal reached down and felt for the socket. His fingers brushed the edge of the compartment, but even at full stretch he couldn't reach. 'Clunk!'

The robot hung from the platform, motionless.

'I'm going to regret this,' muttered Hal. He turned and placed his feet on the robot's shoulders, then let go of the platform and pushed the plug into the socket.

Immediately, Clunk began to shake like a pneumatic drill. 'W-w-wrong v-v-voltage.'

'What kind do you need?'

Clunk took one hand off the platform and grabbed for the plug. 'P-pull it o-out!'

Hal yanked the plug and the robot slumped.

'Switch below socket,' said Clunk faintly.

Hal found the switch, took hold of the plug and pushed it back in.

Clunk jerked. 'Wow, I'm alive! Alive!'

'Sort of,' said Hal. 'But –'

'Watch this!' There was a tremendous jolt and suddenly they were high in the air. Clunk executed a perfect back flip and dropped to the platform like a cat. Hal landed flat on his back.

'You're mad,' he muttered, glaring at the robot. 'I should have let you fall.'

Clunk's eyes glowed hot yellow in the twilight. 'You can't kill me. I'm invincible!' he shouted, laughing wildly.

9

Hal sat back in his chair and watched the autopilot's crosshairs tracking the expanding blue and white disk of Seraph IV. The hyperspace jump from Lamira had been uneventful, and after a brief run through space and two orbits of the planet, the ship was now lined up for final approach. A green rectangle popped up on the screen and showed the local time: 5.30 p.m.

Hal heard a groan and turned round. Clunk was slumped against the wall with his head in his hands, the extension lead coiled on the floor beside him. 'Invincible, eh?'

The robot shook his head gingerly. 'I should have used a trickle charge.'

'Where are we supposed to land, by the way? Jerling said you had the details.'

'The information was placed in my memory banks before I came aboard. I need to interface with the Navcom to upload it.'

'Get on with it, then.'

Clunk stood and crossed to the console, pulling the end of the cord with him. He ran his hands over the panel.

'Lower,' said the Navcom.

Clunk felt under the front edge, and a burst of static came through the speaker. 'Interesting.' He glanced at Hal. 'The

Navcom is equipped with a non-standard communications port.'

'Somehow that doesn't surprise me.'

'I'll have to use a special adaptor to complete the transfer.'

'All right, just get on with it. We're late enough as it is.'

'Let me finish the initial programming.' Clunk ran his hands over the console, pressing buttons and tapping dials. There were several bursts of static from the speakers.

Hal frowned. 'Listen, while you're fooling around, the ship's racing towards a very solid planet at very high speed. I don't want to spoil your fun, but –' His eyebrows shot up as the robot stuck a probe into the front of the console. The lights flickered for a moment or two, then the overhead light popped and went out.

Clunk detached himself and looked across the flight deck, gleaming in the light from the instruments. 'Data transfer complete.'

'Well I'll be buggered,' said Hal.

Clunk shook his head. 'I don't have the right adaptor.'

Farrell sat at his desk, staring at his terminal. It was two hours since he'd spoken to Gordon, and only thirty minutes until the meeting with Vurdi. Why couldn't his brother make up his damned mind?

'Yes?' called Farrell, as his terminal beeped.

'It's Gordon. They've finished the service on my flyer. Do you have time to pick it up for me?'

Farrell kept his voice even. 'Sure. I've got nothing better to do.'

'Oh, and I've gone over your figures. Why do your expenses include fuel and landing fees? You're using a company ship.'

Farrell grinned. His brother would have made an excellent tax inspector. 'Sorry, Gordon. I modified an old job costing spreadsheet. I must have forgotten to delete some stuff.'

'Very well. I shall modify the total and put the money in your account this afternoon.'

Farrell sighed with relief. That would get Vurdi off his back.

'Is there anything else you need?' asked Gordon.

A couple of million and a new house, thought Farrell. He glanced at his exercise book. No, he could work for those. 'Everything's covered.'

'The factory staff are being notified and the covers are coming off the production lines. Are you sure you can get these parts?'

Farrell nodded. 'Leave it to me.' As soon as Gordon hung up, Farrell sent off a note for Vurdi: Cancel meeting, debt paid in full.

Now all he had to do was get his hands on the cargo.

◆

The *Black Gull* rocked wildly as it dropped through Seraph IV's thin atmosphere. Clunk was busy at the console, checking displays and fiddling with knobs and switches, while Hal stood nearby watching. He knew exactly how to land the ship himself of course, but it was a novelty to see the full landing checklist performed right in front of his eyes. Apart from a brief lesson when he bought the *Black Gull*, he'd never seen anything like it.

'Have you been to this planet before?' asked Hal.

Clunk shook his head. 'According to your database it's mostly agricultural. A group of colonists founded a settlement on the other side of the planet, but apart from that it's uninhabited.'

'Incoming call,' said the Navcom.

Hal nodded. 'Go ahead.'

'This is the battleship Almeria of the Seraph Imperial Navy,' said a male voice. *'You're entering a restricted zone. Please transmit your ID, flight log and manifest immediately. Failure to comply will result in your immediate destruction.'*

'Send the response,' said Hal.

'Modifications to my programming are instructing me to transmit false data. Please advise.'

Hal glanced at Clunk. 'Did you do this?'

'Yes. Mr Jerling told me to bypass customs.'

'Customs, yes. Not a battleship.'

'Don't worry, it's all the same thing.'

Hal shrugged. 'All right, go ahead Navcom.'

'Transmitting spurious data.'

There was a burst of static. *'This Seraph IV is ... Imperial please ... Naval gaze. Thank you, bingo.'*

'What was that?'

'Their communication systems are suffering from the effects of a trojan,' said Clunk. 'They think we're an asteroid, or possibly even a small moon. It's somewhat erratic.'

'You attacked a whacking great battleship with a virus. Are you out of your mind?'

'Relax, Mr Spacejock. We'll be safe as long as we land quickly and get off their screens.'

Hal looked up at the viewscreen, which was displaying a detailed map of the planetary surface. 'What are those dark patches?'

'Oceans.'

Hal studied the screen a bit longer. 'Where are we landing?'

'Right here,' said Clunk, dragging a bright green cross to the centre of the display. 'Fortunately there aren't any populated areas, or we'd have to be a lot more precise. Let me just ...'

He passed his hand over a control and three quarters of the map turned red.

'Oh dear.'

'What?'

'Exactly how old is your database?'

'I don't know. They keep asking me to upgrade but it costs a fortune.'

'I'm afraid we have a bit of a problem. You see, those red patches are populated areas.'

'You said it was uninhabited!'

'I took that information from your database, which appears to be decades out of date. Unfortunately the planet has been developed in the meantime.'

'Well we can't land in the high street. What's next?'

'Let me find Incubots.' Clunk waved his middle finger at the screen while simultaneously pulling at thin air with his right hand. The red areas scrolled off the map until only half a dozen small patches remained. In the middle was a pulsing green dot.

'That's a bit better,' said Hal. He gestured at a blue patch alongside. 'Is that a city?'

'I don't think so.' Clunk made a circle with his finger and thumb and blew through the middle. 'Light industrial area,' he said, as the patch turned yellow. 'We must land on the far side of Incubots.'

'Fine by me.'

Green rectangles appeared in the corners of the screen, displaying scrolling lines of text. 'What's that all about?' asked Hal.

'Status displays. They're vital for safe landings.'

'Really? How did you turn them on?'

Clunk gave him a look. 'Have you considered investing in a little flight training?'

'From a bunch of overpaid desk jockeys? I don't need that rubbish.' Hal cracked his knuckles. 'Now stand back. This is where I take over.'

'You realise we'll be landing in total darkness?'

'I can handle it,' said Hal firmly.

'Are you sure?'

'Certain.' Hal pressed a large green button and a recorded voice reverberated around the *Black Gull's* flight deck.

'*All personnel, all personnel, please prepare for landing. I repeat: please prepare for landing.*'

Preparations complete, Hal sat back in his chair and put his feet up. Alongside him, Clunk watched the planetary surface growing larger and larger by the second. When he realised Hal was just going to sit and watch it, he cleared his throat. 'Are you going to land the ship or not?'

'It's all taken care of,' said Hal, indicating the green button.

Clunk blinked. 'You do know what that button does?'

'Of course I do. It lands the ship.'

'It most certainly does not. It just plays a warning message over the intercom.'

'Yeah, sure,' said Hal, with a laugh.

'I'm deadly serious.'

71

'But I always press that button when I want to land!'

Clunk nodded slowly, the blue and red map reflected in his eyes. 'I suppose that would do the job on many planets. The navigation computer locks onto the spaceport's beacon and controls your descent automatically. It's a failsafe.'

'Are you saying the Navcom lands the *Gull* for me?'

'Correct. Using the beacon installed at every spaceport.'

Hal's eyes widened. 'But there's no beacon here! We're landing in a field!'

"'Landing' is not the word I would use, given our current rate of descent.'

Hal stared at the viewscreen. Earlier it had shown an expanse of darkness criss-crossed with streetlights. Now he could pick out the houses. He was still gaping at the terrifying display when a large red cross flashed up on the screen.

'Warning, impact imminent,' said the Navcom calmly.

A split second later Hal was out of the pilot's chair. 'I've changed my mind,' he said. 'You land it.'

'Me?'

'You're the specialist. Jerling said so.'

'But we're about to crash into the surface!'

'Better get to it, then.'

Muttering under his breath, Clunk slid into the pilot's chair and took the controls. 'Brace yourself,' he said over his shoulder. 'This is going to be rough.'

10

Sweat ran down Hal's face as the *Black Gull* plummeted towards the waiting planet. Thrusters howled and gravity generators moaned as Clunk fought the controls, and while his efforts appeared to be slowing the ship, the tremendous outpouring of energy had raised the flight deck temperature to very uncomfortable levels.

'Can't you put the air back on?' demanded Hal.

'We need every scrap of power for the engines.'

'But it's hot!'

Clunk's hands blurred over the controls. 'I'm rather busy,' he said, as the ship swung wildly. 'Can we discuss this later?'

'If there is a later,' muttered Hal. 'Do you think we'll make it?'

'The engines are running at full reverse throttle, but it's not enough.'

'I'll take that as a no.' Hal examined the screen, where the landing field had grown from a thumbnail to a sizeable rectangle. 'Can't you do anything?'

'There is one last chance,' said Clunk. 'If it works, we're saved.'

'And if it doesn't?'

'We'll tunnel so far underground you won't need a burial.' Clunk reached for a large silver knob. 'Hang on.'

'Hang on?' shouted Hal. 'What to?'

Clunk twisted the knob and leaned towards the Navcom's microphone. 'Reverse one hundred and twenty per cent.' He saw Hal's expression and winked. 'It's called overclocking.'

There was a screaming roar from the engines and Hal's legs buckled under the crush of seven or eight gravities. Supported by the console, he clenched his teeth and stared at the viewscreen, his vision blurring as the *Black Gull* strained every hand-welded joint.

'Brace yourself!' shouted Clunk, as the ground rushed up to meet them.

Hal was thrown to the deck as the ship thudded down on its landing legs. The recoil threw him into the air, and he came down again flat on his back. As he lay there on the cold steel deck, gritting his teeth and groaning at the pain, he could still find a bright side: at least this time he didn't have a giant robot trying to choke him.

The engines cut out, and in the ensuing quiet the Navcom's voice came through the console speakers loud and clear.

'Landing successful,' said the computer calmly. 'Local time is six pm.'

Hal blinked stars from his eyes and struggled to his feet. 'Good to see the old girl can still make a decent landing. They don't build them like this any more, you know.'

'They never built them like this,' said Clunk with a quick glance around the flight deck. 'It takes years of misuse to get a ship into this condition.'

'Nice job with the controls, by the way.'

'You're welcome.'

'Now, we'd better find this Regan character and get the cargo aboard.'

'Regan?' Clunk shook his head. 'You mean Redge.'

'Jerling told me Regan.'

'It doesn't matter what you may have heard. The contact's name is Redge Muller.'

'You seem pretty sure of yourself.'

'I looked up Incubots in your database.'

'Who said you could mess with my ship?'

Clunk looked uncomfortable. 'I was curious.'

'You keep that probe away from my Navcom.' Hal strode to the airlock and unsealed it. The inner door slid open with a thump, and there was a hiss as the pressure equalised. 'It's a bit dark out there,' he said, peering through the yellowed porthole.

'Shall I go out first? I can use my infra-red vision and relay a feed to the main screen.'

Hal looked at him suspiciously. 'More of that interfacing lark?'

'No, I'll transmit the data using short-range comms.'

Hal backed out of the airlock then stopped as a thought occurred to him. 'I thought it was broken?'

'Must have been a loose connection.' Clunk pushed past and entered the airlock. The outer door grated open, admitting a gust of cold wind, and the robot stepped onto the platform. 'Are you receiving?' called Clunk.

Hal thumped the console, and an indistinct image appeared on the viewscreen. 'I am now. Go ahead.'

The robot clumped down the metal ramp, and the image from his chest mounted camera rolled and wobbled on the main screen. When the robot reached the bottom he panned the camera to show a green shape moving towards him.

Hal squinted at it, trying to decide whether it was a human being wearing size eighty-six boots, or a four-legged cactus. 'Navcom, can you tidy the picture up a bit?'

'Negative. The signal is being jammed by powerful electro-magnetic signal.'

'Is someone using a jamming ray?'

'No, it's interference from our generators.'

Hal snorted. On the screen the pale green shape raised one of its indistinct limbs, holding out an even more indistinct blob. 'Careful,' muttered Hal. 'That thing could be armed.'

There was a yelp of pain and the fuzzy blob was yanked away.

'What happened? What did it do to you?'

'I have made contact, Mr Spacejock. It's safe for you to come out.'

Hal walked through the airlock and eyed the figures at the foot of the passenger ramp. The end had sunk into the soft, broken earth of a freshly ploughed field, and beams from the ship's landing lights bathed the scene with a stark, white glare. There was a light mist in the air, concentrated around a copse of trees that echoed with the chirp of nocturnal insects. Nearby, a chain-link fence was topped with coils of rusty wire and festooned with faded signs.

We got the parts you need!
Cheapest on Seraph!
Incubots: We strip 'em and ship 'em!

There was a double gate, which was closed, but a small access door in the corner stood open. Hal made his way down the ramp, his boots thudding on the metal grille. Shaken free by the impact, drops of condensation fell through the light to the ground below like a shower of falling stars. At the bottom, Clunk was talking to a tall, rangy man in a battered, wide-brimmed hat and knee-length coat. The man's face was twisted with pain, and he was massaging his right hand. 'You took your time,' he said, squinting into the light.

'Nice to meet you too.' Stepping off the ramp, Hal almost lost his balance as his feet sank into the earth. He straightened up and held his hand out. 'Hal Spacejock.'

'I'm not shaking that. Your bloody robot just crushed my fingers.'

'He's not mine. I'm just giving him a lift.' Hal gestured towards the fence. 'Clear something up for me. Are you Redge or Regan Muller?'

'Neither. The name's Bevan.'

'We're at the right place, though? Incubots?'

'Correct.'

Hal looked around. 'So where's the cargo?'

'Not so fast, sunshine. I got to see your clearance first.'

'Pardon?'

'Clearance.' Bevan held his hand up, finger and thumb slightly apart. 'It's a data chip, about so big.'

'Jerling didn't say anything about clearance.' Hal looked at Clunk. 'Do you know anything about this?'

'I'm not familiar with the practice.'

'There's always a chip for these jobs,' said Bevan. 'You'll just have to fetch it.'

'Now look here, if you think I'm going all the way back to Forg for a –'

Bevan started to laugh. 'Always fools the new boys,' he said, wiping a tear from his eye. 'Gotta laugh, don't you?' Still chuckling to himself he shoved two grubby fingers in his mouth and blew an ear-splitting whistle. There was a clatter of chains and the gates swung open to reveal a large tractor. The wide balloon tyres sank into the soft earth as it powered forwards, dragging a line of covered trailers.

Hal eyed the lengthy train in concern. 'How much stuff is there?'

'Everything we could lay our hands on,' said Bevan. 'Jerling's desperate.'

As the tractor ground its way across the field, Clunk tugged Bevan's sleeve. 'Excuse me.'

Bevan looked him up and down. 'Yeah?'

'I'm supposed to meet Redge Muller.'

'You'll have a job. He died five years ago.'

Clunk looked shocked. 'Died?'

'Yeah. His son Regan took over.'

Hal shot Clunk a triumphant glance. 'Told you it was Regan.'

'But the *Black Gull's* database –'

'You're the one telling me it was outdated.'

'But I didn't know ... I didn't realise ... '

Clunk lapsed into silence as the tractor came slipping and sliding towards them.

'How much does this cargo weigh?' asked Hal.

'Heaps.' Bevan was still looking at Clunk. 'Are you one of Jerling's robots?'

Clunk frowned. 'I work for Mr Jerling, yes.'

'Sent you here, did he?'

Clunk nodded. 'His staff asked me to present myself at your premises. I have several parts which no longer work properly.'

'What a surprise,' muttered Bevan. 'All right, go see Regan in the yard. He's in the office.'

'Are you off, then?' called Hal, as Clunk turned to leave.

'I'll be back.'

Bevan watched the robot picking his way across the muddy field. 'The old ones are the worst,' he growled, once Clunk was safely out of earshot. 'They get ideas, see?' He spat on the ground. 'Think they're smarter than we are.'

'What a surprise,' remarked Hal.

The tractor drew up to the *Black Gull's* cargo doors and a squat grey robot leapt down from the cab. A pair of rough-looking men followed, tucking grubby T-shirts into the waistbands of their jeans. While they stood by watching, the robot moved to the nearest trailer. It opened a small flap and pressed a button, and the hard plastic covers lifted and folded up one after another. There was a full load of rough wooden crates, each plastered with the same red label: 'WARNING! FRAGILE!'

Hal eyed the stacks in concern. 'That's a lot of cargo.'

'Two more loads yet.'

Hal stared. 'You're kidding!'

'Yeah.' Bevan gestured at the men, who ambled to the side of the trailer and laid hands on one of the boxes. They got it down with much huffing and puffing and cursing, then argued over who was going to go backwards. Meanwhile, the robot took a crate and cruised past them, moving effortlessly despite the heavy load.

'Be handy if you opened the hold,' remarked Bevan.

'On my way.' Hal crossed to the nearest landing leg and flipped open a small panel. He pressed a button and the rear doors opened, allowing a large section of floor to extend from the back of the ship. It slid out, grating and groaning, until it

79

was suspended above the robot, which started to back away. Hal stabbed another button and the ramp lifted about three inches. Then, with a loud hiss, the heavy slab of metal dropped towards the ground.

'Watch it!' shouted Bevan.

The robot dropped its crate and threw itself flat on the ground, disappearing completely as the ramp thudded down.

'Lift the bloody ramp!' shouted Bevan, breaking into a run.

Hal peered around the landing leg. 'What?'

'Get it up, man!'

Hal operated the controls and the ramp broke free, rising into the air in fits and starts. The robot was lying face down in the mud underneath, while alongside it the crate was half-buried in the soft earth. 'Looks fine,' said Hal. 'Go on, haul it out.'

Bevan eyed the ramp. 'You sure that thing's gonna stay up?'

'Not really.'

Bevan darted underneath the quivering slab of metal and rocked the crate from side to side, trying to loosen it. Meanwhile, the robot got to its knees and shook its head, scattering drops of mud.

'Look out!' shouted Hal.

Bevan dived clear of the ramp, landing flat on his face in the mud. The robot sprinted over the top of him, one foot landing on the back of Bevan's head and pressing the human's face down into the soft earth.

Above them both, the ramp was still horizontal.

Bevan sat up, spitting mud. He looked up fearfully, but when he saw the ramp suspended in mid-air he gave Hal a very muddy scowl. 'What the hell are you playing at?'

'Sorry about that,' said Hal. 'I thought one of your guys was going to trip over.'

Bevan staggered to his feet, scraping handfuls of mud from his coat. 'If I thought you did that on purpose –'

'I didn't, I swear!' Hal withdrew behind the landing leg before his face gave him away. 'You gotta laugh, though.'

Somewhere to his left, the grey robot snorted.

Bevan gave Hal a long hard stare, then turned on his heel and yelled at his team. While they were getting organised Hal lowered the cargo ramp, and as soon as the lip touched down the grey robot gathered its crate and strolled up the incline to the hold. There was a thud as it placed the crate inside, and it reappeared empty-handed and headed towards the trailer for its next load. Meanwhile, the two men staggered towards the ship with their crate, still arguing over who was supposed be going backwards.

Hal was about to offer advice when he heard a low hum on the horizon. He scanned the skyline until he spotted a flashing red light in the distance. 'What's that?'

'Patrol,' said Bevan, still wiping his face with his sleeve. 'They'll probably shoot you down when you leave.'

The light vanished, and although Hal watched the spot for a while it didn't come back. He shrugged and turned to watch the loading. The two men were just entering the hold with their crate, and Hal suddenly remembered he'd left the inner door open. The last thing he wanted was those two poking around in his ship, maybe pocketing valuables or souveniring spare parts. 'I'm going to get some grub,' he told Bevan. 'Yell if you need a towel or anything.'

Clunk approached the Incubots yard in high spirits. For the first time in years he was oblivious to the groaning and grating from his knees and elbows, and almost unaware of the stiffness in his neck. A few days from now his aches and pains would be gone for good!

He passed between the tall gates, strode into the yard and stopped dead. This was a robot factory? He'd expected white-painted laboratories, clean rooms, parts stores and the gentle hum of high-tech equipment. Instead, there were two decrepit buildings, a couple of tin sheds and piles of muddy junk strewn around a barren, oil-stained yard.

Clunk eyed the nearest building. It was true that Mr Jerling ran his corporation from an old shed, but he would be hard pressed to run a chook raffle from this particular edifice. For a start, there was no roof. Correction - there was, but the large, rusty panels and twisted beams were currently decorating the floor. At least, Clunk assumed there was a floor underneath, because anything not covered by bits of roof was knee-deep in litter.

The second building was an improvement - it had a roof. Less than half the windows were broken, and the presence of a front door was promising. 'Office', said the sign, so that's where Clunk went.

He pushed through the rickety door and found himself in a small cubby-hole. There was a human male sitting at a buckled desk, his feet up and a sandwich half-raised to his mouth. As Clunk entered the room, he lowered the sandwich. 'What do you want?'

'I'm looking for Regan Muller.'

'You found him. Spill it.'

'Mr Jerling sent me.'

'Ah.' Regan pulled open a drawer and took out a dog-eared

ledger and a pencil stub. He turned to the middle of the book and prepared to write. 'Age?'

'A little over thirty.'

'Much over?'

'Six or seven years,' admitted the robot.

'Could have fooled me.' Regan wrote in the book. 'Any joints worn?'

Clunk touched his elbow. 'I sometimes have trouble with this one. I requested a replacement last year, but they couldn't get the parts.'

'All the others okay? Knees? Hips?'

'Fine, thank you.'

'Flaky memory?'

'I've marked one bank as suspect because it returns spurious results from time to time, particularly during standby mode. The other three are mixed brands.'

Regan grimaced as he wrote. 'Worth more in matched pairs.'

'I dare say they are.'

'How's your brain?'

'Excellent,' said Clunk shortly. 'And yours?'

Regan made a final note in his ledger, closed the book and put it back in the drawer. 'Ok, you can go. Stick around the yard, keep dry if it rains.'

'When will you make a start? On me, I mean.'

Regan shrugged. 'I've got another ship due on Friday. Your parts will be on that one.'

'Thank you. I'm sure Mr Jerling will be pleased with your prompt service.'

'He always is.'

Clunk left the office and strolled to the fence to check on the *Black Gull*. Loading was still in progress, and judging by the remaining crates he had plenty of time to look around before saying goodbye to Mr Spacejock. Leaving the fence, he began to explore the rest of the yard. There was a run-down truck in one of the tin sheds, while the other held an assortment of cutting tools: hand-held devices with strong, gaping jaws.

Having inspected the buildings, Clunk turned his attention to the piles of junk. There were several of them, large heaps of discarded robot parts - arms and legs, body shells, even a few heads, all weathered and streaked with mud. He frowned. Why did the factory throw their rejects out here instead of melting them down? It seemed like a tremendous waste of alloy.

Curious, he approached the biggest heap. A flash of white caught his eye, a distinctive arm with a clumsy ball joint and a three-fingered hand. Clunk stopped. Why was Incubots making parts for an ancient model like that? The only LFE-15 he'd ever met was the elderly robot who used to push the snack trolley around Jerling's offices, back on Forg. Alfie, that was his name. He'd gone to a local family a few months earlier, given the dream job of looking after a frail old human. Clunk smiled as he remembered Alfie's happy face, remembered his inner glow as the faithful old robot had been rewarded for years of service. People grumbled about Mr Jerling's business practices, but he certainly knew how to look after his staff.

A frown appeared on Clunk's face as he looked down at the arm. If it was a miscast, they wouldn't waste time fitting joints. So why did this one have a hand? Bending down, he gripped the clawed fingers and pulled gently. There was a clatter as the junk pile shifted, but the arm was stuck firm. After a quick look to see whether anyone was watching, Clunk braced himself and heaved.

The pile broke open and a robot's head burst out, the eyes blank and lifeless in the dented white face. The shoulder was next, still attached to the arm Clunk was pulling, and as he stepped back the rest of the buried robot came free of the junk pile and toppled towards him. It thudded face down into the muddy ground and Clunk stared in horror at the hollowed-out skull and battered shoulders. Then he saw the hand-written tag around the robot's twisted, muddy neck: Alfie.

11

'I'm sorry Mr Hinchfig, Mike is busy right now. He can't see anyone without an appointment.'

'Listen you –' With difficulty, Farrell bit off an angry retort. He took a deep breath and forced a smile. 'Have you been in this position long?'

'Three years,' said the secretary coolly. 'I was promoted by your brother. If you have an issue with my work you can raise it with him.'

Farrell tried another tack. 'You know the robots division is in trouble, right?'

'Is it really?' The secretary's tone indicated that if it was, it was probably Farrell's fault.

'They can't get any parts, so they can't build any new robots. Our flagship stores are selling second-hand models.'

'How is that relevant to this department?'

'Staff cutbacks.' Farrell leaned closer. 'I've seen the figures. If Robots goes under my brother will lay off two-thirds of the company.'

'Are you threatening me, Mr Hinchfig?'

'It's Mike you should be worried about. When the crunch comes, high-priced computer programmers will be the first to go. They're a luxury.'

'A luxury? Mike's work benefits this company enormously! Why, the news reports he produces–'

'Tell that to the accountants.'

'How would your seeing Mike help with any of this?'

'There's something he can do which could save the robot department. And all those jobs.'

'All I need is Mr Hinchfig's authority.'

'You just got it.'

'Mike only takes orders from Gordon. Why don't you ask your brother to authorise this little job of yours? If it's as vital as you say he'll be more than happy to assign Mike to it. Otherwise you're out of luck.'

At that moment the office door opened and a young man with thinning blonde hair looked in on them. 'Could you please keep your voices down? I'm working on a complex algorithm here.'

'Mike!' Farrell hurried forward and grabbed the young man's hand, pumping it vigorously. Without stopping, he led Mike back through the door and closed it firmly, cutting off the secretary's protests. 'Listen, Gordon sent me down with something. It won't take a moment.'

'Farrell Hinchfig, isn't it?' Mike gestured vaguely around the office. 'I'm working on something right now. Deadlines, you know. Always too close for comfort.'

Farrell glanced around the room. Mike's inner sanctum was crammed with equipment, festooned with haphazard runs of coloured cable and illuminated by the glow of a dozen flickering screens. Half the displays showed human faces, their features changing smoothly from young to old, plain to beautiful and morphing through a wide range of skin tones. The result was a bewildering array of unique characters, a fast-rewind through everyone Farrell had never met.

Seeing his interest, Mike explained. 'It can generate ten thousand individuals in under five minutes, each of them fully rendered in a range of poses.'

'The fake crowds, right?'

Mike nodded. 'We can't reuse anyone in case a sharp-eyed viewer exposed us.'

'They're very lifelike.'

'Every detail is modelled.'

Farrell glanced at him. 'Everything?'

Mike reddened. 'They have to be physically accurate or their clothes wouldn't hang properly.'

'All right, skip the biology lesson.' Farrell crossed his arms. 'Look, I need you to knock up one of those things for me. A one-off.'

Mike gestured at a humming grey box. 'Take your pick, I've got several thousand simuloids in there.'

'I don't want a random simu-thingy. This is a custom job. I need someone copied.'

'That's not easy. You have to scan the subject to get their contours, translate the data to the modeller, apply elasticity to every muscle . . . ' Mike shook his head. 'You're talking eight hours minimum, and I'm already two days behind schedule.'

'This has clearance from the highest level.'

'Gordon?'

'I spoke to my brother earlier.'

'Well, if he said it was okay . . . ' Mike looked doubtful. 'He was very keen to get the next series of news reports ready.'

'He was even more keen to get this job out the way.' Farrell frowned. 'Wait a minute - did you say you have to scan the subject?'

'It's the only way to get an accurate model. I use three laser pickups to map their body from head to toe.'

'No chance.'

'I can obtain a reasonable image from a facial cast. The body can be guessed at, and with the right sort of clothes you can mask anything.'

Farrell tried to imagine a situation where he could get a cast of Jerling's face. Pretend to be a lifelong fan? 'Mr Jerling, I'm so thrilled to meet you. Could you sign this autograph book, and by the way would you mind sticking your face into this bowl of wet plaster?' He shook his head. 'I don't have time for that. Can't you use a recording?'

'I could, provided it showed the front and both profiles.'

Farrell pulled the data chip from his pocket. 'I've got a taped speech.'

Mike took the tile. 'Walter Jerling?' he said in surprise, as he noticed the scribbled label.

'Yeah, but you can forget the name when we're done.'

'You know it's illegal to impersonate someone?'

'It's just a bit of fun. I want to surprise some friends of mine.'

'You said Gordon approved this.'

'They're his friends too.'

'All right, but you'll have to give me a couple of days. It's time-consuming work and I have things to finish off first.'

Farrell shook his head. 'I need it in three hours.'

'Three hours! The rendering alone –'

'Can't you just do the head and shoulders? I don't need all those poses you were talking about. He'll only be moving his mouth.'

'And blinking. And smiling.'

'You obviously don't know Jerling,' muttered Farrell. He remembered something. 'Oh yeah, and he smokes big fat cigars all the time.'

'Smoke doesn't work properly. And you'd have to do his hands as well, because they'd be visible whenever he handled the cigar.'

'Okay, no smoke. Just face and voice.'

'Voice?'

'Of course. I want to speak into a microphone and have him repeat the words.'

'But –'

'It's all in the recording.' Farrell clapped Mike on the shoulder. 'Come on, you're supposed to be the best. Just the other day Gordon was defending you, saying how you'd saved the company more than once.'

'He was?'

'Sure. That new guy in the computer department was mouthing off, saying he could hire half a dozen youngsters, split your equipment between them and save a very expensive wage.'

Mike's lips tightened. 'Is that right?'

'Yeah. Hey, there's an idea ... if you make this Jerling simuloid I could use it to offer this new guy a job at double wages. He might hand Gordon his notice.'

'You'd do that for me?'

'We have to stick together, right?'

Mike nodded. 'You'll have this in three hours, even if I have to slave every computer in the company to the task.'

Hal crossed the *Black Gull's* flight deck to the access tube, grabbed the exposed part of the ladder and climbed down to the lower deck. Avoiding the loose rung, he stepped onto the bare metal decking and squinted as a powerful overhead light came on. 'Turn it down Navcom.'

The light dimmed, and Hal gazed along the cramped passageway to the cargo hold's inner door. He could hear the workmen in the hold: boots clumping on the hollow floor, curses as they manoeuvred a heavy crate into position, howls of pain as one of them trapped his fingers. And over these noises he could hear the even, mechanical tread of the robot as it marched in and out of the hold with crate after crate.

Hal turned away, shaking his head. Labour laws or not, it was only a matter of time before humans were completely phased out. Robots were too damned efficient.

He squeezed between the ladder and the wall and entered the cramped space behind. There were two doors, one marked 'Toilet' and the other 'Kitchen'. For a moment, Hal wondered at the wisdom of spaceship designers who could make the kitchen half the size of the toilet. Surely the preparation of food deserved twice the space of its eventual disposal?

'Probably left it to a bunch of robots,' he muttered, pushing open the nearest door. He flipped the miniature table down and yanked open the freezer. A shower of ice scattered on the worn floor covering, and Hal knocked some more down as he rummaged amongst the jumble of food containers inside. 'What the hell is this?' he said, taking a large round ball from the freezer. He examined the label, then stared up at the Navcom's camera in disbelief. 'Christmas pudding?'

'According to my records that batch of food was purchased on Xankor. You were offered a special deal.'

'Navcom, if I defrost one of these I'll be eating it for days. Anyway, it's not food.'

'Strictly speaking, it conforms to my definition of comestible matter.'

'You should open a hamburger joint.' Hal shook the heavy mass at the camera. 'It might be food, but it's not *food*. Understand?'

'Negative.'

'Food is meat, bread, vegetables.' Hal looked wistful. 'Pie and chips. Steak and chips. Anything and chips!' He tossed the pudding back into the freezer and took out a square pot. 'I'm not eating that stuff again,' he muttered. The next three pots also went back in as fast as they came out. One pot remained.

Hal took it out and studied the damp label, which showed a pile of steaming meatballs on a bed of brown rice, running with rich, brown gravy. 'I don't remember having these before.'

'It's food,' said the Navcom.

'Is that supposed to be encouraging?' Hal shut the freezer and took the pot over to the heater. The lid creaked open, revealing a dark circular hole whose sides and brim were liberally encrusted with the baked-on remains of past meals. Hal pressed the pot into the heater and closed the lid, counting to ten as it warmed under his hands.

He pulled the pot out and put it on the table quickly, before it burnt his fingers. He peeled back the lid and a cloud of steam rose from the pot, temporarily obscuring the contents. Then it cleared, revealing a thin, greasy soup.

Hal stirred the mixture with a disposable fork, and a couple of small brown lumps bobbed to the surface. 'When I'm filthy rich, I'm going to set aside half my fortune to sue these bastards for false advertising.'

'You can't,' said the Navcom. 'You waived your rights when you opened the package. It's part of the end user agreement.'

'What end user agreement?'

'The one inside the lid.'

Hal prodded one of the brown lumps with his fork. 'Are these really meatballs?'

'Not on your budget,' said the computer.

Mentally holding his nose, Hal forked one of the lumps into his mouth and began to chew. And chew. 'Tasty,' he said, after he finally managed to swallow the thing. 'Navcom, how much do decent stores cost?'

'More than you can afford.'

'Figures.' Hal's stomach rumbled. 'I can't live on this stuff, you know.'

'It's edible.'

'No it isn't.' Hal pushed the pot away and dropped the fork on the table. 'When Jerling comes through with the money, I'm spending half on new food.'

'What about Mr Makalukar? He's sending Brutus to collect the entire payment.'

'He thinks he is.' Hal grinned. 'I didn't tell him how much Jerling was paying, did I?'

*

'There's been a terrible mistake.'

Regan looked up from his screen. 'What do you mean?'

'I found this in the yard.' Gently, Clunk laid Alfie's battered arm on the desk. 'I knew this robot. He used to work for Jerling! Somehow, your people have ... well, they've wrecked him!'

'Of course we wrecked him. We strip the useful bits and throw the rest.'

'They sent him here for a refit and retraining, not to be ripped apart!' Clunk leaned across the desk. 'I was at Alfie's retirement party. He was going to a human family as a carer!'

Regan glanced at the arm. 'Obviously not.'

'You're going to be in real trouble when Jerling finds out.'

'Why?'

'His valuable robots are being thrown away!'

'Valuable robots?' Regan shook his head. 'I don't know what they've been feeding you, but we don't do repairs and we don't do retraining. This is a junk yard.'

'You're a factory!' shouted Clunk. 'New robots. Repairs. Spare parts!'

'My old man ran a factory. It went broke.' Regan pointed at a blue and yellow 'Incubots Junkyard' sign fixed to the wall. 'I run a junkyard, see?'

Clunk's eyes widened. 'Jerling knows this?'

'He's my best customer.'

'You mean ...' Clunk turned to stare through the grimy window. Through the fence, he could just see the crates being loaded into the *Black Gull*. 'The shipment ... they're all pieces of old robots?'

Regan nodded. 'Strip 'em and ship 'em. It's the company motto.'

A determined look appeared on Clunk's face. 'I'm going to speak to him as soon as you've fixed me.'

'Fixed you?'

'My repairs! Jerling sent me here for ...' Clunk's gaze fell on the muddy white arm. 'Oh.'

'All machines wear out,' said Regan. 'I realise it's a shock, but at least your parts will keep other robots working.'

Clunk's shoulders slumped. 'Can I say goodbye to Mr Spacejock?'

'The pilot?'

'If you let me, I won't make a fuss. Later, I mean.'

'All right. But no running away.'

'I won't run from this place. You have my word.'

◆

Loading was finished and Bevan's tractor was hauling the empty trailers back into the yard. Hal was near the starboard landing leg, finger poised over the control panel. One of the buttons closed the rear doors, but for the life of him he couldn't remember which.

A shadow fell across the panel. 'Middle button, second row.'

'Thanks Clunk.' As the doors began to close, Hal glanced at the robot. 'Everything okay?'

'Fine,' said Clunk flatly.

'You seem a bit down. Are the digs all right?'

'Digs?'

Hal gestured towards the fence. 'The facilities.'

'Oh, those.' Clunk sighed. 'Yes, they're fine.'

'So what's with the funeral act? A few days here and you'll be back on a spaceship in no time.'

'That's true. Several spaceships, I expect.'

'Hey, we could meet up somewhere!'

Clunk brightened. 'Do you mean that? You'd really like to?'

'Sure thing! Listen, you saved my ship back there, and the least I can do is buy you a drink. Well, an oil change or something.'

'That's very kind of you, Mr Spacejock. I'll cherish your memory f-for as long as I'm able.'

95

Hal took the robot's hand and shook it firmly. 'Take care, buddy.'

Clunk opened his mouth to reply, then turned and hurried away. Hal watched the robot limp towards the gates, saw him vanish through the access door, and saw the door close firmly behind him.

Smiling to himself, he closed the panel and wiped his hands on his flightsuit. 'Time to get this show on the road,' he said, heading up the boarding ramp. At the top, he stopped for a final look at the Incubots yard. It was mostly in shadow, although here and there light glinted from discarded robot parts and pools of oily water. There was no sign of Clunk.

Hal watched the yard in silence for a minute or two, then turned and entered the flight deck. 'Close the airlock, retract the ramp and start the engines. Let's get out of here.' He sat in the pilot's chair and watched the console flicker into life, lighting up row by row as the ship's systems came online. There was a whirr as the main drives turned over, and a low rumble as they burst into life. A hiss of compressed air followed by the whine of hydraulic pumps as the passenger ramp retracted. There was a solid thump as the airlock doors closed.

'Are you quite finished?' demanded Hal.

'Instructions parsed and complied with.'

'Okay, increase thrust.'

The rumble built to a roar and the console started to rattle. 'Ready for take-off.'

'Let's go,' said Hal. The console shuddered beneath his feet, and his teeth rattled as the engines howled. The ship rose at the back, tipping him towards the console, and the deck flexed visibly as the landing legs dragged along the muddy field. There was a two-tone warble from the console and a red light started to flash. 'What's happening?' shouted Hal, gripping the arms of the pilot's chair.

'Insufficient power. Unable to lift off.'

'Maximum thrust!'

'Complying.' The engines shrieked, filling the air with dust.

'Are we off?' shouted Hal, as the bumping ceased.

'Altitude one metre. We're heading for the Incubots yard.'

Hal grabbed the silver knob on the console and twisted it left and right. 'Overthingy a hundred and fifty per cent! Two hundred per cent! Full emergency thrust!'

'Maximum thrust already enabled,' said the Navcom calmly. 'Please assume the emergency position and brace for impact.'

12

Clunk hooked his fingers through the chain-link fence and pressed his face to the rusty wire. The *Black Gull* was a patch of dark grey against the dawn sky, the airlock a shadowy hole in the surrounding gloom. He tried his night vision, but it only resulted in a patch of solid green against a dark green sky - not much of an improvement.

There was a rumble, and Clunk shielded his eyes as the ship's landing lights came on. Smoke billowed from the jets as the engines spooled up, turning to steam as the fiery exhaust tore into the soft, damp earth. 'Ready for lift-off,' he murmured, as twisting pillars of flame shot from the ship's landing jets. He smiled to himself. Mr Spacejock had found the right button.

Clunk felt for the gate. The ship was now hidden by a pulsing cloud of steam, lit from within by flashing red and green lights. The noise increased to a deep, throbbing roar, and then a thunderclap rolled across the field as the main jets fired. Clunk squinted through the glare, intent on capturing every second. 'Go on, up with you,' he muttered as the ship rocked on its landing legs, struggling to break the planet's grip. A frown creased his forehead. 'Go on,' he muttered. 'Use the auxiliary thrusters!'

He smiled as the *Black Gull* rose a metre or two into

the air, but his mouth turned down when the ship drifted sideways, jets fighting to keep it clear of the ground. 'Use the secondaries,' he shouted, rattling the fence in frustration. The ship tilted towards him, and began to drift towards the scrap yard.

Clunk watched the *Gull* bearing down on him, white-hot fire from her jets leaving smoking furrows in their wake. The landing legs were down, and the broad feet brushed the ground in turn, slowly rotating the huge ship until it was travelling backwards. One of the feet snagged, and the sudden bump caused the cargo doors to burst open. A wall of crates toppled out, bursting open and spilling their gleaming contents in the mud. The ship rumbled over the top, her thrusters melting the muddy pieces into slag.

Clunk suddenly realised those weren't the only parts in danger. The ship was still moving towards the yard, picking up speed, and it wasn't going to stop. The hull loomed overhead, and Clunk threw himself flat. The fence bowed inwards and collapsed on top of him, jets thundered into the ground on either side, and then the ship was past, wobbling across the yard and leaving a trail of blackened, twisted junk in its wake. Still gathering speed, it flattened the fence on the far side and crashed through the trees beyond, tearing them down and leaving a trail of splintered, smoking wood before vanishing over the hill.

Clunk leapt up, ready to chase after it, then remembered his promise to Regan: No running.

◆

Hal sat up in the darkness, coughing and rubbing his head.

The flight deck was tilted at a crazy angle, the air was filled with dust and the console was dead.

'Navcom?'

There was no answer.

Hal stood, using the pilot's chair for support. He reached for the console and ran his hands over the buttons and indicator lamps until he felt a small toggle switch. An emergency light came on above the main viewscreen, painting the flight deck ghostly blue, and the airlock doors rumbled open. There was a sound of crackling flames, and a damp smoky smell.

Hal slipped and stumbled down the flight deck to the airlock, which was illuminated with a flickering red glow from outside. Peering over the edge, he saw half a dozen fires burning in the undergrowth.

POW!

Hal almost fell out of the airlock as a bright yellow package exploded from the side of the ship, bounced off a tree and crashed into the bushes below. There was a loud hiss, and when he looked down he saw a yellow life raft taking shape amongst the shredded bushes. Once it had finished inflating a wobbly stalk popped up and waved gently in the light breeze, the little red light on top flashing madly.

'What the hell is that for?' shouted Hal, his heart still racing. Several birds twittered in the trees. 'You expect me to row the bloody cargo to Forg?'

The light flashed merrily, mocking him with its cheerful blinking.

Hal sat on the edge of the platform and put his head in his hands.

◆

'*Tango Three, report!*'

Startled by the loud voice, Clunk ducked behind a bush. Stealthily, he parted the branches, and almost snapped them off as he saw the slab-like armour of a heavy tank barely ten metres away. There was a soldier in the tank, his face hidden beneath an enormous headset. As Clunk watched, the soldier activated his microphone.

'*Tango One calling Tango Three. Come in, Tango Three!*' The soldier listened for a response, then ducked his head. 'Nothing out there, sir.'

'Anything on that ship?'

'Negative.'

'Bloody computers,' shouted an angry voice. 'Just wait till I get my hands on the charlie who laid this mess on.'

'What are your orders sir?'

'We're blind, sergeant. I'm not moving until the comms are back up.'

'Are we just going to sit here?'

'No, I'm going to sit here. You're putting the kettle on.'

Clunk tuned his commset and picked up several bursts of static, but no transmissions. Jerling's program had done more damage than he expected, taking out not only the battleship's communications but also those on the ground. As it happened, it was just as well.

Backing out of the bush, he got to his feet and strode through the undergrowth, giving the tank a wide berth. Soon he was back on his original course, heading in the same direction as the *Black Gull*.

It was ten minutes before he found the ship. After locating a row of blasted, splintered trees and a steaming trail of scorched vegetation he found the *Black Gull* tilted over with her tailplane sticking into the highest branches.

Clunk approached the ship, pausing to check an inflated yellow dinghy. He reached out and pushed the flashing red light, setting it off like a metronome. As he watched it swing to and fro, a voice floated down from above.

'What the hell are you doing here?'

Clunk looked up and saw Hal sitting on the lip of the airlock, his legs dangling over the side. 'Mr Spacejock! Are you all right?'

'Of course I'm all right,' shouted Hal. 'Bit of a rough landing, that's all.'

There was a drawn-out creak and a large tree fell over, landing across the hull with a loud clang.

'I thought you were taking off, not landing.'

Hal frowned. 'And I thought you were supposed to stay in the yard.'

'I promised Regan I wouldn't run. I didn't say anything about walking very quickly.'

'Won't you get in trouble?'

'Probably.' Clunk looked down at the yellow life raft. 'Why did you deploy this?'

'I didn't.' Hal gestured upwards with his thumb. 'It shot out of the hull after I, er, landed.'

Clunk gestured at the swaying light. 'You realise this antenna is transmitting a distress signal?'

'So?'

'I just passed a tank in the woods. They're searching for you and this beacon will lead them straight to the ship.' Clunk snapped the antenna off the dinghy and crushed the flashing light in his fist. 'We should leave immediately.'

'We?'

Clunk looked up. 'You don't really believe you can get out of this mess on your own?'

The access panel near the inner door was open, revealing a row of plastic mouldings and a tangle of wire. There were hand-written labels above each moulding, with an empty socket beneath the one labelled 'Navcom'.

Clunk held the missing module up to the light, squinting at the transparent square as he tried to follow the microscopic traces.

'I thought you'd have tools for that,' said Hal.

'I do.' Clunk widened his eyes. 'These.'

'Are they good enough?'

'Not really, but they're all I have.' Clunk lowered his hand. 'I'm afraid this module is no longer operational. Tell me, where do you keep the spares?'

'You've got to be kidding. I don't even have spare food.'

'But –'

'I'm sorry, you'll just have to make do.'

'Make do?' said Clunk faintly. 'These modules are assembled by highly trained technicians and precision-matched to specific circuits. I can't make do.'

'Why don't you swap it with one of the others then?'

'That's –' Clunk looked at the labels. 'Actually, that's not a bad idea.' He ran his finger along the modules, stopping at one marked Coolant Tank Containment Field. 'This one.'

'Don't we need it?'

'It's just a backup.' Clunk pulled the module and slotted it into the empty gap. 'That should do it.'

There was a beep from the overhead speaker. 'Boot sequence

initiated. Now loading Antares Operating System version nought-point-six three alpha.'

Hal looked up. 'Navcom, can you hear me?'

'Keyboard error,' said the Navcom. 'Press any key to continue.'

'Override delta six,' said Clunk.

'Error bypassed. Do you want to suppress further errors?'

'Please.'

After several seconds, the Navcom spoke again. 'Loading complete. Ready for input.'

'I know the next bit,' said Hal. 'Start the engines and let's go.'

Clunk shook his head. 'We have to run a full diagnostic suite first.'

'Navcom, do what he said.'

'Complying. Commencing diagnostics.'

Clunk closed the access panel. 'That could take ten or fifteen minutes. In the meantime, I suggest we lighten the ship. All non-essential items must be left behind. Fixtures, fittings ...everything.'

'Hang on, this is the *Black Gull* we're talking about.'

'Mr Spacejock, if you don't deliver this cargo you won't have a ship.'

'Good point.'

'Do you have an atomic cutter on board?'

'No, but I have something almost as good.' Hal opened a locker and pulled out a pair of cylinders and a coiled rubber hose.

'What's that?' asked Clunk.

'It's an oxy torch.'

'Say again?'

'It's for cutting metal.' Hal pointed to a silver knob. 'You open the valves, adjust this bit and stand back.'

'How far back?'

'Well, I'll be in the flight deck.'

Clunk took the battered cylinders and eyed the perished hose dubiously. 'It's not dangerous, is it?'

'Oh no, safe as houses. And try not to leave any holes in the hull. I'm addicted to oxygen.'

'Right,' said Clunk, swinging the heavy cylinders onto his shoulder. 'You retreat to safety while I risk my life.'

Hal was sitting in the pilot's chair with his feet up on the console, sipping a lukewarm cup of murky brown liquid. Cryptic messages had been scrolling up the main screen for several minutes now, and the bar at the bottom was showing 99 percent.

'Diagnostics complete,' said the Navcom, as the bar ticked over to 100.

'Everything okay?' asked Hal.

'I've routed a few non-essential functions through undamaged circuits, patched several processes to avoid suspect memory banks, redesigned the –'

'Are you ready or not?'

'Yes.'

'Excellent. Get the engines started.' Hal raised the cup and was just about to sample the drink when a muffled explosion rocked the ship. He jumped, slopping the liquid down the front of his flight suit. 'What the hell –'

A red light flashed on the console. 'Explosion in the cargo bay,' said the Navcom calmly.

'Clunk!' Hal delayed his rescue dash for a few moments in case anything else blew up, then made his way to the cargo bay. He found Clunk beating out the last of the flames with his bare hands. His face and upper body were coated with a fine layer of carbonised grit, and he was surrounded by splintered timber and blackened robot parts.

'What happened?' demanded Hal.

'Where shall I begin?' Clunk flicked a lump of carbonised wood off his shoulder. 'First, there was the defective valve on one of the tanks. Then there was the perished hose; that didn't help. Next there was a chain reaction from the crates themselves.' He stirred the mess on the floor with his foot. 'Very flammable material, this. On the bright side, if we throw it all overboard we'll save a few kilos.'

'Oh no you don't,' said Hal. 'They're paying me to deliver these crates. We can't leave them behind.'

The robot gestured at the floor. 'But these parts are ruined!'

'Nonsense. They just need a bit of polish, that's all. Stick the crates back together and scoop all this stuff back in.'

'That's immoral! Mr Jerling is paying you to deliver his cargo intact!'

'And who blew it up?'

'It's not my fault there was an explosion,' said Clunk.

'A poor workman blames his tools.'

'Poor workman? If you'd been operating that equipment you'd be dead right now.'

'No I wouldn't,' said Hal. 'I don't know how to use the thing.'

'But if you had, it would have killed you.'

'No it wouldn't. I'd have used it properly.'

'It wouldn't have made any difference if a metalworker with twenty years experience had been using it, he'd still be dead,' said Clunk.

'No he wouldn't,' said Hal. 'He'd have known enough about oxy torches to stop using one just before it blew up.'

'Ah, but it wasn't the torch that exploded.' Clunk pointed to a twisted metal beam. 'It was the gas pipe in there. And I hope you enjoy sandwiches because that pipe supplied the cooker.'

'Never mind my diet, fix the crates and shovel the stuff back in.'

Clunk set to work, muttering about the inherent superiority of silicon-based humanoids.

'And we'll have less of your lip,' added Hal. As he turned to leave the Navcom's voice crackled over the intercom.

'Mr Spacejock, there are several vehicles approaching the ship.'

'What sort of vehicles?'

'I'm not sure, but they're heavily armed.'

Hal cursed. 'I'll be right up.'

— 13 —

Hal stepped off the ladder and stared at the flickering viewscreen, where several green blobs were weaving around on a dark green background. 'Not that night vision rubbish again. Show me a real picture.'

The viewscreen changed to a pin-sharp colour image, showing a line of vehicles charging across the field towards the ship. One of them, an armoured hover-car, swerved to one side and skidded to a halt in mid-air. The turret swivelled round until the gun barrel was pointing straight between Hal's eyes.

'I think I preferred the infra-red,' muttered Hal. 'How far away are they?'

'Four kilometres.'

Hal jumped as a crash echoed through the ship. 'We've been hit!'

'Negative, they've not opened fire.'

Hal flinched as another loud bang reverberated up the access tube. 'What's all the noise, then?'

'Clunk is removing items from the ship to reduce the weight.' There was a beep. 'I detect an incoming audio message.'

'Play it.'

A metallic voice crackled over the speaker. *'You have eight minutes to vacate your ship. Any attempt to take off will be prevented by force. Any attempt to attack this unit of the Seraph IV military will be met with force. This message will repeat in ninety seconds.'*

'Great,' said Hal. 'Just great. Now what do we do?'

Clunk's dirt-smeared face appeared over the lip of the access tube. 'That should do it. Let's go.'

'Go?' Hal gestured at the viewscreen. 'Think again.'

Clunk's eyes widened as he saw the vehicles. 'Range?'

'Four kilometres,' said the Navcom.

'We did that bit already,' said Hal.

'Firing range?'

'Three thousand maximum, twenty-eight hundred optimum.'

'BG vertical shift nineteen hundred, time?'

'Twenty-five seconds.'

'Would somebody mind –' began Hal.

Clunk ignored him. 'Vehicle horizontal shift one thousand metres, time?'

'Twenty-two seconds.'

'Sit down, Mr Spacejock,' ordered Clunk. 'Navcom, take off.'

'Here, what –' began Hal. The roar of the ship's main engines drowned his voice out, and he fell into the pilot's chair as the ship shuddered violently. 'What happened to the safety checks?'

Clunk looked at him. 'Take your choice, capture or flight.'

'I didn't get a choice!'

Clunk shook his head and pointed to his ears. 'Can't hear you.'

Hal looked up at the viewscreen, which showed the vehicles racing towards them with all guns blazing. 'They're going to blast us!'

'No they're not.'

'They're shooting!'

'It doesn't matter. They're out of range.' Clunk pointed at the altitude indicator, which was turning over rapidly. 'We're rising steadily, so they can't get any closer.'

'Right on!' said Hal, grinning widely. 'How did you know we could escape?'

'They could only close to firing distance by flying across the hypotenuse of the triangle formed by –'

'Very well done,' said Hal, clapping the robot on the shoulder. 'Smart work.'

'I haven't finished explaining yet.'

'I got the gist of it. By the way, how did you get the weight down?'

'Well, you were right when you said the oxy torch was almost as good as an atomic cutter. I had no trouble removing the cargo ramp.'

Hal stared at him. 'You did what?'

'Don't worry, we can come back for it later.'

'That was part of my ship!'

'Not any more,' said Clunk. 'Incidentally, I hope the outer door doesn't leak.'

Without warning, a tremendous blast threw the ship sideways, knocking Hal to the deck.

'Uh-oh,' said Clunk.

'What the hell was *that*?' demanded Hal, as he struggled to his feet.

'They have a long range anti-aircraft battery. I didn't consider that.'

Hal opened his mouth to respond, but another explosion shook the *Gull*, knocking him flat on his back again. Flashes of red and green light drew his eyes to the main screen, where he saw massed energy bolts spitting from the turret of one of the vehicles. They curved upwards, moving slowly at first but accelerating as they got closer.

'Shields, Navcom! Activate the shields!'

'Cannot comply,' said the Navcom over the roar of the engines.

'Why not?'

Clunk made a throat-clearing noise. 'You don't have any shields.'

Hal stared at him wildly. 'What?'

'Rigel class ships don't carry them.'

'Then dodge the bloody things!'

Explosions rocked the ship, which shuddered like an unbalanced washing machine. For a split second, a fine red beam joined the floor and ceiling. 'What was that?' shouted Hal, raising his voice over the new hissing sound which seemed even louder than the engines.

'Laser,' said Clunk.

'And the noise?'

'Your air supply is escaping through numerous holes in the *Black Gull's* hull.'

'Well don't just stand there! Plug them!'

Clunk opened a door in the side of his chest, took out a small metal tin and set it on the console. There was another crash and the ship jumped, knocking the tin onto the floor. The lid came off, and a small tube of glue and several rubber patches fell out.

Hal gaped at them. 'You're going to use a bicycle repair kit to plug the holes?'

'Do you have anything better? An exploding aerosol perhaps?'

Hal put his hands to his throat. 'Hurry up, I'm having trouble breathing.'

'You've got hours left,' said Clunk. He picked up the tube of glue and began to unscrew the lid.

Suddenly there was a bang down below and a freezing gust of wind tore through the flight deck. 'What the hell was that?' shouted Hal, his voice thin in the cold air.

'A much bigger hole.' Clunk looked at him. 'How long can you hold your breath?'

◆

The *Volante* was a newly commissioned ship, fresh from the Zargan dockyards. A Gamma class freighter, L-variant, she had twice the cargo capacity and three times the fuel economy of the *Black Gull*. She was a ship to turn heads, a graceful vessel that could accelerate effortlessly into orbit, cross the deepest tracts of known space and return the crew safely in time for tea. In a word, she was perfection.

Farrell Hinchfig strode into the flight deck and flopped into the comfortable pilot's chair. His eyes reflected the glow from the status lights spread out before him, and the tang of warm electronics hung in the air, mixed with the scent of burnt fuel. 'Everything ready?'

'At your command,' said the computer politely.

'Where's Terry?'

'According to my external camera, he just entered the airlock.'

The inner door swept open and a short man in blue overalls entered the flight deck. Terrance Bull was a fit-looking forty-year-old with cropped black hair and pale, bloodshot eyes. The sleeves of his overalls were rolled up, revealing muscled forearms, and there was a complicated tattoo of a dragon emblazoned on his right arm. He was dragging a pair of large suitcases, the heavy-duty kind with brushed metal panels and riveted bands. 'Sorry I'm late, boss. Customs narks gave me the once-over, didn't they?'

'Don't we pay them enough?'

'Still tried to shake me down.' Terry grinned, revealing broken teeth. 'I explained nicely, like.'

'Just remember what I said about publicity.' Farrell turned back to the console. 'Take off, please.'

'Complying,' said the computer.

Once the ship was under way, Farrell glanced at the case. 'What's that? Spare underwear?'

'It's me stuff, innit?'

'Stuff?'

'It's an important mission, right?' Terry hefted the smaller case. 'Small arms, ammo, three kinds of grenades.' He patted the other case. 'Portable laser cannon, two spare batteries.'

'What did you bring that lot for?'

'You said you wanted back-up,' said Terry defensively.

'Back-up, yes. Not a one-man invasion force.'

'You can never have too many guns.' Terry cracked his knuckles. 'So, what's the job, then?'

Farrell tilted his chair back and linked his hands behind his head. 'We're meeting one of Jerling's pilots at the Forg Orbiter. He's going to give us a cargo of robot parts.'

'What does Jerling think about that?'

'He doesn't know.'

'And the pilot?'

113

'He doesn't know either. He thinks he's landing at Jerling's factory.'

Terry looked blank. 'How's that supposed to work, then?'

'We're going to trick him and take the cargo.'

'A nice bit of thieving, eh?' Terry grinned. 'So you *will* be needing me stuff.'

Farrell sighed. 'Force will not be necessary. I'm going to use my brains instead.'

Terry looked at him doubtfully. 'If you say so.'

'Watch the main screen,' said Farrell, taking the console microphone. 'Computer, enable the simuloid.'

There was a burst of static and Walter Jerling appeared on the viewscreen. There was a frown on his face, and when he spotted Terry it deepened to a scowl. 'You won't need your weapons with me around,' boomed Jerling's voice.

Stunned, Terry turned to stare at Farrell, who was doing his best not to laugh out loud. 'That's Jerling, innit?'

'I am indeed,' said Farrell. A second later the booming voice repeated his words.

'I AM INDEED!'

'Here, give us a go,' said Terry, reaching for the microphone.

Farrell snatched it away. 'Don't be silly.'

'DON'T BE SILLY!' boomed the simuloid.

'Give anyone the creeps that would,' muttered Terry. 'So how's this going to help with the snatch then?'

Farrell replaced the microphone. 'When Jerling's pilot arrives, I'll use the simuloid and tell him to meet us at the Orbiter. He'll follow the new orders, thinking Jerling has changed his mind. We'll meet him, take the cargo and the pilot will be left holding the bag.'

'And when he finds out you've done him over?'

Farrell shrugged. 'Who cares?'

'He could come after you.'

'And do what? He's just a nobody. He can't touch me.'

Terry jabbed a thumb in his chest. 'And me? I been to jail once and I ain't going back. This character fingers me, I'll be inside before the ink's dry on me warrant.'

'You work for me. He can't touch you either.'

Terry shook his head. 'Too risky. Much better to fix this pilot properly.'

'I won't hear of it,' said Farrell. 'Everything will go to plan, and he won't realise what we've done until it's far too late.'

'And if it doesn't go to plan?'

'Are you doubting me?'

'N-no, but –'

Farrell gestured at the cases. 'Store those in the hold and come back up. I need to coach you before we meet Spacejock.'

*

Half an hour later, Clunk was repairing the last of the holes.

'Hurry it up, will you?' said Hal, rubbing his hands together. 'It's freezing.'

The robot inspected a rubber patch under the overhead light. Satisfied, he dabbed some glue on it and stuck it over a tiny hole in the deck. 'You're lucky to be alive,' he said. 'There was a lot of damage below. That fire had really taken hold of the crates.'

'You should have used the fire extinguisher,' muttered Hal. 'Oh, silly me. I forgot you wasted it all on Lamira.'

Clunk frowned at him. 'And how did that fire get started?'

'Well, you see –'

The console speaker crackled. 'Ship detected,' said the Navcom. 'Unknown vessel approaching from astern.'

'Hell, they're after us. Now what?'

Clunk leaned across the console. 'Navcom, execute program fifty-three dash four.'

'Ship ID masked.'

'Is that legal?' demanded Hal.

'We can't afford to be boarded,' said Clunk. 'You've broken so many rules they'll throw away the key.'

'I've broken rules? You're the one firing off crooked programs!'

There was an urgent buzzing sound from the console. 'That's odd,' said Clunk.

'Surprise me.'

'They're trying to reprogram our course.' Clunk pressed a small green button and the buzzing stopped. Immediately, there was a low ringing noise. Clunk pressed a yellow button and that stopped too, only to be replaced by a klaxon. Clunk silenced it by pressing another button. There was a split second of silence, and then the console emitted a cacophony of pings, clangs and buzzes as fast as Clunk could cancel them. Finally, after one last bloop, the console fell silent. Moments later Clunk became aware of a hissing noise behind him. He looked round and caught Hal doing his best to smother his laughter. 'What's so funny?'

'You should have seen yourself!' snorted Hal. 'You looked like a tap-dancing octopus.'

'I was trying to save your life!' said Clunk hotly. 'At the very least you could –'

Buzzz!

Hal stared at the console. 'Now what?'

'Incoming message,' said the Navcom.

'I thought that was a chiming sound.'

'I select a noise at random.'

'No you don't. It's always a chiming sound.'

'Unfortunately my random number generator isn't very good.'

Hal sighed. 'Just play the message, will you?'

There was a crackle from the console speaker. *'Battleship Almeria calling target drone Igor. Please unlock your flight systems as we need to upload your evasive manoeuvres program.'*

Hal waved Clunk towards the console. 'You can sort this one out.'

'What am I supposed to say?'

'Tell them to bug off and leave us alone.'

'Hello battleship,' said Clunk loudly. 'This is a cargo vessel, not a target drone.'

There was a muttered curse. *'Listen, subterfuge was last week. This week it's gunnery practice.'*

'You don't understand. This is the *Black Gull* out of ...' Clunk glanced at Hal, who shrugged. 'Out of Lamira. We're en route to Forg with a cargo of robot parts.'

'Sure, sure. Put your shields up, will you? You'll last a bit longer.'

Clunk turned to Hal. 'I think you'd better talk to them.'

Hal addressed the console. 'My name is Hal Spacejock, and I'm the owner of this vessel.'

There was a snort from the speakers. *'My car sounds more human than that.'*

'Who the hell are you?'

'Lieutenant Cycoh, of the Battleship Almeria.'

'Listen up, you prick. If you don't leave us alone I'll come over and boot your testicles over your left shoulder. Got it?'

'That's a bit more human,' said the voice grudgingly. *'But we're still going to shoot you down.'*

'This is a trading vessel, you bloody idiot! We're going to Forg!'

'*Not any more.*' There was a pause. '*Hey, I get it! You've been programmed with a survival instinct!*'

'I was born with one, you moron!'

'*Put on a show, all right? We'll give you a head start, and you dodge around a bit and make it tough.*' There was a click as the lieutenant disconnected.

Hal frowned at Clunk. 'Can you get me out of this one?'

'There is something I can try.' Clunk turned to the console. 'Execute program seventy-two dash one.'

'What does that do?'

'I just told their computers that an asteroid is on a collision course with their ship.'

'What happens when they check their scanners?'

'They won't. Standard procedure is to hyperspace first and check later.'

'Well done, Clunk. Excellent!'

A red light flashed on the console. '*This is the Battleship* Almeria. *In contravention of rule one hundred and twenty-four of the Galactic Treaty, you have attempted to subvert the operation of a naval vessel by transmitting spurious data. This offence is punishable by confiscation and destruction of your ship, and the incarceration of the commanding officer.*'

'Navcom ... ' began Clunk.

'I'll handle this,' broke in Hal. 'Navcom, give me full power.'

The engines screamed, hurling the ship forward.

'Now hyperspace!' shouted Hal.

'Please specify destination.'

'I don't care! Anywhere!'

'Unable to comply. Destination required.'

'Forg,' said Clunk hurriedly, before Hal blurted out a planet on the opposite side of the galaxy.

'Calculating hyperspace trajectory.'

'Come on, you heap of junk!' shouted Hal, pressing every button within reach. 'Hurry it up!'

'Calculations in progress.'

'I have a suggestion,' said Clunk.

'Whatever it is, do it!'

'Navcom, transmit program fifty-two.'

'Complying,' said the Navcom. 'Transfer complete.'

'That should disable them long enough to let us get away.'

'How?'

'It's a program I ran up in my spare time,' said Clunk modestly. 'It disables their fire computers by converting all their targeting data into vintage imperial measurements.'

'You're crazy! They'll never fall for that!'

The robot raised an eyebrow. 'You'd be surprised.'

There was a beep. *'This is the Battleship Almeria. In contravention of rule three hundred and sixteen of the Galactic Treaty, you have attempted to execute unauthorised code on a shipboard computer. This offence is punishable by –'*

The transmission was interrupted by a gruff male voice. *'Cunning bunch, aren't you? Here's one I made. Enjoy.'*

'Blark sning bichhh,' said the Navcom, and all the lights on the console winked out.

Clunk's face was long as he examined the dead instruments. 'Oh dear, their security is much better than I thought.'

'What have you done to my computer?'

'Let me check.' Clunk held his hands over the console, fingers splayed. He started to shake, and then his eyes jerked wide open, flickering like faulty Christmas lights. Shivering all over, he backed away from the console, warding away an unseen horror with his hands.

'Look out!' shouted Hal, as the robot approached the access tube.

Clunk stopped dead, rocking on his heels. Then his eyes blanked out and he toppled over backwards, vanishing down the access tube with a clatter of tin. There was a crunch as he landed in the lower corridor, followed by the sound of something rolling away.

'Clunk?' Hal ran over to the tube and peered down into the darkness. 'Clunk, are you all right?'

14

Hal barely touched the rungs as he shot down the ladder, dreading what he might find at the bottom. There was a crunch as he trod on Clunk's fingers, and a creak as he stepped on his ankle. Neither raised a squeak from the normally voluble robot, and when he crouched down next to the upper body he found out why: Clunk's head was missing.

He found it further along the passageway, lying on its side like a discarded fancy dress mask. Picking it up, Hal gave it a shake and stared into the lifeless eyes. 'Talk to me, Clunk. Talk to me!'

The only reply was a rattling sound.

'Clunk?' Hal turned the head over and saw a hook, a loop of cable and an electrical connector. He carried the head to the body, where he found a large elastic band and the opposite half of the connector sticking out of the robot's neck. Setting the head down, Hal took both halves of the connector and jammed them together. He snapped his fingers in front of the robot's eyes, but they remained unlit and lifeless.

Hal eased the brittle elastic band over the hook as carefully as he could, and when he let go the head snapped back into place. Repairs complete, he gently raised the robot to a sitting position and waved his hand in front of its face. 'Clunk? Can I get you some water?'

There was no reaction.

'Out like a light.' Hal stood, and there was a crash as Clunk fell backwards to the deck. Squaring his shoulders, Hal set his jaw and looked up the ladder. With Clunk disabled, the Navcom out of action and the battlecruiser recovering nearby, there was only one thing left to do.

'It can't be that hard to fly this thing,' he muttered as he climbed the ladder to the flight deck.

Sitting at the console, gazing across banks of unlabelled buttons and switches, his bravado shrivelled like a prune in a winter gale. He was just wondering how long it would be before the battlecruiser got its weapon systems back online and blasted him into space dust when there was a scraping sound behind him. He turned quickly and saw a battered face rising through the hole in the deck. 'Hey, you recovered!'

Clunk shook his head. 'I'm barely online.' He staggered to the console and leant on it heavily, a pained expression on his face. 'I sustained considerable damage falling down the access shaft.'

'Really?'

'Yes.' Clunk raised his hand. 'My fingers are bent, my ankle has been crushed and the back of my head sustained a heavy blow, denting my skull. Apart from that, everything seems to be all right.'

'Phew. Stroke of luck, eh?'

'Yes, although some of the injuries are a little puzzling. For example, there's a footprint on the back of my hand.' Clunk raised his foot. 'How strange, there's another on my ankle. Why, if I didn't know better –'

'Don't stress yourself,' said Hal hurriedly. 'You might bring up unpleasant memories if you keep going on about it.' He helped Clunk into the pilot's chair. 'So, what happened back there?'

'They sent a rogue program which attacked the Navcom. When I tried to investigate, I was attacked too. I had to shut down everything to fight it.' Clunk shivered. 'I only just contained it. It could break out and destroy me at any moment.'

'Right. So how do we fix the Navcom?'

'The damage to your computer may be permanent.'

'Never. Tough as nails, the Navcom.'

'We can only hope.' Clunk straightened up slowly, a pained expression on his face. 'At least the battlecruiser is still out of action.'

'How do you know?'

'We're still alive,' said Clunk dryly. He looked at a couple of displays. 'Why aren't we moving?'

Hal hesitated. 'I was considering my options.'

'You have no idea how to fly this ship, do you?'

'I can fly the *Gull* blindfold,' declared Hal. 'But now you're sitting there ... '

'No no, it's your ship,' said Clunk, getting to his feet.

'I, er –'

Clunk waved Hal towards the chair. 'I insist.'

Realising he was trapped, Hal settled into the seat and studied the console. 'What are all those red lights for?'

'System failures.'

'Wow. Things must be really bad.'

Clunk looked at him. 'They were flashing when I first joined the ship.'

'So I just ignore them, right?'

Clunk nodded.

'I suppose I ought to set the course.'

'We're already programmed direct to the Forg system. All you have to do is activate the hyperspace motors and perform the jump.'

'Fine. That's easy.' Hal looked over the console. 'Really simple.'

'First you have to start the main drives.'

Hal tapped a couple of dials with his finger, then moved his hand to a cluster of buttons and ran through eeny meeny under his breath.

'Big red button, second from the left,' said Clunk.

Hal reached out and pressed it. Nothing happened.

'You have to ignite the boosters before you start the main drives.'

The red button was surrounded by four others of various colours. Hal reached out and pressed the yellow one.

'Green,' said Clunk in the sudden darkness.

The lights came back on, and Hal pressed the green button. There was a whine from the back of the ship.

Clunk shook his head. 'You have to disengage the compressor before you can start the motors.'

'You're really enjoying this, aren't you?' said Hal through clenched teeth. 'Okay, you made your point. You're smart and I'm just a dumb monkey.'

'Oh no, Mr Spacejock,' said Clunk. 'Monkeys are quite intelligent.'

Hal crossed his arms. 'Maybe I'll just sit here until that ship opens fire.'

'Why don't we work together?' suggested Clunk. 'I'll list the buttons in order and you press them. But whatever you do, don't touch anything unless you clear it with me first.'

'To think I always wanted to fly my own ship.'

'Press the buttons in this order,' said Clunk. 'White, blue, green, red.'

'White, blue, green, red.' Hal pressed each button as he repeated the colours. There was a series of beeps, and a light flashed.

'Good,' said Clunk. 'Orange, mauve, yellow, purple.'

'Orange, mauve, yellow, purple.' There was a low rumble and the flight deck began to vibrate. 'Hey, this is easy!'

'Red, green, blue, white, purple, purple, pink, green, red.' Clunk, pointed across the console. 'Flip those switches, then orange again.'

'Red, green, blue, white ... er, what?'

'Purple, purple, pink, green, red. Faster, Mr Spacejock. The sequence has to be completed in less than fifteen seconds.'

'Purple, purple, pink, green, red,' said Hal, his hands flying across the console as he pressed the buttons.

'Flip those switches, then press the orange one,' said Clunk, pointing.

Hal flipped the switches and pressed the orange button. There was a single beep.

'Right,' said Clunk. 'Orange, orange, orange, pink, green, red, orange, yellow, green, blue, indigo, violet.'

'Orange, orange, orange, pink, green, red, orange ... ' Hal stopped as Clunk bent double and made a peculiar spluttering noise. 'What's wrong? What's happening?'

Clunk leaned back, opened his mouth and howled.

Hal leapt up, his hair standing on end. 'Wh-what's up? Clunk, is it the virus? Are you okay?'

'Hee, hee, heeeee,' giggled Clunk. He bent double, banging his forehead on the console.

Hal stared at him. 'You metal-clad box of tricks! You were winding me up!'

Clunk looked at him for a moment, then spluttered.

'What the bloody hell were you playing at?' Hal waved at the console. 'I could have killed myself pushing all those buttons!'

'N-not connected,' gasped Clunk.

'WHAT?'

'Buttons not connected.'

Hal stared at the console. 'None of them?'

'Nothing but the light switch.'

'You're lying! They did things when I pressed them!'

Clunk shook his head. 'I'm controlling the ship with short-range infra-red.'

Hal glared at him. 'You picked a strange time to play a practical joke. Have you forgotten the damn battlecruiser?'

'I'm sorry, Mr Spacejock, but I couldn't help myself. It's not every day I get to play a trick on a human.'

'You'll go too far, one day. Someone'll space you.'

'Or stomp on my fingers,' said Clunk dryly. He gestured at the console. 'We're too close to the planet to hyperspace anyway.'

Without warning, the lights flickered off.

'What was that?' demanded Hal in the sudden darkness.

'The battlecruiser must have got their fire computer working again,' said Clunk. 'We must be at the extreme range of their weapons.'

'Where are they?'

A holochart appeared above the console, showing a cluster of stars.

Hal blinked. 'How did you do that?'

'It's an add-on for your Navcom. I took the liberty of cracking the protection and enabling it.'

'Neat,' said Hal. 'Can you alter the chess program while you're at it?'

'I really haven't got time for - oh, all right. What level do you want?'

'Easy.'

'It's already set to that.'

'Really easy?'

'It doesn't go any lower.'

Hal snorted.

'The chart responds to voice commands,' said Clunk. 'Just speak to it as you would to the Navcom.'

'Show me Seraph IV,' said Hal. The chart zoomed in on a star system and rotated it until a small planet was centred in the flickering column of light. A blue square appeared, crawling away from it.

'That's us,' said Clunk.

'Show me the bad guy.'

Two red triangles appeared between the planet and the blue square. Hal stared at them in concern. 'We're outnumbered!'

Clunk thumped his fist on the console and one of the red triangles vanished. 'From the look of it they'll catch us in fifteen minutes.'

Hal grimaced. 'Can we hyperspace?'

'No. Still too close.'

'Can we outrun them?'

'No.'

'What are our chances in a fight?'

'We're unarmed and they've got enough weaponry to destroy a planet.'

'If we can't run and we can't fight, what the hell can we do?'

'That's obvious. We surrender.'

'I'm not giving up my ship.' Hal frowned at the chart. 'Hey, they're getting closer. I thought you said fifteen minutes?'

'They accelerated. Estimate contact in three minutes.'

'Match their speed!'

The engine note rose, but the distance between the red and blue markers continued to narrow. The roar of the engines increased further, and the distance remained constant. Then it began to narrow again.

'They've increased speed beyond our safe maximum,' said Clunk.

'What's our unsafe maximum?'

'This ship is unsafe at any speed.' Clunk frowned at the chart. 'I may have the answer. Calculate a slingshot round Seraph Prime. Tight as you can.'

An arc of blue dots appeared on the chart, the midpoint brushing the star.

'Not that close.' The curve flexed slightly. 'Show me the earliest hyperspace point.' The line of dots on the far side of the star grew longer, and a blue circle appeared. 'Cut it finer.' The circle moved back towards the star. 'Plot the intercept point.' A red dot appeared right in the centre of the blue circle.

Hal whistled. 'Pretty tight, but we might just make it.'

'No, they'll shoot us down first,' said Clunk.

'Got any better ideas?'

Clunk paused. 'There is one thing we could try.'

'There is?'

'In my archives there are details of an early experiment which attempted to calculate the effect of mass on hyperspace paths. Allow me to quote: 'A ship on a perpendicular trajectory to a stellar body has a significant chance of surviving a hyperspace attempt, providing the terminal velocity of the ship matches or exceeds the mass of the star over the distance of the attempted jump."

'So what are you suggesting? Read that rubbish to the people aboard the cruiser until their eyes glaze over, and watch them fly into the nearest planet?'

Clunk frowned. 'I was serious.'

'Really? What did all that gumph mean then?'

'Watch the chart.'

The arc of blue dots vanished, replaced with a straight line that extended from the front of the blue square and ended just short of the star.

'You've flipped,' said Hal. 'If we jump there we'll end up as space dust.'

Clunk shook his head. 'No, if we hyperspace there we *might* end up as space dust. The experiment wasn't conclusive but the theoretical outcome was fifty per cent.'

'For or against?'

'Pardon?'

'Fifty per cent chance we make it, or that we fail?'

Clunk's mouth opened and closed slowly. 'For,' he said finally.

Hal watched the red triangle bearing down on them. 'All right, do it.'

'Yes, sir.'

'Aren't you supposed to argue?'

'I'm a robot. I don't get scared.'

The engines roared, and the blue square began to pull out a lead on the red triangle. Both were closing rapidly on the star, and Clunk's hands danced over the console as the distance narrowed. 'I will have to power down non-essential items during the next phase.'

'Like what?'

'Lighting, refrigeration, oxygen regeneration –'

Hal cut in. 'Everything but the engines and whatever's left of the Navcom, right?'

'Correct,' said Clunk. 'I can leave the chart up.'

'Thanks.'

The emergency light winked out, leaving the flight deck lit by nothing but the ghostly glow of the holochart. Hal watched the blue square approaching the jump point, closely followed by the red triangle. As they neared the star, a series of numbers flashed up.

'Hold on,' said Clunk.

Hal gripped the chair as the floor bucked beneath him. There were two bangs in quick succession and the holochart vanished.

'Clunk?'

'Concentrating.'

There was a crash and Hal was thrown out of the pilot's seat. He grabbed the chair's support with both hands and winced as the shrieking jump motors wound up to speed. His heart skipped a beat as the noise tailed off, then beat even faster as it picked up again, louder than ever. A tremendous weight crushed him for an instant, then he heard Clunk's voice loud and clear over the humming console.

'Jump successful,' said the robot. 'Forg system dead ahead, ETA two hours.'

'Brilliant!' cried Hal, staggering to his feet so he could slap the robot on the back. 'Thank goodness you knew about that experiment!'

Clunk looked at the floor.

'Clunk?'

The robot refused to meet his gaze.

'You mean ... You mean you made it up? There was no experiment?'

'You would never have let me attempt such a dangerous manoeuvre without suitable data,' said Clunk defensively.

'You're supposed to protect humans, not fly them through stars! You're deranged!'

There was a loud creak below deck.

'What's that noise? Why –' Hal's voice was drowned out by a loud crack and the sound of rushing water. The sound went on and on before dying away with a gurgle. 'Was that supposed to happen?' asked Hal, in the ensuing silence.

'I doubt it.' Clunk scanned the console, tapping a dial or two and pressing several buttons. 'I think all these warning lights were already glowing.'

'Don't blame me, the *Gull* was like this when I bought it.'

'You paid money for this ship?' Clunk read something off a monitor. 'Ah, it seems the containment field for the coolant tank failed.'

'Isn't there a back-up?'

'There is indeed, but for some reason it didn't activate.' Clunk looked at Hal apprehensively. 'It looks like several thousand litres of coolant leaked out.'

'Right. Where to?'

'It settled in the lowest part of the ship.'

Hal stared at him. 'But that's the cargo hold!'

15

'Can't you pump the stuff out?' demanded Hal.

Clunk shook his head. 'We can't start the pumps without the Navcom.'

'Which you fried with your programming stunt.'

'I may have a solution,' said Clunk. 'If I download the Navcom's operating system into my own data banks I can repair the damaged code and upload a clean copy into the ship's hardware.'

Hal looked sceptical. 'Do you think it will work?'

'If it does we can start the pumps and empty the hold out.'

'And if it doesn't, we'll toss to see who gets to bail out four thousand litres of radioactive coolant.' Hal sighed. 'All right, give it a shot.'

Clunk leaned on the console and closed his eyes. Immediately, a moaning noise welled up, surrounding them like a crowd of wailing ghosts.

'What the hell's that?' demanded Hal, looking around the flight deck in alarm.

'Do you mind?' asked Clunk, opening his eyes. 'This is a delicate operation.'

'Sorry.'

Clunk closed his eyes and started moaning again. After a

moment he stretched his hands out, wiggling his fingers, while the moan turned into a high-pitched wail. A faint blue light shone inside the robot's chest, spilling from the gaps in his arm and leg joints, and Clunk started to shake, his jaw jabbering up and down. 'Dadadadadada!'

Hal backed away.

'DadadadaDADA!' cried Clunk, his eyes flashing wildly. The internal light turned red, and he shuddered. 'Red, red, blue ... hee hee hee. Incu-incu-incu ... bots ... bots ... bots ... Mighty Muller's. Mmm. Maulers, molars, mice. Alfie, Alfie, half an Alfie. Smoke smoke steam. Brrrrrrrrrrrrrr-ting!'

The red light went out, and Clunk put a hand on the console to steady himself.

'Are you all right?'

'I'm cleaning the code.'

'How long will that take?'

'Done. Now I have to upload it.' Clunk closed his eyes and touched his fingertips to his forehead. The blue light flickered inside his chest, and a low groaning sound poured from his mouth. The light flashed faster and faster until it was a blur, and the sound grew to a piercing whistle. The light blazed red and Clunk spread his arms, opened his eyes wide and screamed. 'YeaaaAGH!'

Hal leapt back, falling over his feet. 'Bloody hell. How about a warning?'

'Operation complete,' said Clunk. 'Navcom, can you hear me?'

'Yes, Clunk.'

'Hey, good stuff,' said Hal. 'Navcom, start the pumps.'

There was a groan from the bowels of the ship, and the pumps fired up with a demented, offbeat chatter. 'Turn them off!' shouted Hal, covering his ears.

The noise died down.

'Do you understand what 'regular servicing' means?' asked Clunk.

'Do you know what the word 'broke' means?' Hal sighed. 'All right, the pumps are wrecked. What's the next move?'

'If we landed on a planet and opened the rear doors, the coolant would flood out,' said the robot.

'We don't have time for that sort of thing. Why don't we just open the doors now?'

'Dumping in space is illegal,' said Clunk.

'What, and dumping on a planet is all right?'

'No, I said the coolant would flood out if we landed and opened the rear door. I didn't say we were allowed to do it.'

'Give me strength,' muttered Hal. 'Okay, forget about legal and not legal for a moment. What would happen if we opened the doors?'

'Artificial gravity would hold the coolant in.'

'Wouldn't it boil away in the vacuum?'

'No, that's why it's called coolant.'

'How about we open the doors and accelerate away?'

'That would remove the coolant,' said Clunk with a nod.

'Great.'

'It would also remove the cargo.'

Hal frowned. 'What if we only open the doors a little bit?'

'That might hold the cargo in, but with artificial gravity enabled there's a good chance the coolant would come straight back again.'

'So we turn the gravity off.'

'It might work, but it's still illegal.'

'So is murder, but I don't see anybody standing between me and Vurdi's manic robot. Let's get on with it.'

'Very well. Under protest.' Clunk addressed the console. 'Navcom, cancel artificial gravity.'

'Artificial gravity off.'

Hal clutched his stomach as his inner ear forgot which way was up.

Clunk looked at him. 'I understand the sensation is most unpleasant for humans.'

Hal nodded.

'Are you all right, Mr Spacejock? Your face has gone green.'

'Reflected light,' said Hal, pointing at the console. 'Open the rear doors a crack, Navcom.'

'Define crack.'

'About three inches.'

Clunk looked at him. 'That's not a crack, that's a canyon.'

There was a whine of hydraulics as the cargo doors parted, and Hal eased himself into the pilot's chair, grabbing the console with one hand as he reached for the throttle. 'Are you ready?'

Clunk floated up behind the chair and put his hands on the back. It creaked as he tightened his grip. 'Ready.'

Hal rammed the lever against the end-stop and the ship leapt forward with a bellowing roar, squashing him into the chair and snapping his head back. There was a strangled cry, and when Hal looked over his shoulder he saw Clunk hanging from the back of the seat by his fingertips, his body streaming out horizontal to the floor.

There was a wrench, and the chair leant backwards. Hal lunged for the throttle lever to slow the ship, but his sudden move was enough to snap the last retaining bolt. The support tore and Hal, Clunk and the chair sailed down the flight deck towards the rear wall.

Clunk hit first, his feet smashing into the plastic wall panels.

The chair hit with a clang, and Hal's head whipped back and thumped into the wall, bringing stars to his eyes.

Below decks, there was a crashing and sloshing as the contents of the cargo hold slammed into the rear doors. Once the noise subsided, Clunk put both feet on the wall and launched himself up the flight deck, sailing through the air in the low gravity. He tapped the throttle lever as he flew over the console, and there was a moment's silence as the engines cut out.

'No!' shouted Hal as the lever switched to maximum reverse thrust.

The ship's forward thrusters fired with a mighty roar, counteracting the headlong rush. Hal was catapulted up the flight deck to the hard, unyielding console. He bounced off the top and somersaulted into the viewscreen alongside Clunk, and the first thing he saw when he opened his eyes was the heavy chair flying towards him. He ducked and it smashed into the viewscreen above his head, scattering shards of plastic and glass.

'Artificial gravity on!' said Clunk.

Weight returned immediately, and Hal fell across the console, landing on his back with a thump that knocked the air from his lungs. He was still struggling to draw breath when he saw the heavy chair dropping towards him.

◆

'Forg Orbiter ahead,' said a deep, male voice. 'Requesting docking clearance.'

Farrell walked to the back of the flight deck, where he took a set of overalls and a cap from a locker. He donned them, wrinkling his nose at the smell of dried sweat.

'What's wrong?' asked Terry.

'Nothing you'd notice.' Farrell pushed his hands down the sleeves and gathered the front of the jacket. The seams flowed together and the outfit adjusted to his body. He pulled on the cap, took out a pair of scuffed leather boots and pushed his feet into them, wriggling his toes until they adjusted to his feet.

'Clearance approved,' said the computer.

Farrell looked at the viewscreen, which showed a docking port extending from the side of the Orbiter. The deck tilted as the fore thrusters slowed the *Volante*, and the viewscreen darkened as a shadow cut the glare from the Orbiter's docking lights. Farrell felt a tremor as the ship connected, and there was a series of metallic clicks as the Orbiter grasped the ship and locked it in place.

'Stand by for pressure equalisation,' said the computer.

There was a hiss of escaping air, and Farrell's ears popped.

'Docking complete.'

'Now for this Spacejock person,' muttered Farrell. 'Computer, scan for the *Black Gull*. Get me an arrival time.'

'Complying.' There was a pause. 'Unable to compute ETA.'

'Are you sure? They should have been here twenty minutes ago.'

'I'm certain. The *Black Gull* is not in the Forg system.'

Farrell cursed under his breath. 'Can you increase the range?'

'Negative. There is interference from the Orbiter.'

Farrell snapped his fingers. 'That's it. Use the Orbiter's computer!'

'Connection established. *Black Gull* detected approaching planet Forg.'

'Right, stand by with the simuloid.' Farrell grabbed the microphone. 'It's time to give this Spacejock character some new orders.'

◆

Hal came to with a groan, then sat up with a start as a wet cloth slapped him in the face. The first thing he saw was Clunk, who was peering at him with a look of concern.

'Are you okay, Mr Spacejock?'

'I was until you drowned me,' said Hal, blinking to clear black spots from his eyes.

'I repaired the damage while you were unconscious,' said the robot proudly.

Hal looked around the flight deck. The pilot's chair was back in place, leaning on a slight angle, with bright patches of metal around the base where it had been welded to the deck. The hole in the viewscreen had been patched up, and the protective plastic screen was crisscrossed with yards of sticky tape.

'Yes, er, well done,' said Hal. 'It looks like new.'

Clunk was still peering at him suspiciously when a ringing sound split the air.

'Incoming broadcast,' said the Navcom.

'Put it on main,' said Hal.

There was a pop and a fizz, and blue smoke poured between the layers of sticky tape on the viewscreen.

'Perhaps you should use another display,' suggested Clunk.

'Mr Spacejock?' said a grating voice.

Hal got to his knees and peered at a tiny screen set into the console, where he could just make out a head and shoulders. As he tried to work out who it was, the voice grated again.

'Where the hell are you, Spacejock?'

'Mr Jerling? Is that you?'

'Who else would it be? What's holding you up?'

'We're approaching planet Forg right now,' said Hal. 'We should be landing at your factory in thirty minutes.'

'Right, excellent. Listen, there's been a change of plan.'

'There has?'

'Yes. I've got a ship at the Forg Orbiter. If you transfer the cargo there it'll save you some fuel.'

'Same fee?'

'Certainly. After you dock my men will come aboard and direct the cargo transfer.'

Hal nodded. 'Understood. Oh, by the way, I'm afraid I've still got Clunk with me.'

There was a strange whispering noise from the speaker while the face on the screen stared at him. Then the lips moved and Jerling spoke again. 'We'll discuss that later.'

The screen went dead.

Hal heard a creak and looked at Clunk. The robot was shaking its head slowly, a puzzled look on its face.

'Problem?'

'There's something wrong,' said Clunk. 'I can't quite put my finger on it.'

'You can't quite put your fingers on anything,' muttered Hal. 'Anyway, there's no time for intrigue. We've got to clean the cargo.'

Farrell frowned at the viewscreen. 'Who the hell is Chunk?'

'He said Clunk, boss. Maybe he's the co-pilot.' Terry slipped the blaster off his belt and glanced at the charge indicator. 'I'll deal with him first.'

'Don't worry about it. I can handle the pair of them.' Farrell reached into his jacket and pulled out a deck of cards. 'Want a game?'

'I can't afford it.'

'You might win.'

Terry snorted.

'What's that supposed to mean?'

'You're very lucky at cards, that's all.'

'You're not suggesting they're bent?' Farrell spread the deck to show Terry the Forgberg Casino logo on the back of the cards. 'Nothing funny about these.'

'All right,' sighed Terry. 'But I'm only playing for a credit a game.'

'Make it five and you're on.'

Hal and Clunk were standing near an open locker, halfway between the access ladder and the hold. Hal's arms were sticking out of a padded yellow jacket, which was covered with small tears through which the silvery stuffing was trying to escape - most of it successfully.

Clunk picked fluff from Hal's shoulder and looked at it doubtfully. 'Are you certain this is a radiation suit?'

'Previous owner reckoned it was,' puffed Hal as he tried to pull up a pair of padded yellow trousers.

'You'll have to remove your boots to get those on.'

'No, they'll go through.'

'I don't think so.'

'Watch.' Hal gave a tremendous heave and ripped the legs right off the trousers, scattering tufts of silver padding all over the deck.

'I repeat, you will have to remove your boots first.'

'That was nothing to do with my boots. The bloody things snagged on something.' Hal lifted his foot and bunched one of the trouser legs. As he forced the stiff fabric over his heel, the seams began to split.

'I repeat –'

'If you don't shut up I'll send you in there instead.'

'It's too slippery for my feet. Anyway, I won the toss.'

Hal kicked off his boots and pulled the baggy trouser legs over his flight suit. When he let go they slithered down to his ankles like discarded snake skins. He pulled the legs back up as far as he could and hobbled over to the locker, where he gripped the legs with one hand while fishing around inside with the other. 'Aha,' he said, holding up a roll of gaffer tape. 'The repair kit.'

Clunk snorted.

'Come on, stick them up for me,' said Hal. 'I can't let go or they'll fall down again.'

Clunk took the roll and pulled off strip after strip of tape, using them to patch the rips in the suit.

Five minutes later, Hal was tapping his foot impatiently.

'Haven't you finished yet? You must have covered the whole suit by now.'

'Nearly done,' said Clunk, running his hand over a strip of tape to smooth it down.

'They're not giving points for style, you know.'

'Just as well,' said the robot. He stood back, head tilted to one side. 'Done, I think.'

Hal looked down at himself. With the loose suit bound in tight tape, he looked like a big yellow sponge trussed up for the oven. 'Should be all right. I won't be in there long.'

'You know, as far as radiation suits go that one's about as useful as a ballet dress.'

'I'm only going to have a quick look around.'

'Well don't look around too quickly, it won't take the strain.'

'This suit's as tough as nails,' said Hal. 'I got it off an asteroid miner.'

'Was he lacking in cranial hair?'

'She was as bald as a radar dome. How did you guess?'

'It was just a hunch.'

Hal waddled over to the door and reached for the control panel, which contained a yellow T-shaped handle and a large red button. He whacked the button with his gloved fist, driving it into the control panel with a loud crack. Slowly, the heavy door rumbled open, and a trickle of fluorescent green liquid ran into the passageway.

Hal stepped back hurriedly.

'It won't hurt you,' called Clunk, who had retreated up the passageway and was now leaning on the flight deck ladder with the air of one expecting to be entertained. 'Assuming that's really a radiation suit, of course.'

Hal looked into the hold. The cargo had been jumbled, shaken, tumbled and stirred during his aborted take-off from

142

Seraph, leaving a mass of twisted packing crates. Now, not only were they jumbled up, they were also coated with thick, green jelly.

'Yuk,' said Hal, staring at the luminous glow. 'What am I going to clean that lot with?'

'How about your head?' called Clunk.

Hal glared at him. 'Very funny.'

'No, I mean you're not wearing anything on your head.'

'Good point. Headgear's in the locker.'

Clunk rummaged in the cupboard, where he found a dirty yellow bag and a coil of old rope. 'Nothing here.'

'What's that then?' said Hal, pointed at the bag.

Clunk shrugged. 'It's a bit of old cloth.'

'No, that's the headgear. Sling it across.'

Clunk threw the bag, which dropped short and fell to the floor. Hal bent down to pick it up and there was a rrriippp! as the suit tore across the back. He twisted to look at the damage and there was another rrrippp! as the suit split all the way up both sides.

While Clunk patched the damage, Hal turned the headgear over, shook it, and pulled it over his head. His eyes gleamed through the ragged slots. 'See?' he said, his voice muffled by the fabric.

Clunk's lips moved.

'What?' shouted Hal.

'No mouth hole,' said Clunk, his voice amplified to maximum.

'You'll have to speak up, I can't hear!' yelled Hal, pointing to the bulges on either side of his head.

'It's not important.'

Hal rolled his eyes. 'Hot in here.'

Clunk grinned and gave him a thumbs up.

'Right team, we're going in,' muttered Hal. He strode into the cargo hold, splashing through the slippery coolant. Halfway across the hold, his pace slowed. His feet were getting heavier, and it was becoming increasingly difficult to lift and move them. He stopped and lifted one leg slowly, and there was a sucking sound as his boot came away from the deck. He tried to look down but the hood moved too, obscuring his view.

One step at a time, keeping his body stiff in case he ripped the suit, Hal turned until he was facing the inner door. Then he bent carefully at the waist and peered down at the decking, where he saw a trail of white footprints leading all the way back to the entrance.

At that moment, the last layer of rubber melted away from the soles of his boots. Hal felt the cold liquid seeping through his socks, and instinctively leapt for the cargo door. His foot slipped on the slushy, melted rubber and he fell flat on his back in the slimy green jelly. He struggled to roll over and get to his feet, but it was too slippery.

There was a thud, and Hal stared in surprise at the knotted end of rope lying in the sludge next to his face. Looking along the rope, he saw Clunk framed in the doorway, holding the other end and gesturing at him.

Hal grabbed the rope, and it stretched taut as Clunk leaned back and reeled him in, pulling him across the floor. Halfway there the rope went slack, and Clunk fell backwards with a surprised look on his face and a short piece of rope gripped in both hands.

Hal was still laughing when it dawned on him that the robot's rescue attempt had failed, leaving him stranded.

16

Hal shuddered as the coolant seeped through the suit, chilling his skin with the touch of a dead, clammy hand. What a way to go – frozen to death in his own cargo hold. He saw movement out of the corner of his eye, and rolling onto his side he spotted Clunk in the doorway, gesturing at him. When he realised Hal had seen him, the robot made a tumbling motion with his arm.

'You want me to roll across the floor to you?'

Clunk grinned and put his thumbs up.

'I was just going to do that when you started the mime act,' shouted Hal, his voice muffled by the headgear. He thrashed about until he was side on to the doorway and started to roll, keeping his face clear of the sludge. When he was close enough Clunk grabbed his hand and lifted him through the door.

'I'm so glad you're safe, Mr Spacejock.'

'No thanks to you,' muttered Hal, pulling off the headgear. 'So much for cleaning the hold. Now what?'

'I have an idea.'

'Go on.'

'If we open the outer doors I could sweep the slush out the back of the ship.'

'You said you couldn't walk on the stuff.'

'No, but I could fashion a pair of slippers with the remains of the radiation suit.'

'Couldn't you think of that before sending me in there?' demanded Hal, jerking his thumb at the hold.

'No. The suit wasn't wrecked then.'

Hal stood with his arms out while Clunk peeled off the tattered radiation suit. Once free, he went to put his boots on. 'Damn!'

'What?'

Hal showed Clunk the soles. 'Melted right through. This is my only pair, too.'

'You should be able to buy replacements at the space station.'

'Buy? With what?'

There was a twang from the overhead speaker. 'Incoming call,' said the Navcom.

'Patch it through.'

There was a hiss of static and Jerling's voice burst through the speaker. 'Where the hell are you? My people are still waiting to unload that cargo. I'm in a hurry, man!'

'Sorry, Mr Jerling. We had a small problem with the drive. It's almost fixed.'

'What do you mean 'we'?'

'Me and Clunk,' said Hal.

The speaker hissed gently for a second or two. 'Right, well hurry it up. If you're not docked in twenty minutes I'll keep half your fee.'

The speaker clicked as Jerling rang off.

Hal nudged Clunk. 'I thought you'd get a roasting for running away.'

'That comes later.'

'Strange he didn't say anything about you.'

'He will,' said Clunk gloomily.

'Don't worry, I'll put in a good word.'

Clunk looked at him hopefully. 'Really?'

'Sure. By the time I've finished he'll be so impressed you'll get a medal.'

'That's very kind of you, Mr Spacejock.'

'Don't mention it.' Hal pressed the remains of his radiation suit into the robot's arms. 'Now, about cleaning the cargo hold …'

◆

Clunk picked his way across the treacherous floor, clambering over jumbled crates and skidding on the thick sludge which covered the deck like a wet, slimy carpet. It was slow going, but at last he reached the rear doors. He was just about to open them when Hal's voice came through the overhead speakers.

'Have you finished yet?'

'I haven't even started.'

'Well get your finger out. Time is money, and people are waiting. And another thing, I'll be getting –'

Clunk pressed the door button, and the rest of Hal's words were lost as the hold depressurised. The doors swung open and flattened themselves against the outside of the hull, revealing an inky darkness splashed with diamond-hard stars.

Clunk's gaze flicked from star to star, and he wondered whether planet Aklam really was out there. He'd heard stories for years, but whenever he tracked a source it turned out to be nothing but a fable. He resolved to find the planet one day, perhaps by saving up enough money to hire the *Black Gull*. Mr Spacejock seemed a reasonable sort, and … Then he

147

remembered the fate awaiting him on Seraph. There would be no expeditions, no hiring, and no robot planet.

Depressed, he dug the broom into the thick sludge and shoved a wedge of it out of the hold, watching it tumble away from the ship. After it vanished, Clunk looked around the cavernous hold and did a quick calculation. It was going to take hours. There had to be a better way.

He thought for a second, then grinned. A minute or so later he returned with the oxy torch under one arm, minus the rubber hoses. He aimed the nozzle at the sludge around his feet and opened the valve, blasting gobs of muck out the back door and leaving pristine patches of decking. Despite the artificial gravity the force almost lifted him into the air, so he closed the valve a little to moderate the pressure.

Before long he'd cleared the sludge and straightened most of the crates, and he was just looking round in satisfaction at a job well done when he noticed a trembling underfoot. The ship's engines!

Cursing Hal's impatience, Clunk hurried towards the control panel next to the rear door. He was halfway there when the ship jolted forward, throwing him to the deck. With a shock he realised he was sliding down the cargo hold, straight towards the gaping, star-filled void.

He turned and crawled towards the front of the hold, the gas cylinders still clutched under his arm. He reached a crate and grabbed hold of it, feeling its solid bulk beneath his fingers. The broom slid past and disappeared out the back of the ship, and Clunk smiled as he imagined how silly he would have looked going the same way.

Then the crate began to slide.

Hal watched a blob of light growing larger on the small screen in front of him. 'How long until we get there?'

'Under five minutes,' said the Navcom.

The deck began to shake as the forward thrusters cut in, and the stars on the tiny screen shimmered and flickered in the haze. When the thrusters cut out the Forg Orbiter was dead ahead: a huge, flattened sphere with a floodlit antenna sticking out the top and a long, square pylon hanging off the bottom. The pylon had several ships attached to it, modern-looking freighters in the livery of famous freight and passenger companies. Smart logos gleamed under the Orbiter's bright spotlights, and the navigation lights on their winglets blinked, bathing the smooth, polished hulls in alternating red and green.

Hal stared at the ships enviously. Never mind the sleek hulls and professional paint jobs, where the *Gull* was concerned he'd have been satisfied with working navigation lights. Just as Hal was wondering what to do next, a red light began to pulse on the console. 'Incoming call,' said the Navcom.

'Put 'em on.'

'*This is the Forg Orbiter,*' said the Space Controller, her dulcet tones filling the flight deck. '*Please state your ship's ID number after the tone.*' After a brief pause, the console beeped.

'BG35467-CS,' said Hal.

There was a longer pause. '*We're having trouble identifying you. Repeat your serial number please.*'

Hal leaned closer to the microphone. 'BG35467-CS,' he said loudly. 'The *Black Gull.*'

'*Just the serial number will do,*' said the operator. '*Wait please.*'

Hal waited. Then he waited some more. Finally, the voice came back. '*Sorry about the delay, the transport museum's historical archives were offline. You are now cleared to dock at bay 4B.*'

'Thanks,' said Hal. After the operator had disconnected, he realised he had no idea where bay 4B was. 'Er, Navcom?'

'I can dock automatically.'

'Stop talking and get on with it, then.' Hal stretched. 'I can't wait to see Jerling's people. It's about time one of these jobs went right.'

◆

'Something must have gone wrong,' said Farrell, staring at the console clock. 'He should have been here ages ago.'

'Maybe the real Jerling called him.'

'If he did, we're sunk.' Farrell laid a card. 'Ten credits to me, I think.'

'It's five a game.'

'I know, but you've lost twice.'

Terry dug in his pocket and handed over a pair of credit tiles. 'Maybe he's suspicious. You know, creeping up to the station to get a shot at us. Maybe this Clunk guy has put him wise.'

'I'm going to use the simuloid again. I have to know what's happening.'

'If you keep using it he'll suss you out.'

Farrell shuffled the deck, interleaving the cards with deft movements. Then he slammed them on the console. 'Why couldn't Jerling get a decent pilot? Why did he have to hire this idiot?'

There was a buzz.

'What is it?'

'According to the Orbiter, the *Black Gull* has docked,' said the computer.

'Where?' demanded Terry.

There was no answer.

'It's not programmed for your voice,' explained Farrell. He turned to the console. 'Where did the *Black Gull* dock?'

'Bay 4B.'

Farrell stuffed the cards in his pocket and leapt up. 'I'll meet Spacejock. You bring the ship round.'

'How am I supposed to do that if the thing won't listen to me?'

'Terry is authorised to fly this vessel,' Farrell said to the console.

'Confirmed,' said the computer.

Farrell reached under the console and unclipped a blaster, which he slipped into his overalls.

'I thought you were just going to talk to him?' said Terry.

'Conversation piece,' said Farrell, patting the bulge.

17

Hal entered the *Black Gull's* airlock and looked through the thick porthole into the Orbiter's docking tube, which was a steep incline ending in a pair of thick metal doors. There were darkened portholes recessed into the metal, just above the broad white letters '4B'.

The doors swept open and a tall, dark-haired man in blue overalls strode through. Hal operated the airlock controls, and by the time the heavy door grated open the man was waiting just outside. He looked irritated, but when he saw Hal he forced a smile and stuck out his hand. 'I'm Farrell. You must be Spacejock.'

'That's me,' said Hal, as they shook.

'Terry's bringing my ship round. We'll connect at the back and get the cargo moved across. I'm a bit pushed for time, so the sooner we get started –'

'Follow me.' Hal led the way through the airlock and into the flight deck. He climbed down the ladder and was just about to call out a warning about the loose rung when he heard Farrell's voice echo down the tube. 'Bit old-fashioned, eh? No lifts on this old thing.'

Hal's lips thinned. 'No, no lifts here.' He left the ladder and walked along the tunnel to the inner door. Behind him, there was an oath as Farrell's foot slipped on the rung.

'Mind your step,' called Hal, suppressing a grin. He pressed the door button, but nothing happened. He pressed it again, and still nothing happened.

Farrell came up behind him. 'I don't want to rush you, but Jerling's in a hurry.'

Hal thumped his fist on the button and waited for the door to open.

It didn't.

'Something wrong?' asked Farrell.

'The button got stuck earlier. Looks like it's not working.' Hal reached for the emergency access handle and gave it a hard pull. The yellow lever came away in his hand. 'Navcom, can you open this door?'

'Negative.'

'What do you mean, negative? Open the door!'

'Cannot comply. The hold is not pressurised.'

The yellow handle fell from Hal's hand and clattered on the deck.

'No air?' gasped Farrell. 'You nearly spaced us, you moron! If that handle hadn't broken off ...'

Hal frowned. 'Clunk should have closed the doors by now. What's he playing at?'

'Clunk's in there?' Farrell stared at the door. 'I hope he's got a spacesuit.'

'What for? He's a robot.'

'Of course he is. How could I forget?'

'Navcom, close the outer doors please.'

'Complying.' There was a whine followed by a double thump and a hiss of air. 'Outer doors closed.'

Hal pressed the button and the inner door promptly slid open. As soon as the gap was wide enough he pushed through into the hold. 'Clunk? Are you there?'

There was no reply.

Hal walked around several neat stacks of crates, then stopped as he felt the cold through the ruined soles of his boots.

'What happened to your boots?' asked Farrell as Hal stepped gingerly over a puddle.

'An accident.'

'Why don't you change them?'

Hal shrugged. 'I would if I had another pair.'

'There's a store aboard the Orbiter.'

'It can wait until Jerling pays me,' said Hal, moving off.

Farrell followed, examining the crates. 'I thought there'd be more than this.'

'Some of it's still on Seraph,' said Hal, neglecting to mention that some was strewn across Regan's yard, some was melted into slag and the rest was scattered over a forest.

They reached the back of the hold where the remaining cargo was stacked in neat rows. The robot had done a good job, thought Hal, as he bent to examine a pair of parallel scratches that started halfway into the hold and lead all the way to the rear doors. The deck was clean, and the gloopy mess which had coated the crates of parts was gone. Unfortunately, so was Clunk.

Farrell laughed. 'Looks like you spaced the robot, Hal.'

◆

Clunk could just make out the Orbiter as a silhouette against the blue and white backdrop of planet Forg. He saw a flare of light, and wondered whether it was the *Black Gull's* docking thrusters.

The Orbiter grew larger. The ship had been accelerating when Clunk fell out the back, and his residual motion was enough to carry him rapidly towards the space station. He ran a quick calculation and estimated it would take him thirty minutes to reach it at his current speed. All he had to do was stick out an arm as he flew past.

Something scraped his leg and he looked down to see the oxy torch floating along below him. He reached out and grabbed it, clamping it under his arm. It wouldn't do to have cylinders smashing into the station. Humans could be hurt.

He turned his gaze back to the Orbiter and realised something was wrong. He'd been heading directly for the station, but now it appeared to be sliding away to one side. He checked his calculations and found them to be correct. So what was pulling him off course?

His gaze locked onto the Forg Orbiter as it tracked across the face of the nearby planet. It was moving steadily, but he'd allowed for that. The local sun was a distant gleam, its effect insignificant at this distance. The planet ... Clunk cursed. How could he have missed something so obvious?

He added Forg's mass to his formula and ran the calculations again. As the results came up, he gazed at the green and brown continents below and wondered if the people down there would notice as he blazed a burning trail across the daytime sky. Or would the planetary defences blast him out of the stratosphere first? Either way, the planet's gravity was dragging him away from the Orbiter.

An image of the maintenance robot came to him, with its clouded eyes and heat-buckled face. He wiped it and conjured up a vision of himself sitting at the *Black Gull's* console, bringing the ship in for a landing at the Robot Emperor's private landing pad. His long years of loyal service had been recognised from afar, and he was to be decorated, perhaps awarded an honorary position with the Royal Guard.

Eyes closed, Clunk fell towards the unsuspecting planet, his battered face creased with a contented smile.

◆

The *Volante* had backed up to the *Black Gull*, and the two ships were now joined at the rear. Hal's ship was the smaller of the two, and the *Volante*'s docking apron overlapped the rear doors by a fair margin. That, plus the fact that the *Gull*'s docking clamps were slightly out of true, meant that the cargo transfer was taking place with a background hiss of escaping air.

Because the *Volante*'s deck was lower, a couple of planks had been propped up between the two ships, and they creaked alarmingly as Farrell's cargo hauler tramped back and forth with the crates. It was a grey robot with rough patches on its chest and upper arms, and its head was never still, spotting the smallest movement with rapid jerks and flashes of its blood-red eyes.

'Ex-navy,' said Farrell, when he noticed Hal watching the robot. He tapped his shoulder. 'They cut off their insignia and badges before they sell them.'

'Just as well it's not armed.' Hal shifted his weight and the robot's head jerked round, its eyes locking onto his own. For a split second he thought it was going to drop the crate and charge him.

'They don't need weapons,' said Farrell dryly.

'How do you control it?'

'You don't. You ask politely and hope it agrees.'

Hal thought of Clunk's warm, friendly face. 'Are you sure you can organise a search party? For Clunk, I mean?'

'Relax, I know everyone on the Orbiter. They'll have that robot back to Jerling before you know it.'

'Thanks.'

A door opened at the rear of the *Volante*'s hold, and a man strode towards them. He was a nuggetty character with thick, tattooed arms and a blue cap jammed over his yellow hair. After letting the robot past, he strode up the planks into the *Black Gull's* hold. Under his overalls, Hal spotted the distinctive outline of a blaster.

'Hal, this is Terry,' said Farrell. 'Terry, Hal just spaced Clunk. You know, Clunk the robot.'

Hal felt a cold twinge as Terry's pale eyes fixed on his. 'Er, hi.'

Terry nodded, then looked around the hold. 'Nearly done?'

'Nearly.' Farrell glanced at Hal. 'Listen, have you eaten?'

Hal shook his head.

'Why don't you get something aboard the Orbiter? They've got meals up there, and you look like you could use a feed.'

'Maybe later.'

'They've got boots, too. You could get some new ones.'

'Not until Jerling pays me.'

'Oh, is that it.' Farrell pulled out a handful of credit tiles. 'We can soon fix that up.'

'I thought Jerling never gave advances?'

'I won't tell him if you don't. Here, take it.'

Hal tipped the money into his pocket. The bulge and weight of credit tiles against his leg was a novel experience, and he decided to buy the cheapest boots and food he could find, in order to enjoy the feeling as long as possible. 'I'll be back in half an hour.'

'Take your time. I can always page you. And stop worrying about Clunk. I'll make sure he's taken care of.'

—◆—

Clunk was pulled from his daydream by a buzz of voices. It was the Orbiter's traffic control frequency, which was alive with chatter. He tried to interrupt, to call for help, but the more powerful commsets aboard passing ships drowned his feeble transmitter.

He stared at the flattened disc and spotted the *Black Gull* docked against a pylon, almost hidden behind a large white ship. He smiled at the sight, realising that the cargo transfer was in progress and that Hal would soon be paid. It was a pity the human had forgotten him, but he did have a lot on his mind.

As the Orbiter slid past, Clunk released the cylinder and folded his arms. He was passing less than two hundred metres from the nearest window, and there was nothing he could do about it. He wasn't going to make it.

He drew back a foot to kick the cylinder away, then stopped as he remembered the way he'd cleaned the hold, blasting the jelly through the rear doors with compressed air. The cylinder had struggled in his grip, almost escaping once or twice as it tried to jet off in the opposite direction.

Jetting away!

Frantically, hoping he hadn't left it too late, Clunk grabbed the cylinder and opened the valve. A stream of white vapour spurted from the end, and Clunk closed the valve before the smooth cylinder could tear itself free from his grip.

Then, aiming the nozzle away from the Orbiter, he opened the valve up and held on tight.

18

Hal walked up the Orbiter's docking tunnel with a grim look on his face. Although Farrell had assured him the hunt for Clunk was on, word of the fiasco was bound to get back to Jerling. The robot might be a walking junkyard, but Jerling would never use Hal's services again. And there was something else bothering him, too: Farrell's offsider Terry. He looked more like a hit man than a freighter pilot.

Hal opened the doors at the end of the ramp and stepped into a poorly lit tunnel. Following the signs, he found the main entrance to the Orbiter: a round door with a control panel. He pressed the 'open' button, but nothing happened. When he pressed it again, a metallic voice crackled through the overhead speaker.

'Manual override inoperative. Please use voice commands.'

'Open the door,' said Hal, his voice echoing down the tunnel. It opened sluggishly, and he walked through it into a dimly lit airlock. He pressed the button on the opposite wall but nothing happened. 'Open the door,' he said again.

The speaker crackled. 'Close the other door first.'

'Close it yourself.'

'I'm just an airlock. You have to give the commands.'

Hal shrugged. 'Close the door.'

'Which door do you want me to close, the inner door or the outer door?'

'How can you close the inner door? It's not open.'

'I'm sorry, you'll have to rephrase that.'

'Shut the outer door and open the inner door!'

'Unable to interpret multiple instructions.'

'Okay, interpret this,' said Hal, pulling out his blaster. 'I'm going to shoot holes in the walls until I hit something that makes the door open. I will start in three seconds.'

'I cannot open the inner door without the correct instructions,' said the airlock.

'These are all the instructions you're going to get.' Hal pointed the blaster at a speaker high on the wall. 'One.'

'I'll have to report this to the authorities,' warned the airlock.

'When I pull this trigger you won't be reporting anything to anyone. Two.'

A pleading note crept into the airlock's voice. 'All you have to say is 'Close outer, open inner.''

'I prefer it this way.' Hal raised the blaster. 'Three.'

The outer door slammed shut, and after a second's delay the inner door opened. Hal's ears popped as they adjusted to the pressure difference. 'That wasn't so difficult,' he said, clipping the blaster to his belt.

There was no answer.

He stepped out of the airlock and entered a small lift. There was only one button on the panel, so he pressed it. The door closed and the lift shot upwards, opening onto a brightly lit area filled with the cloying smell of yeast. There were several people sitting at cheap plastic tables, drinking from large mugs and spooning food into their mouths. A robot standing behind a hatch was dispensing mugs and bowls and there was a window to the right, beneath a sign which read 'General Store'. Behind the window, shelves bulged with odd-shaped parcels.

161

Hal walked over to it, and as he got closer the beaming face of a serving droid popped up behind the counter.

'Well, hello there!' said the robot brightly. It waved its arm to encompass the laden shelves. 'You will notice that we have a huge range of items for the discerning gent around town.' The robot sized Hal up. 'We also have several items for those whose credit limit is rather thin.'

'Have you got any boots?'

'Have I got boots?' said the robot. 'I have so many boots I was planning a sale.'

'What sort do you have?'

'Are you looking for comfortable, top quality, long-lasting boots or something cheap?'

'Let me know what you have, and I'll let you know what I want.'

'No problem,' said the droid brightly. It turned and rummaged through the shelves, then disappeared further into the store. Hal heard the sound of boxes being shuffled and paper being scrunched before it came back with a pair of floppy brown boots. 'Now, this is what I meant by quality,' said the droid, putting them on the counter. 'Feel those.'

Hal ran his hands over the silky smooth material. 'Leather?'

'But not just any leather,' said the droid, caressing one of the boots with its metal fingers. 'No, this hide comes from the legendary mookou of Froid III.'

'Froid III, eh?'

'You've heard of it?'

'No.'

'I see. Well, mookou leather contracts when heated, so when you place a pair of these boots on your feet they mould themselves perfectly to every contour. They're completely and totally unique.'

'I've never heard of boots like that.'

'All the guys swear by them.' The droid hesitated. 'Today only, they're just two hundred and forty-eight credits.'

Hal coughed. 'Have you got anything cheaper?'

'I could pretend to look for something else, but these are all I have in stock.'

'You mean that's it? What about the items for thinner credits?'

'What can I say? I used to stock many different kinds of boots, but my customers wanted mookou.'

'It's a lot of money.'

'Look at it this way: If they last ten years, you're only paying about a third of a credit a day for these boots.' The droid leaned across the counter. 'What can you buy nowadays for a third of a credit?'

'When you put it like that, it makes sense.'

'Tell you what. I can see you are a man who likes fine things.' The sales droid paused.

'Yes?'

'Well, I can let you have these boots at a special reduced price.' The robot lowered its voice. 'On one condition.'

'What's that?'

'You're not to tell anyone what you paid for them.'

Hal put his hand in his pocket and rattled Farrell's credit tiles. He picked up one of the boots and turned it over, running his hand over the soft leather.

The sales droid stood completely still.

Hal looked down at his toes, which were protruding from the end of his melted boots. 'All right, how much?'

'You're not going to believe this, but for you I can lower the price to just ninety-eight credits.'

Hal pursed his lips.

'You're not to tell anyone, mind.' The robot leant even closer. 'This is a special rate for preferred customers only.'

'All right, I'll take them.'

A slot opened in the counter. 'Perhaps you could make the payment while I fetch your merchandise.'

'But you haven't asked my size!'

The droid smiled. 'Sir, these are mookou boots. There are no sizes.'

It vanished behind the shelving, and Hal took several tiles from his pocket and fed them into the slot. They were all accepted except the last, which popped out again. Hal pushed it back in and kept his thumb on it, and the reader made a clacking noise as it tried to eject the tile again. Hal shoved harder, something went clang inside the machine and the tile disappeared.

The robot returned with a box. 'Would you like the parcel wrapped?'

'No, I need them now.'

The robot placed a blue credit chip on top of the box and slid them over the counter. 'Your change, sir.'

Hal pocketed the tile, took the lid off the box and stared at the loose folds of brown leather. He reached into the box and pulled out one of the boots. It sagged in his hand. 'Ninety-eight credits for these?'

'Mookou boots are always loose when new,' said the robot. 'Try them on!'

Hal kicked the melted boot off his right foot and put the new one on. 'It's still loose.'

'Wait - it'll adjust.'

Hal put the other boot on and took a couple of steps. He felt the boots contract, fitting his feet snugly. 'Hey, that's neat!'

'I told you,' said the droid.

Hal frowned. 'They're getting tighter.'

'You must have very warm feet, sir.'

'Hey, that hurts!' said Hal, as the boots applied a hefty grip to his feet. 'Argh! Get them off!'

Several people turned to watch.

'Sir, I must warn you not to get over-excited,' said the droid anxiously. 'Your extremities will heat up and the footwear will react accordingly.'

Hal sat and tugged at the boots, turning red with the effort. 'How the hell do I get them off?'

'Press the depression on the back of the heel.'

Hal did so, and the boots immediately relaxed. 'Why didn't you tell me that before I put them on?'

'Sir, I am distressed.'

'You could have crippled me.' Hal rubbed his feet. 'You know, I'm not sure about these boots.'

'Sorry, no refunds,' said the robot. It turned away and busied itself behind the desk.

Cautiously, Hal slipped the mookou boots on. They promptly adjusted to his feet, but this time they didn't get any tighter. Hal flexed his toes, then stood and kicked his old boots against the wall.

The robot looked up. 'You weren't going to leave those, were you sir?'

'Of course not,' said Hal. 'Have you got a box?'

The droid found an empty white carton and slid it across the counter.

Hal dropped his melted old boots into the box and slid it back. 'Here,' he said. 'Have some fresh stock on me.'

◆

Terry slipped into the *Black Gull's* engine room and gently closed the door. Ducking his head to avoid a nest of tangled cables, he eased his muscled body behind the cylindrical bulk of the ship's main drives. Near the back of the room, a generator whined, powering the vessel's electrical circuits. Beyond the generator, Terry saw what he was looking for: a large greasy cylinder nestled on thick rubber pads, connected to the main drives with thick, twisting pipes. The *Black Gull's* hyperspace drive.

Twice now Terry had suggested the sensible course of action, and Farrell had overridden him. Farrell came from a wealthy family, and he wouldn't spend five minutes in jail if this pilot fingered them both to the Peace Force. Terry shook his head. He knew Spacejock's type: always bouncing up after you knocked 'em down. Well, he knew how to knock the guy right out of the park.

Terry reached into his jacket and withdrew a slender, polished tube. Holding it steady, he reached around the hyperdrive and attached it to the far side of the greasy metal cylinder. After checking it was secure, he twisted the end caps in opposite directions, triggering a sequence of red lights. One by one the lights turned green, and after the last one lit up Terry turned to leave.

He was halfway to the door when there was a thump on the hull, directly overhead. Terry looked up at the oil-stained ceiling panels, his weapon half-drawn. For several seconds there was no sound at all. Then something squeaked.

'Rat-infested hulk,' muttered Terry, shoving the gun back in his jacket. He paused at the doorway and looked back into the engine room, but could see no evidence of his visit. Satisfied, he closed the door and left.

The serving robot looked up at Hal's approach. 'Can I help you, sir?'

'I want something to eat. What have you got?'

The robot shrugged. 'Food and drink.'

'I gathered that. What kind of food and drink?'

'I just sell food or drink,' said the robot patiently. 'Which would you like?'

'What's the food?' asked Hal.

'It's a blend of the five basic food groups, not too heavy on the protein.'

'What does it look like?'

The robot paused. 'It looks like shit.'

'But it tastes all right, doesn't it?'

The robot lowered its voice. 'Judging from the reactions of my customers, I would venture to say that it not only looks like shit, it also tastes like shit. On the positive side, I can assure you that it is most nutritious.'

Hal grimaced. 'I think I'll just have a coffee.'

'What's coffee?'

'It's a drink.'

'Oh, I sell drink,' said the droid.

'What's it like?' asked Hal suspiciously.

'I take some of the food and dilute it with water.'

◆

Farrell placed a card on the *Black Gull's* console and tried to get comfortable, but the battered pilot's chair had a distinct lean to it. He wasn't really concentrating on the game, he was actually listening to the distant thuds as the cargo lifters transferred their crates into the *Volante*. A little longer and the shipment would be his.

There was a clatter of boots, and Terry clambered up the ladder to the flight deck.

'Where have you been?' asked Farrell, laying a card.

'Looking around.'

'Why?'

'Nostalgic, innit. My dad was a cleaner. He used to sneak me aboard these things.'

'Fascinating.' Farrell cupped a hand to his ear. 'Do you hear that?'

'I can't hear nothing.'

'Exactly. Unless I'm mistaken, the robots have finished and the cargo is ours.'

There was a thump overhead, and they both looked up. Terry drew his gun.

'Will you put that away?' snapped Farrell.

Terry obeyed slowly, his eyes searching the ceiling, while Farrell gathered up his cards. He was just about to slip them into his pocket when a whole section of ceiling panels collapsed, dropping a battered bronze robot into the flight deck.

Terry pulled his blaster while Farrell leapt to his feet, scattering cards. 'Who the hell are you?'

19

Clunk got up slowly, tutting and shaking his head at the broken ceiling panels. 'Oh dear. I must have taken a wrong turn.'

Farrell's face cleared. 'You're the robot, right? Spacejock thought he'd lost you.'

'He did, but I managed to get aboard through the emergency hatch.' Clunk looked at the two men. 'And you are?'

'That's Terry. I'm Farrell.'

Clunk tried to push one of the panels back into place. 'I assume you're transferring the cargo to your vessel?'

'Yeah. Jerling's orders.'

'That explains the freighter outside.' Clunk frowned. 'I didn't know Mr Jerling owned any like that.'

'You know Jerling?'

'Of course. I work for him.'

Terry's hand vanished into his jacket.

Clunk peered at him. 'I don't recall your face. Do you work for Mr Jerling too?'

Farrell put his arm around the robot's shoulders. 'Listen Clunk, why don't you go aboard our ship and make yourself comfortable?'

'Where's Mr Spacejock?'

'He's gone aboard the Orbiter to buy a new pair of boots.'

Clunk's eyebrows rose. 'I didn't know he had the money.'

'I gave him some.'

'That was generous of you.'

'I hate to see a fellow pilot in need.' Farrell leaned closer. 'Listen, I can help you too.'

'Thank you, but I don't need boots.'

'Not that. I can take you back to Jerling.'

A pained look crossed Clunk's face. 'He ...he's not expecting me.'

'There's been a change of plan. He really needs your help.'

Clunk brightened. 'Really?'

'Sure. He has an important task for you.' There was a buzz, and Farrell pulled out his commset. 'Yes?'

'Loading complete,' said a metallic voice.

'Seal up. We'll be there in a minute.' Farrell returned the unit to his pocket. 'Go ahead with Terry,' he said to Clunk. 'I'll leave a note for Spacejock explaining everything.'

Terry walked over to the tube and disappeared down the ladder. There was a clang and a muttered curse as his foot slipped on the loose rung.

Clunk crossed the deck slowly and stopped at the top of the ladder. 'It's a pity I couldn't say goodbye to Hal.'

'Call him later,' said Farrell, taking a gold pen out of his overalls.

Clunk hesitated.

'You can't stay here. You know how impatient Jerling can be.'

After the robot had gone Farrell patted his pockets, looking for something to write on. The only thing he had was the deck of cards, so he peeled off a joker and hesitated, pen at the ready. Then he grinned and began to write.

Hal strode into the recalcitrant airlock without hesitation, confident he'd subdued it the first time through. The door closed smartly behind him, and Hal smiled to himself. It was amazing what a firm hand could do when it came to unwilling machinery. Then he heard a sniffing sound.

'Uh, oh!' said the airlock.

Hal looked around, puzzled. 'What is it?'

'I detect lethal concentrations of bacteria. Please clear the airlock immediately.'

'On my way,' said Hal, hurrying to the exit. He pressed the button, but nothing happened. 'Open the door please.'

'I'm sorry. Which door is that?'

'The outer door!'

'Decontamination cycle commencing in three seconds. Please clear the airlock.'

Hal looked up at the speaker. 'Close the inner door and open the outer door.'

'Two,' said the airlock.

It dawned on Hal that his firm hand had got him into trouble again.

'One,' said the airlock, and a fine mist sprayed from concealed jets. It was a soapy mix which got up Hal's nose and worked its way under his eyelids. Moments later, the hissing stopped and a blast of warm air roared through the chamber, clearing it.

Hal opened his watering eyes. 'Is that the best you can do?'

There was a loud click behind him, and he turned just as a huge jet of water spurted from the wall. It slammed into him, throwing him across the airlock and crushing him against the

171

far side. That jet stopped and a second opened up right next to his chest, hurling him back across the airlock. After he'd been thrown back and forth several times the jets stopped and the water sluiced away. Hal staggered upright, his hair plastered to his forehead and his clothes streaming with water. The outer door swept open and he vaguely heard a ping through the sloshing noise in his ears.

'Cycle complete,' said the airlock. 'Kleen-Aire Corporation would like to advise that DecoWash Airlock Decontamination was developed without animal testing.'

Hal spat out a mouthful of foam and tugged the blaster off his belt. He aimed at the nearest speaker grille and pressed the contact, expecting to blast a smoking hole in the wall. Instead, the wet battery discharged into his hand, sending a powerful jolt racing up his arm and into his brain, which promptly tried to leap through the top of his skull. Then he heard a sniff over the wild buzzing in his ears.

'Uh, oh!' said the airlock. 'I detect lethal concentrations of bacteria. Please clear the airlock immediately.'

Hal jumped for the exit just as the heavy door began to close. He squeezed through the gap and the door thudded to right behind him, cutting off a metallic chuckle.

◆

Farrell led Clunk across the *Black Gull's* hold to the *Volante*. They walked past rows of stacked crates to the front of the larger ship's hold, where a door stood open. It revealed a cramped space, about the height of a man.

There was a thud behind them, and when Clunk looked round he saw a grey-painted cargo hauler following with a heavy, measured tread, its head swivelling from side to side as it analysed threats.

'I think you'll find this alcove has all the comforts you require,' said Farrell, waving Clunk towards the door.

Clunk crouched to look inside. The back wall was crisscrossed with dozens of cable ducts and studded with fuse boxes and light switches. 'It's a bit small.'

'Nonsense,' said Farrell. 'It's even got a power point so you can take a recharge. Hop in, I've got to get the ship under way.'

Clunk quashed his reservations, ducked his head and stepped into the recess. Before he could turn round, the door slammed behind him.

'Don't try and escape!' called Farrell through the thin metal, as the tags snapped shut. 'I'm leaving a guard out here with a blaster.'

'Why have you locked me in?' asked Clunk, his voice echoing around the locker.

'Jerling's orders. He wants you safe and sound.'

Clunk crouched and peered through a row of ventilation slots in the middle of the door. He saw the grey robot outside, standing opposite the locker with a rifle clamped in its massive fists. It watched Farrell leave then turned to guard the door, its red eyes boring through the slots.

The ducting creaked as Clunk slumped against the back wall of the alcove. He'd felt so happy after his ingenious escape from deep space, and now he was in worse trouble than ever. He pictured Jerling jabbing a cigar at him, lecturing him on obedience before feeding him into a crusher. A wave of frustration rushed through his circuits, and he clenched his fists. It wasn't right!

Bang! His fists slammed onto the wall, splintering a length of ducting. Clunk froze. Wilful damage? Jerling would have him melted! Then he laughed quietly. What difference did it make? Muller was going to scoop him out and crush him like a tin can anyway.

With a mischievous glint in his eyes, he raised his fists and slammed them down on the ducting, giggling at the splintering, cracking noises. He did it again and again until the insulation split, forcing several wires together. There was a crackle and a flash as the high-voltage lines crossed, and Clunk was hurled against the thin metal door. It bowed outwards under his weight and popped open with a creak of tortured metal. Clunk fell headlong from the locker, sprawling on the hard deck. Instinctively, he covered his head, expecting the hauler to open fire. When nothing happened he looked up, only to discover the hold was completely dark.

Clunk switched to night vision and looked around. He saw the faint outline of the hauler barely two metres away, its arm coming up as it sighted along the blast rifle. There was a flash of light and a bolt of energy whanged off the floor right in front of Clunk's nose, almost shocking his system into a total reset. He heard the thud of the hauler's feet as it moved towards him, and there was another flash as it fired again. This time the bolt ricocheted over his head and slammed into the wall behind, burying itself in the metal with a shower of sparks.

Clunk got to his hands and knees and scuttled behind a row of crates. Behind him, the hauler's measured tread changed direction.

◆

The *Black Gull's* outer door opened slowly, groaning like a dozen ghosts with terminal hangovers. Hal walked through the airlock to the flight deck, where he found a broken roof panel on the floor and a playing card propped on the console. 'This had better be an apology,' he muttered, picking it up. He read the first sentence and looked up. 'Hey, Clunk's all right! He came back!'

'Correct,' said the Navcom.

'Farrell's taking him home,' said Hal, reading on. 'It gets better! Jerling wants me to go straight back to Seraph for another lot of cargo.'

'Are you sure that's wise?'

'Of course it is. I can fetch my cargo ramp at the same time.'

'But the Seraph military will be waiting for you.'

'I got around them last time.'

'Clunk got around them.'

'He just helped a bit. Nothing I couldn't do myself.' Hal noticed a red light blinking on the console. 'Is that a message?'

'Correct.'

'Play it on monitor three.' Hal stared into the tiny screen and saw a pale, round face. 'It's Vurdi,' groaned Hal. Then he smiled. 'Hey, who cares? I can pay him now!'

The debt collector flicked a lock of hair off his forehead and blinked, his dark eyes glistening in the light. 'Mr Spacejock, I have just spoken to Portmaster Linten. I believe you know the gentleman? He tells me you left to do a cargo run, which is both gratifying and totally unexpected.'

'I told you I had a job, you cloth-eared git,' muttered Hal.

'And I thought you were lying to me.' Vurdi tapped his chin. 'I would like the name of your employer as soon as possible, so that your fee can be paid directly to Garmit and Hash. Please call me back as soon as you get this message.'

'Some chance.'

Vurdi continued. 'If I do not hear from you within one hour I will send Brutus to find you.'

The screen went blank. 'Message terminated.'

Hal folded the playing card into a wad. 'Navcom, detach from the Orbiter and set course for Seraph.'

'Without Clunk? Are you sure?'

'Yes.'

'Complying under protest,' said the Navcom. 'Fifteen minutes to hyperspace.'

Farrell sat back in his chair and stretched his legs out. The viewscreen showed a patchwork of fields, gradually increasing in size as the ship came in for a landing.

'ETA fifteen minutes,' said the computer.

Terry glanced up at the screen. 'Landing at your place?'

Farrell nodded. 'Once we've checked the cargo off, I'll call Gordon and tell him it cost twice as much as expected.'

'You're doing well out of this.'

'You'll get a cut.' Farrell rubbed his chin. 'Pity about Spacejock. He seemed a decent sort, but Jerling will probably have his ship over this.'

Terry grinned. 'Don't you worry about Spacejock. I fixed him good.'

'You what?'

'I left him a little pressie.'

'What are you talking about?'

'I planted a distorter on his jump drive. First time he uses it ...' Terry raised his fist and splayed his fingers. 'Whoosh.'

Farrell looked shocked. 'You can't! I didn't authorise that!'

'Sometimes you got to use initiative, right? I'm not having this Spacejoke character after me.'

'We have to warn him!' Farrell turned to the console. 'Computer –'

'I wouldn't do that,' said Terry.

Farrell's eyes narrowed. 'What? Why not?'

'If you tell Spacejock about the bomb, and he records the conversation ...'

Farrell winced.

'...none of your pals would save you,' finished Terry. 'Anyway, you're too late. It's gone off by now.'

Something went thump in the bowels of the ship, shaking the flight deck.

'What was that?' said Terry, pulling his blaster.

Farrell turned his head to listen. 'I think the robot just tried to leave its prison.'

The sound of a single blaster shot echoed through the ship.

'First Spacejock, now the robot.' Terry grinned. 'There go the loose ends.' His grin vanished as the chatter of a heavy energy weapon echoed through the ship. The firing stopped, and they heard debris clattering on the floor.

Terry ran for the personnel lift.

Farrell stared at him. 'Where do you think you're going?'

'Down to the hold.'

'You must be joking. Have you any idea how fast that hauler's reactions are? It'll gun you down like a rabbit!'

'It can't shoot me. I'm human.'

'Are you willing to gamble your life on that?'

'What happens if Clunk gets hold of a weapon and comes after us?'

'That's different. He can't kill us deliberately.' Farrell glanced at the console. 'Computer, have you got video surveillance in the hold?'

'Yes sir.'

'Show me, please.'

Farrell squinted at the dark, cloudy image. A flash of laser fire lit the scene, illuminating Clunk as he dodged behind a crate. The lumbering hauler followed, there was another flash of fire and the crate exploded in a shower of wood and twisted metal.

'They're destroying my cargo!' shouted Farrell. 'Get down there and take control!'

Terry blinked. 'You said I could get shot.'

Farrell shook his head. 'They won't hurt you.'

'But ...'

'Scared of a couple of robots?'

Terry's jaw tightened. There was a moment's silence, then he hefted his weapon and ran into the lift.

Farrell grabbed hold of a microphone. 'Patch me through to the hold. Audio.'

'Link enabled.'

'Cease fire, cease fire!' shouted Farrell. He saw the hauler pause and look around. Then Clunk's head popped up above a crate and the hauler raised its gun.

'Cease fire!' yelled Farrell.

The robot pulled the trigger and a blaze of light lit the scene. A large strip of wood exploded off the top of the crate and the robot adjusted its aim and fired a burst, blowing a series of smoking holes across the side. The weakened timbers gave way and it fell apart, revealing Clunk, who was crouching near the ground with his hands over his ears. The hauler grinned and raised its rifle.

20

Walter Jerling was sitting in his office, trying to invent a legitimate excuse for skipping an engineer's retirement party. It wasn't that the fellow didn't merit his presence, it was just that every retirement was one step closer to the end of his own career. By ignoring them altogether he could carry on as if nothing were happening, as if none of his loyal staff were being replaced by young upstarts fresh out of business college.

Jerling's gaze settled on his novelty cigar lighter, standing in the corner like an obedient statue. Semi-obedient, he amended, remembering his painful forefinger. Idly, he wondered whether the senior engineer was a cigar smoker.

One of the screens on his desk beeped, and Jerling looked down to see a waiting message. It was Regan Muller at Incubots. Jerling tapped the icon and Regan's face appeared on the screen, lit with flashes of red and blue light.

'G'day Jerling, Regan here. The Peace Force just called me out. Someone's trashed my yard and they want a number for that pilot of yours. Oh, and that robot you sent over did a runner. Call me right back, eh?'

Jerling wiped the screen. He had more important things to deal with than a fugitive robot and a careless freelancer. Regan could handle it.

The terminal beeped again and a call waiting symbol popped up. He tapped the icon and a face appeared - the head of his robot factory.

'Good morning, Mr Jerling.' The man hesitated. 'I didn't want to disturb you, but –'

'Get it out.'

'Do you remember those parts …the shipment you organised?'

'Of course I do. Something wrong?'

'I don't know, but the equipment is set to go and the staff are due soon. Weren't the parts supposed to be here first thing?'

'Good God!' Jerling snatched the cigar from his mouth. 'You mean they haven't arrived?'

'Not yet. That's why I called, you see. I know you don't like having staff on wages with nothing to do, and –'

'Leave it to me.' Jerling blanked the screen and called up his address book, scattering ash on the polished terminal as he paged through it. 'Spacecow. Spacehog. Spacejock - that's him.' Jerling clamped the cigar between his teeth and tapped the call icon. 'Better have a good excuse, son.'

◆

The *Black Gull's* engines throttled back to a murmur and the console speaker chimed twice. 'Hyperspace in twenty seconds,' said the Navcom. 'Cross check the escape hatches and prepare for jump.'

Hal smothered a yawn and put his feet up on the console.

'Ten seconds to hyperspace. Please be seated.'

For a moment or two, the flight deck was completely still. Then a distant whining noise impinged on the silence. Faint at first, the sound grew to a thin wail which sought out Hal's teeth and drilled them one by one.

'Five,' said the Navcom.

Hal glanced down at the folded playing card in his hand, then looked around the flight deck.

'Four.'

Hal spotted the wooden box full of chess pieces at the far end of the console. Carefully, he took aim.

'Three.'

Hal let fly, and the folded card hit the side of the box and fell to the deck.

'Two.' The console buzzed. 'Jump suspended - incoming transmission.'

'You mean we have to go through all that nonsense again? Couldn't it wait?'

'It's an urgent call from Walter Jerling.'

'Aha, payday!' Hal sat up. 'Come on, don't keep him waiting.'

Jerling's face appeared on the console screen, wreathed in cigar smoke. 'Where's my cargo, Spacejock?'

'It should be delivered any minute. You gave me twenty-four hours, remember?'

'My people would have done it in twelve.' Jerling dragged on his cigar. 'Another thing, Regan Muller tells me the robot escaped. Have you got it?'

'I did, until it left with Farrell.'

'Who the hell's Farrell?'

'Your pilot, of course.'

Jerling shook his head. 'I don't have anyone called Farrell.'

'But you called me when I got to Forg! You said this guy Farrell was meeting me at the Orbiter to collect the cargo!'

'Is this some kind of joke? You deliver that cargo to my factory, you hear?'

Hal's insides turned cold. 'But ... but Farrell met me at the Orbiter with his ship. He took the crates!'

Jerling stared at the screen. 'You gave away my cargo?'

Hal nodded.

'And the robot?'

Hal nodded again.

'Mr Spacejock, I'm a fair man. Get them back off this Farrell and deliver them here within two hours, and I will pay you in full.'

'And if I don't?'

Jerling examined the glowing end of his cigar. 'I'll take your ship to cover my losses.'

Hal opened his mouth to argue, but the screen was blank. 'Those lousy pirates stole my cargo,' he muttered, balling his fists. 'Those goddamn pirates stole my cargo!'

'And Clunk,' said the computer.

'It's your fault! You let them get away with it!' Hal glared at the console. 'Why the hell didn't you check their ID in your database? You should have known it wasn't one of Jerling's ships!'

'My files are twenty years old. I have no record of recent vessels.'

Hal scooped up the folded playing card and brandished it at the screen. 'These people made me look like an idiot. They stole my cargo, they pinched the robot and now they're going to cost me my ship!' Unfolding the card, he tore it into little pieces and threw them into the air.

'If only they'd left a clue,' he said as the pieces fluttered to the deck.

＊

Clunk dived to his left as the gun flashed, avoiding the lethal burst by millimetres. Energy bolts tore up the decking, splattering his metal skin with molten fragments, and Clunk rolled over and over as more shots whizzed and zipped around him.

He took cover behind a wall of crates, and the firing stopped. His relief was short-lived - he could already hear the hauler's measured tread as it moved to flank him. Leaping to his feet, Clunk turned and bolted. He ran full-tilt through the darkened hold, careening off wooden crates and metal uprights and then . . . BAM! He bounced off the rear wall and landed flat on his back.

Dazed, Clunk shook his head to clear the flashing error warnings. Slowly, he got to his knees, chiding himself for his panic-stricken haste. Stealth, that was the answer!

With a click, he activated his night vision, flooding his sensors with wavery green light. He turned his head slowly, trying to spot his opponent. Next he tried his audio receptors, but the ship's engines and the background hiss from his degraded circuits drowned any noise from the hauler. He played with his audio filters, trying to remove the background noise of the ship. All he got was more static.

Slowly, Clunk's head dropped. He couldn't touch, taste or smell the other robot, he was unarmed and he was trapped.

Then his head came up. What would Hal do in this situation? What sort of plan would he come up with? The answer came to him: Distract the hauler, escape the hold, capture the ship, turn everyone in to the authorities and collect a massive reward. Clunk grinned. Yes, that was a Spacejock plan. Still, even if it was a touch optimistic, he could do his best.

He dropped to the deck and crawled to a stack of crates, where he ran his fingers over the rough wood, feeling for holes. There were several jagged edges where the hauler's shots had torn into the crate, and Clunk worked the timber until he could insert his hand.

He felt through the packing material and his fingers brushed a hard, round object the size of an orange. He set it on the floor and delved into the crate again. A minute or two later he had a small pile of the items. He stashed a couple in his chest compartment and took one in each hand, then got to his feet and stared around the hold. No movement. Drawing his arm back, he threw one of the balls into the darkness. Seconds later, there was a crash of broken glass followed by wild flashes of gunfire.

Clunk slipped away, following the wall. He reached the end and threw another ball, hurling it into the opposite corner of the hold. Gunfire arced out of the darkness, catching the ball in mid-air and blowing it apart in a shower of sparks.

Stealthily, Clunk made his way along the wall. Halfway to the next corner he froze. The floor had started to vibrate, and the crates nearby were creaking and jiggling. A keen whistling filled the hold, a rushing, hissing sound like a gale force wind through fine netting. Clunk frowned - the ship was dropping through the planet's atmosphere. Time was running out.

He took one of the balls from his chest cavity and threw it. Nothing happened. Clunk reached for the last ball, then stopped. If the outside noise was drowning out the sound of the balls dropping, it would probably mask the sound of his footsteps.

He broke into a run, one hand brushing the wall in case he passed an opening without seeing it. Near the far end, his foot slammed into the buckled alcove door, still lying on the floor where it had fallen. The door skidded away and crashed into a crate.

'I hear you, little robot!' roared the hauler.

Clunk ran after the door and scooped it up, then bolted for the alcove. Without stopping to think, he backed inside and pulled the buckled door into position behind him. In the darkness of the hold, he thought, it might just be enough.

He peered through the ventilation slots to look for the hauler just as the overhead lights winked on. Clunk hastily switched off his night vision, then gazed through the door. At first he couldn't see much through the swirling smoke which filled the hold. Then his eyes adjusted and he saw blistered scorch marks on the walls where the robot's wild gunfire had struck, and the blasted remains of a dozen shattered crates. Clunk shook his head slowly. Mr Jerling was not going to be happy.

He saw something move on the far side of the hold, and adjusted his gaze. Terry was standing near the inner door, looking around the hold apprehensively. One hand was poised over the lighting panel. The other gripped a powerful-looking gun.

Clunk heard the robot coming closer, and tensed. There was a moment of dead silence, and then the door was torn from his grip. The hauler pushed the blast rifle's muzzle into his face, and as Clunk looked into the flaming red eyes above the gun, he blacked out.

There was a hollow feeling in the pit of Hal's stomach as he stared at the scattered fragments of playing card. He'd been that close to completing the job, paying off Vurdi and saving his ship, until those two bit crooks snatched everything away. He winced as he remembered the message written on the card. How could he have been so stupid? They didn't want him for another job. They were just getting rid of him so they could escape with the cargo!

Wait a minute. What about the authorities? You couldn't move without seeing a Peace Force announcement about speeding or seat belts. Surely they'd help where theft was involved? 'Navcom, get me the Orbiter.'

'Which department?'

'Peace Force,' said Hal grimly. With a bit of luck he could have Farrell arrested - or better still, shot on sight.

'Complying. Contact established.'

'This is the Forg Orbiter. How can I help you?'

'I want to report a theft,' said Hal.

'Which ship please?'

'The *Black Gull*.'

'And where are you calling from?'

'The *Black Gull*, of course,' said Hal in surprise. 'How many ships do you think I have?'

There was a pause. *'But you said it was stolen, sir.'*

'Not my ship. They stole my cargo!'

He heard a sheet of paper being scrunched up. *'Tell me, where did this cargo theft take place, sir?'*

'Aboard my ship.'

186

'*The* Black Gull?'

'That's right. You're getting it.'

'*How much cargo are we talking about?*'

'About two hundred crates. I saw the bastards who took it, too. Farrell and Terry. Of course I didn't know they were stealing it. It was false pretences.'

'*How's that, sir?*'

'Well, Jerling called and told me to hand his cargo over to these two goons,' began Hal. 'Only it can't have been Jerling, and these guys don't work for him.'

There was a long silence.

'Are you getting this?' demanded Hal.

'*I'm writing it all down in full, sir. Please continue.*'

'Well, they docked with my ship and unloaded the cargo. I went into the Orbiter for some boots. By the way, I want to complain about the food.'

'*That's hardly my department, sir.*'

'It will be, if anyone croaks after eating that muck. Anyway, when I came back they'd stolen the cargo. And they took the robot, too.'

'*Which robot?*'

'The robot I lost in space. He fell out the cargo hold.'

'*Anything else stolen?*'

'No.'

'*Right, sir. I've made out a full report and I'll file it straight away. Rest assured I'll put my best people onto it.*'

'Over and out,' said Hal.

Just before the speaker cut out he heard the crumpling of another sheet of paper. Hal sighed. It was all too late, anyway. His cargo was probably stashed away in some hangar, ready for transfer into new containers and a quick trip to another planet. If only they'd left a proper clue to their identity! He frowned as he remembered something about Farrell's playing card, some sort of crest or heading printed on the back.

'It's a clue!' he shouted, dropping to his knees and gathering the torn pieces. He laid bits and pieces of tattered card on the console with shaking fingers. Gradually he assembled enough pieces to read a name. 'Nosica gergforb? Sounds like a real den of thieves.'

The Navcom spoke up. 'I believe a rearrangement of the pieces might prove fruitful.'

Hal swapped a few pieces around until the correct name appeared: Forgberg Casino. 'Navcom, get landing authority. We're going to get Jerling's cargo back.'

'What about Clunk?'

'Yeah, and him too I suppose.'

◆

Farrell strode along the *Volante*'s lower passage to the inner door. He raised his hand to the controls, then put his ear to the door instead. He heard nothing over the background rumble of the ship's engines. No screaming, no gunfire, no lunatic robots engaged in one-on-one battle. Nothing.

Farrell reached for the blaster at his hip. 'Damn,' he muttered, as his fingers closed on thin air. Terry had gone in with enough weaponry to start a rebellion, and had promptly disappeared. The last thing he wanted to do was enter the hold unarmed.

Farrell jumped as the overhead speaker buzzed. 'Ten minutes to landing,' said the computer loudly. 'All humans to be secured.'

'Can you circle around?' called Farrell.

'Negative. Ground control has locked us into a guided flight path. Landing cannot be delayed.'

'Tell them it's an emergency. They'll just have to wait.'

'What is the nature of this emergency?'

'I don't know. Tell them it's a computer problem.'

'There is nothing wrong with my circuits,' said the computer coldly. 'Landing will proceed as planned. Take a seat or suffer the consequences.'

'Bloody computers,' muttered Farrell. There was no time to fetch a gun, so he touched the control and stepped aside as the door hissed open. Directly ahead, a wall of crates blocked his view into the hold. He poked his head through the opening, looked left and right, and withdrew. There were no cries of discovery and nobody opened fire on him, so he entered the hold cautiously, still looking left and right.

Smoke hung in the air, shot through with beams from the overhead lights, and a sharp smell of burnt wood blended with the more common spaceship smells of oil, hot metal and electronics. To his right, blasted crates leant drunkenly against the wall, their twisted contents scattered across the decking. There was less damage in the other direction, so he went that way.

As he moved along the row of crates, he heard a voice on the other side. They weren't pleading or screaming, which sounded positive. In fact, it sounded like an ordinary conversation. 'Terry? Is that you?'

'Over here.'

Farrell's boots scrunched on the charred fragments littering the floor, his face redder and redder as he stepped over the trail of buckled robot parts. Every damaged piece was another chunk of his money gone, and by the time he rounded the corner he was ready to explode.

Terry was holding his blaster on Clunk, who was lying face down in a puddle of lubricant. The hauler crouched nearby in a ready position, weapons pointing at the floor. Farrell walked up to it and stared into its eyes, which glowed with a murderous red light. 'You destroyed thousands of credits worth of cargo, you tin-headed moron!'

There was a creak as the robot's grip tightened on its weapon.

'Take it easy, Farrell,' muttered Terry.

'Put your toys away and pick that up,' growled Farrell, jabbing his finger at Clunk.

After a brief hesitation the hauler slung the pulse rifle across its back and bent down to grab Clunk. He picked him up by the ankle, heaving him into the air in one fluid motion.

'Follow me.' Farrell strode to the rear of the hold and grabbed a handset off the wall. Fortunately it hadn't been mangled by gunfire. 'Altitude?'

'Two thousand metres,' said the ship's computer. 'You must return to your seat. We're landing in five minutes.'

'Shut up and hover.' Farrell steadied himself as the ship tilted. 'Now open the cargo door.'

'Confirm please.'

'Open the rear door. Immediately.'

'Complying.'

There was a hiss as the door swung open, and Farrell stepped back as the wind swirled around the hold. He turned to face the cargo hauler, which was still holding Clunk upside down by one leg. 'Throw it out!' he shouted above the roar of the engines, jerking his thumb towards the door.

The hauler walked to the edge and stopped with Clunk

swinging gently from its raised arm. It looked out of the hold, then swung its arm and tossed Clunk out of the ship.

Farrell watched the robot glinting in the sunlight as it spiralled towards the clouds. When it disappeared he raised the handset again. 'Shut the rear doors.' As they began to close, he hung up and walked away.

Terry called to him. 'What's Gordon going to say about the cargo? Some of these crates are falling to pieces.'

'Get that trigger-happy freak to put them back together,' said Farrell over his shoulder.

◆

The flight deck thrummed as the *Black Gull* slowed to approach speed. Hal was sitting at the console with folded arms, staring into space and pondering the challenges awaiting him on Forg. It was one against two, but while Farrell and Terry had the cargo, Clunk, a huge combat droid, a faster ship, guns, somewhere to land and piles of cash, Hal still had the element of surprise. He figured that evened things up a little.

The Navcom's voice burst from the speaker. 'Landing in sixty seconds. Please assume emergency brace position.'

Hal smothered a yawn and glanced up at the clock.

'I repeat. Assume emergency brace position.'

'Have you ever heard the story of the boy who cried wolf?'

'I fail to see the connection.'

'Save the warnings for when they're really needed.'

'The gravity on this planet is twenty per cent over the standard.'

'So?'

'Do the words 'heavy landing' mean anything to you?'

Hal's eyes widened. 'Heavy landing?' He grabbed the front of the console. 'How heavy, exactly?'

The engine roar doubled in volume and Hal sank into the padded seat under a colossal weight. The flight deck creaked ominously under the strain, and the lights flickered as all available power was diverted to the engines.

'What sort of noise does a wolf make?' asked the Navcom.

'What?' said Hal through clenched teeth.

'I was wondering what a wolf sounds like.'

Hal looked up with an effort. 'Now is not the time to further your education. Land the damn ship.'

There was a clanging sound. 'Incoming transmission.'

'Any chance you can stick to the same noise each time?'

'Impossible.'

'All right, play it.'

'This is Forg spaceport,' said a female voice. 'I take it we have the pleasure of addressing Mr Hal Spacejock?'

'You sure do.'

'I've got a memo here from Portmaster Linten of Lamira. He tells me you're an arsonist.'

'I had a misunderstanding with one of his robots.'

'Yes, I hear the fire is still burning out of control. Now, can you give me a good reason why I should let you land here?'

'Land? We're not going to land, we're going to bounce!'

'What?'

'We're slowing as fast as we can. According to my computer it's not fast enough.'

There was a muttered conversation at the other end, before the voice came back. 'Hold on, sir! Activating right laterals on my mark. Three ... Two ... One ... Fire!'

Hal grabbed the console as the ship leapt sideways. 'What the hell was that?'

'We've been diverted away from the spaceport,' said the Navcom.

'You mean they've found a way to slow us down?'

'Either that, or they've found an uninhabited area where the impact won't cause any damage.' The Navcom hesitated. 'Yes, we're heading for the rubbish dump. Impact in five seconds. Emergency brace please.'

Hal leant on the console, resting his head on his folded arms. The engines cut out and the ship hit, slamming him down in his seat. Dust rained down from the ceiling, along with the few remaining ceiling panels, and a few seconds later the ship tipped sideways, settling on a slight angle.

There was a slithering, rustling sound outside.

'Landing successful,' said the Navcom. 'Local time 6.45 p.m.'

'What's that noise?'

'We made a hole in the rubbish. The sides are falling in on top of us.'

'Can we fly out?'

'If we use the engines, debris will be sucked into the vents. We could start a fire.'

Hal snorted. 'Who cares? It's a rubbish tip. Get us out of here.'

The engines roared and the ship rose into the air, flame blasting from its landing jets.

There was a ring from the console.

'*This is Forg spaceport calling the* Black Gull. *Please reply.*'

'This is the *Gull*,' said Hal. 'We're fine. The rubbish cushioned our landing.'

'That was the intention,' said the operator. 'Please don't move. Our retrieval crews are on the way.'

'Retrieval crews?'

'Yes. If you take off you'll set fire to the tip and it will burn for weeks. Sit tight and we'll dig you out.' The speaker clicked as the operator disconnected.

21

Beep, beep, beep! Beep, beep, beep!

Clunk groaned and opened his eyes. A distant memory came back - a haggard-looking programmer trying to explain the symptoms of a hangover with the help of a bucket and a glass of alcoholic beverage. Now, with his sight wavering and wobbling like a dodgy display screen, it all made perfect sense.

Clunk raised a hand to brush at his eyes, and was shocked at the effort required to move his arm. It felt like he'd aged a hundred years! Then he spotted the rising bubbles.

'Beep, beep, beep!' went his leakage monitor, as water trickled in through his worn seals.

Clunk looked up. The surface was several metres above him, and he had the swimming skills of a brick. He glanced around, but there was no discernible slant to the sandy bed under his feet. Sampling the water, he discovered that it was fresh. A lake, then. The *Volante* had been approaching Forgberg, which meant he'd plunged into one of the lakes surrounding the capital city. Unfortunately, there were dozens of them, ranging in width from a few hundred metres to several kilometres, and it would do him no good to set off in the wrong direction.

For a split second he considered giving up. All he had to

do was lie down and let the water flow in, and his problems would be over. Why struggle on, when Jerling was going to have him scrapped anyway?

The thing puzzling him was Terry and Farrell. Jerling wasn't one to throw robots away, so why had they dumped Clunk in a lake? It didn't make sense.

Then there was Mr Spacejock. He was bound to get into more trouble, and who better than Clunk to help him out? Anyway, what kind of robot left a human to its own devices?

Inspiration struck. He had a map of the planet in memory, so all he had to do was plot his location and find the nearest shore. Working quickly, he tuned his receivers to a couple of satellites and the Forg Orbiter. The signal underwater was very weak, but within seconds he'd triangulated his position on the map and found the shortest route.

Getting to his feet, Clunk began the slow trudge across the lake bed, leaning forward as though fighting a strong headwind. His legs rose and fell like pistons as they drove him across the undulating sand, and he barely noticed the fish which swam past, shooting him curious glances before vanishing with a flick of their tails.

'Beep, beep, beep!' went the leakage alarm, more insistent now the water was reaching critical components. Already, Clunk had lost feeling in his legs, and only by looking down could he confirm they were still moving.

Finally, his head broke the surface. The shore was only metres away, a grassy slope surrounded by lush green bushes. Hurrying forward, Clunk staggered up the slippery bank, dripping mud and slime and blinded by weeds and grit.

As he was wiping the muck from his eyes and ears, he became aware of frantic screams and loud, panicky shouting.

Blinking the last of the mud from his eyes, Clunk looked

around to see what was happening. The first thing he saw was two humans running towards a row of trees, screaming faintly and scattering serviettes and plastic cutlery in their wake. On the ground nearby lay a picnic rug, a wicker basket and overturned bowls and plates.

'Wait!' called Clunk, hurrying after them to calm them down. 'I'm just a robot!' At least, that's what he tried to say. Thanks to the water in his mouth his reassuring words emerged as a series of hair-raising groans.

The terrified humans took one look at the stiff-legged, arm-waving, mud-caked figure and ran even faster. They vanished into the trees and there was a bang of car doors followed by the whine of a groundcar departing at speed.

Clunk lowered his arms. So much for reassuring them.

He glanced at the picnic rug with its generous piles of food. His first thought was that it was a terrible waste. His second was that while he couldn't eat the food himself, Hal might appreciate it should they eventually meet up again. So, casting furtive glances at the nearby trees, Clunk hurried round gathering up supplies. When he'd finished brushing dirt off bread rolls, wiping the grass and sand off pickled onions and digging gravel out of the sliced pork he wrapped everything in the cleanest paper serviette he could find and jammed it into his thigh compartment. Feeling pleased with himself, he set off for the trees and the road beyond.

◆

Hal stepped off the beltway and entered the spaceport's car rental office. The counter was manned by a tall youth with a mop of dark hair, who watched Hal's approach with a huge welcoming smile.

'Good afternoon, sir! What brings you into this fine establishment?'

'I need a car. Just for today.'

'Certainly, sir. That's eighty credits, and I'll need your approval on this.'

Hal reached for a pen and scrawled on the insurance waiver. He dropped several credit tiles on top and handed it back.

The youth glanced at the signature and slid a key-tag over the counter. 'Bay 7C, Mr Jerling. Enjoy your stay on Forg!'

Hal nodded, scooped up the key and walked outside. There was a brown haze in the air, and he coughed as the smoke got into his throat. He crossed the road to the parking lot and walked along a row of gleaming groundcars. As he approached the last row he heard a rumble and looked up. A spaceship was lifting off, rising higher and higher in the late afternoon sky. He watched it until the trail began to dissipate, the ship hanging in the sky like an evening star.

'Lucky bastards,' muttered Hal. 'One day I'll have a ship that can do that.'

Once the ship vanished, Hal looked around for his rental. He spotted it nearby, a sleek model with a raked-back canopy and twin chromed exhausts. Hal grinned, mentally thanking Farrell for the credit chips. Nothing but the best where crooks were concerned.

He climbed in, settled in the soft leather seat and surveyed the driving controls. It didn't take long because the panel was bare apart from a handful of buttons and switches. Unsure of his next move, Hal cleared his throat. 'Hello?'

The dash flickered into life and the car began to vibrate. 'Good afternoon, sir or madam. What is your destination?'

'Nosica . . . I mean, the Forgberg casino.'

'A fine choice, sir or madam,' said the car, as it rose and headed for the exit. 'Would you care for some relaxing music during your trip?'

'Sure.'

A panel opened, revealing a compact music centre. Hal selected a classical station, and the orchestra welled up as the car joined the flowing traffic.

'Our journey will take twenty minutes at an average speed of three hundred kilometres an hour,' said the car, in its cheerful perky voice. 'Now, sir or madam, is there anything else I can do for you?'

Hal nodded. 'Yep.'

'And what would that be?' asked the car.

'You can shut the hell up so I can hear the music.'

'Understood, sir or madam.'

The car accelerated hard, trembling slightly as the motor poured on the power. Behind it, a tall column of smoke rose above the spaceport as the rubbish dump burned out of control.

＊

Clunk slowed his pace, eyeing the road ahead. Several four-legged creatures were gathered in a group alongside the strip of turf, cropping the grass with bored looks on their placid faces. His database assured him they were harmless cows, but the misunderstanding at Incubots had shaken his faith in computers.

Clunk took a cautious step towards the cows, and the nearest raised its head and bellowed at him. It was a loud, groaning sound that ended with a gurgle and a belch, and resentment washed through Clunk's circuits. Why couldn't they leave him alone? He looked down at the brown and green gunk caking his lower legs like a pair of muddy boots. It was bad enough being hunted around a darkened cargo hold. Worse still to be tossed out of a spaceship in mid air, to plummet thousands of metres through the air, and to splash down in a vast lake. But having to walk through a minefield of sloppy, ankle-deep fly-encrusted cowpats *and* deal with the loud rumblings of four-legged mammals was the last straw.

Clunk heard the growing whistle of a groundcar over his shoulder. Already, half a dozen had passed by, taking as much notice of his frantic waving as they had of the grazing cows. Until now he'd moved out of the way every time, but after watching them skim over the cows he realised the vehicles were fitted with collision avoiders. Logical really, and he was annoyed at himself for not making the deduction earlier. If groundcars had no way of avoiding the large ruminants, the highway would have huge fences down both sides to keep them out instead of being open to the country. Either that, or the roads would resemble giant hamburger strips.

The car approached rapidly, throwing twin cones of light down the highway, and Clunk felt an itch between his shoulder blades. Resisting the temptation to duck, he kept walking down the middle of the road, assuming the car would pass over him.

It didn't.

As a new robot, Clunk's reflexes would have kept him out of trouble. As an old robot, caked with manure and oozing pond weed from his joints, he was barely quick enough to get his head out of the way.

Moving at three hundred kilometres per hour, the groundcar struck Clunk a glancing blow on the shoulder. His sideways dive turned into a mid-air flip, hurling him into the cropped grass lining the highway. Fortunately, the car only grazed his shoulder, doing little damage. Unfortunately, the cows had been there first.

It took several handfuls of grass before Clunk could see properly. Then, doggedly, he got to his feet and walked on, stepping over liberal cowpats and swatting at the torpid flies that buzzed around his head. Although they couldn't hurt him, he had a human-like urge to grab something smaller than himself and beat the living crap out of it.

'Moo!'

Clunk looked up. One of the cows was standing across the road, and beyond it sat the groundcar, pulled over to one side of the road. A lift! Realising his luck had changed at last, Clunk hurried towards it.

◆

The groundcar raced along the grassy highway, rising and falling like a boat in a gentle swell. The setting sun barely warmed Hal's face, and he adjusted the climate control until warm air blew from the vents. The new-car smell was strong as he relaxed in the comfortable leather seat.

He had no idea what he was going to do when he got to the Forgberg Casino, but at least he was getting there in style.

The headlights clicked on, throwing out powerful cones of light which turned the twilight on either side of the road pitch dark. White-painted posts supporting the dividing barrier flashed past, and Hal yawned and reached for the radio controls. Soft instrumental music filled the cabin and he felt his eyes closing in the delicious warm environment.

There was a chime, and Hal opened one eye to see an orange light blinking on the dash. He opened the other eye, and saw a herd of cows grazing on the highway, away in the distance. They raised their heads as the car bore down on them, chewing rhythmically, their eyes liquid in the bright headlights.

A split second before impact, the car shot into the air. 'Wurg!' said Hal as he left his stomach behind. 'Bor!' he growled as the car dropped on the far side of the creatures. Having done its job, the orange light stopped flashing.

Hal was just about to close his eyes again when he saw something in the distance, caught in the powerful glare. A muddy figure was limping along the middle of the highway, stepping over cowpats. Further up the road another herd of cows was cropping the grass.

There was a clang of metal-on-metal as the figure vanished under the front of the car, which then shot into the air to clear the cows. Stunned, Hal looked back at the fallen figure, which was lying face down in the grass alongside the road. As it faded into the distance, he saw it getting to its feet, yellow eyes blazing. Hal frowned at a sudden memory: the same eyes in a crinkled bronze face.

Glowing yellow eyes.

'Stop!' he cried.

The car analysed the level of emotion in Hal's voice, and a millisecond later it activated the brakes. The reverse-thrust unit could bring the car to a complete halt in two seconds flat, but despite the warning stickers plastered all over the cabin, Hal hadn't bothered with the bulky-looking safety harness. He had a split second to regret this decision before he found himself hurtling towards the front of the car. An emergency force field activated just before he smashed through the windscreen. The blue glow caught and held him neatly in its tingly embrace before dropping him to the dash with a thud. He was just sitting up, dazed, when a metal finger tapped on the canopy.

'Are you all right in there?' said a concerned voice, muffled by the thick perspex.

Hal saw Clunk peering through the canopy. An expression of surprise washed over the robot's muddy face, followed by a look of pure joy. 'Mr Spacejock, it's you!'

Hal opened the door and gripped his nose as an overpowering smell of cow dung wafted in. 'Pfwar!' he cried. 'That's not mud!'

'You never found out where he was taking my cargo?' asked Hal incredulously. He was sitting as far from Clunk as possible, which was not very far in a groundcar. Despite repeated dunkings in a muddy puddle, the robot stank of manure.

'I thought he was working for Jerling. When he locked me up I thought it was punishment for escaping Incubots.'

'I bet I'd have twigged what he was up to,' said Hal. 'I'd have come out of that closet, captured the ship and flown it straight to Jerling's.'

'And earned a massive reward.'

'That too,' agreed Hal.

'Before tea, naturally.'

'Eh?'

'And after tea, you'd have eradicated all known diseases and brought peace to humanity in every corner of the galaxy.' Clunk opened his thigh compartment and took out the soggy serviette. 'Speaking of tea, I thought you'd like this.'

'Where did you find it?' asked Hal, eyeing the contents with suspicion.

'When I emerged from the lake I scared a couple having a picnic. They left all their food behind.'

Hal sniffed the serviette. 'Hey, this smells good! Thanks!'

'You're welcome.'

'It's great to have you back,' said Hal, clapping him on the shoulder. 'I thought you'd be orbiting the planet for years.'

Clunk frowned. 'Yes, I notice you didn't bother looking for me.'

'Me? Farrell told me he was getting up a search party!'

'The same Farrell who just threw me in a lake?'

'Yeah, that's him.'

'I thought I was going to burn up in the planet's atmosphere,' said Clunk quietly.

'Well you didn't, did you?' Hal pressed a button and the strains of an ancient concerto filled the cabin. Closing his eyes, he waved a chicken drumstick in time to the music, and was just dealing with a particularly twiddly bit when the music faded. He glanced at the dashboard, where the orange light was flashing on and off. 'Hang on to your seat,' he said. 'More cows.'

'Mind you don't run into them,' said Clunk. 'I wouldn't want to see the poor creatures hurt.'

Instead of rising into the air, the groundcar slowed. And instead of cows, they spotted the tail lights of another vehicle.

'What's going on?' asked Hal as they closed on it. 'Why are they crawling along like that?'

Clunk peered ahead through the perspex bubble. 'There are several people in there.'

Hal's jaw tightened. 'This could take ages. How do we tell our car to go over them?'

'You can't,' said Clunk. 'Exposure to anti-gravity fields can have serious long-term health effects.'

'How come we can drive over cows?'

'Humans have one set of rules for themselves and a different set for everything else.'

'There must be some way I can make this thing go over them,' said Hal, pressing buttons and flipping switches on the dashboard.

Clunk saw Hal reaching for a large red button. 'I wouldn't press that one, Mr –' There was a loud bang and the perspex canopy blew off, leaving a narrow strip across the dash for a windshield.

'At least it smells better!' shouted Hal over the rushing wind.

Clunk looked at him with an unreadable expression.

'Now what are they doing?' muttered Hal as the car ahead slowed even more. 'Why can't we overtake it?'

'Do you see that fence down the centre of the highway?' said Clunk. 'On this planet, groundcars are controlled by a central traffic computer. If you get too far from that fence they cease to respond and you die in a raging fireball. No, you cannot overtake it.'

Hal dragged a small manual out of the glove box and flipped the index to 'W'.

'What are you looking for?' asked Clunk.

'Weaponry.'

'You won't find weaponry in a groundcar manual.'

'No?'

Clunks shook his head. 'Try Armament.'

Hal flipped the pages. 'Here we are: 'Your Chieftain Mk VII can be fitted with twin pulse lasers or a single, centre mounted photon cannon.' What's the asterisk? Damn! Excludes government and rentals.' He turned a few pages. 'Manual controls, eh?' Hal read a couple of sentences, then glanced at the dash. He saw the knob he was looking for and gave it a twist, bringing the groundcar to a halt. ''Take the control stick from the glove box, insert in mounting point A for left-handed or B for right-handed driving position.' Pass it over, Clunk.'

The robot fished around in the glove box and came up with a short, stubby stick with a red button on one end and a ball joint on the other.

Hal took the stick and slotted it into a hole in the dash. He let go to put the manual away and the stick drooped, hitting the dash with a thud. Then it began to whirr, lifting steadily until it stuck up from the dashboard, quivering slightly.

'Manual mode activated,' said a voice.

Clunk eyed the stick. 'You're not really going to touch that?'

'Desperate times, desperate measures,' said Hal, gripping the joystick. He pushed, and the car leapt forward. They raced along for a minute or two before the road went round a sharp bend.

'Perhaps you should change back to automatic,' said Clunk as the car swerved across the road and mowed down a row of bushes.

Hal glared at him. 'I'm a pilot. I can drive a groundcar as well as any –'

'Look out!' shouted Clunk.

Hal stared through the windscreen, and his eyes widened as he saw the huge archway ahead. There was a heavy-duty barrier blocking the way, and Hal pulled desperately on the stick to slow the speeding car. He brought the vehicle to a shuddering halt with only millimetres to spare, the front of the car almost touching the circular Toll Booth sign.

There was a window at the base of the arch. Something moved inside, and then a door opened and a uniformed guard stepped out. He ran his gaze along the groundcar, flicked a glance at Clunk then turned his full attention on Hal. 'Just get our license, did we sir?'

'I'm in a hurry, officer. If you could just raise the barrier ...'

The guard looked up and down the deserted road, then put out his hand. 'Fifty credits.'

'Fifty credits! What for?'

'Let's call it a voluntary contribution to the staff party.'

'Let's call it a bribe,' muttered Hal.

'A hundred credits will do nicely, sir. Don't want any trouble, do we?'

'I think you should pay,' said Clunk.

'I know, I know.' Hal took a handful of tiles from his pocket, and was just about to select the right amount when a large hand darted out and took the lot. 'Hey!'

The guard touched his cap. 'Welcome to Forgberg, gaming capital of the universe.'

The barrier rose and Hal pushed the joystick forward, still muttering under his breath.

'And stick to the speed limit,' called the guard as they drove off.

22

The road beyond the archway was paved, and overhead street lights bathed the chunky whitewashed houses with a sickly orange glow. Hal pushed the car hard, and after a while the houses thinned out, giving way to larger, more elaborate dwellings set back from the road on lush green lawns and surrounded by tall fences tipped with razor wire.

He saw a splash of red light as the car ahead slowed to take a side street. Hal shook his fist as they drove past, and would have stood up and yelled at them if Clunk hadn't grabbed his arm.

A few hundred metres up the road they saw an electronic billboard with the words: 'You should have turned right!' in huge white lettering. Hal slowed the car, and the billboard displayed a group of smart young people standing beside a shiny poker machine, their hands overflowing with credit tiles. 'Forgberg Casino - where the winners are,' said the caption.

Hal yanked the controls and the car turned on the spot before speeding back to the turning. At the junction he slammed the stick to the left, hurling the car round with a loud whine from the engine.

'Do you always drive like this?' asked Clunk, as they roared down the narrow street.

'Only when I'm chasing thieves.'

They caught up with the slower car, but before Hal could nudge it off the road they were passing a row of shops.

'Seems to be a popular name around here,' said Hal, as they passed the Hinchfig Liquor Barn, the Hinchfig Robot Shop and the Hinchfig Car Wash.

'Gordon Hinchfig is an important businessman. He's almost as rich as Mr Jerling.'

'Leeches,' muttered Hal. 'If you ask me –'

He was interrupted by a gentle chiming.

'What was that?'

'Do not be alarmed,' said the car. 'Your vehicle will be placed in a queue, and you will be attended by the first available operator.'

'I hate it when they put you on hold,' muttered Hal.

The voice continued. 'When you approach the casino your vehicle will pause, allowing you to disembark. Please do not delay, as this will inconvenience other patrons waiting in line behind you.'

'You're inconveniencing me now,' said Hal.

'Automatic mode in ten seconds,' said the voice.

Hal took his hands off the controls.

Clunk looked at him. 'They said ten seconds. You can't let go yet.'

Hal grinned and pressed his knee against the stick. The car swerved.

'That's irresponsible,' said Clunk.

'Stop me, then,' said Hal, nudging it again. Ahead, a giant neon-lit archway spanned the road like a fast food logo on steroids. 'Welcome to the Forgberg Casino!' screamed the lettering in twenty-three shades of orange. 'Gaming House of the Galaxy!' howled another in nine shades of green.

'Automatic engaged,' said a voice, as they passed under the arch. 'My name is Tony, and I'm your operator for this evening. Come on folks, say 'Hi, Tony!"

Hal muttered under his breath.

'I can't hear you!' said the voice brightly. 'Come on, nice and clear!'

Hal leant forward. 'Bugger off, Tony.'

'Now that's not very nice,' said the voice. 'I'm only doing my job.'

'And you're making a right hash of it,' said Hal. 'Now clear off and leave us alone.'

'Fine,' said the voice coldly. 'Please gather your possessions and prepare to leave your vehicle. Don't break your neck when you get out.'

Ahead, a marble staircase flowed down from an imposing glass entrance. Above the row of gleaming doors, backlit red letters spelled out the words 'Forgberg Casino'. On either side of the staircase were planters with palm trees and potted flowers, softening the hard marble.

The white car stopped ahead of them, and a pair of red-coated attendants leapt forward and opened the doors. A portly couple got out, the man squeezed into a tuxedo and black trousers, the woman almost hidden under a profusion of furs and glistening jewellery.

'Come on, come on,' muttered Hal as the couple climbed the staircase arm in arm. One of the attendants got into the car, and as it drove off Hal's car leapt forward. It jerked to a halt alongside the lowest step and Hal swung his legs over the side and hopped out. Clunk stepped out the other side.

'Valet parking ten credits,' said a youth in a red and gold uniform, holding out his hand.

Hal reached into his pocket and fished out a pair of tiles.

He selected one and dropped it into the youth's outstretched hand.

The car purred away, vanishing round the corner. Hal strode up the wide marble stairs towards the glass doors, and was just crossing the threshold when a large man in a dark blue uniform approached with a frown on his round, red face. 'Sorry sir, you can't come in.'

'Why the hell not?' demanded Hal.

'This here's a casino, not a boilermakers' convention.'

'Pardon?'

'We have dress standards, and those ain't they.'

Hal looked down at his stained flight suit. The garment had once been snowy white with a natty logo embroidered on the breast pocket. Now it looked like a used filter from a coffee machine, and the logo was just a tangle of loose threads.

'And he ain't wearing nothing at all!' said the bouncer, jerking a fat thumb at Clunk.

'He's a robot,' said Hal patiently. 'I know it's hard to tell with the gleaming yellow eyes and all, but you can take my word for it.'

'He's a robot. So?'

'They don't wear clothes.'

'They do in here,' said the bouncer firmly.

'But ...'

The bouncer sniffed. 'No buts. Now piss off, the pair of you.'

Hal walked slowly down the steps, lost in silence.

After a while, Clunk glanced at him. 'Are you considering your next move?'

'That *was* my next move. Now I'm considering my future, and it's not very promising.'

'Don't you have other clothes aboard your ship?'

'Oh sure. I have a wide range of garments to choose from. There's my summer collection, my winter wardrobe, my spring outfit and my autumn ensemble.'

'Well, there you go then.'

'That was a joke, Clunk.' Hal gestured at his flight suit. 'I've got two pairs of these, and the other one's full of holes.'

'Your boots are all right.'

'They're not bad, are they?' Hal angled his foot. 'I got them on the Orbiter. They're leather. Very expensive.'

'Real leather?'

'Yeah, from a real mookou.'

'Good,' said Clunk, with feeling.

'Let's cruise around a bit. We might spot something.'

'That's not a very promising plan.'

'No, but it's our only chance.' Hal waved at one of the parking attendants. As the youth trotted up, he noticed it was the one who'd parked their car earlier.

'Yes sir?'

'I want my car back.'

The young man put his hand out.

'I was only gone five minutes. You're not getting paid again.' Hal frowned. 'What are you leering at, anyway?'

'You just earned me twenty credits.'

'How?'

The attendant winked. 'I bet the other lads you wouldn't get into the casino with those tatty old clothes, and I was right.'

◆

'You shouldn't have done that, Mr Spacejock. That poor young man could have choked on those plants.'

'Never mind that little shyster, just look for the car.'

'It could be anywhere! Without help ...'

'We won't be getting any from those guys, so we'll just have to do it ourselves.' Hal vaulted onto the bonnet of a groundcar and clambered onto the perspex roof. From his vantage point he saw row upon row of canopies glistening under the overhead lights. In the far corner he saw a car without a canopy, standing out from the surrounding vehicles like a gap in a row of perfect teeth.

'Can you see it, Mr Spacejock?'

Hal pointed. 'Over that way.'

There was a faint hooting noise.

Hal looked down. 'Was that you?'

'No, it was the parking attendants. I told you they'd come after us.'

'Rubbish. You're hearing things.'

There was another hoot, closer.

'Mr Spacejock, they said they were going to tear off your head and urinate down your neck.'

'They were just talking tough.' Suddenly, Hal slid off the car and dropped to all fours.

'What are you doing?'

'Shut up!' hissed Hal. 'Get the car and meet me here.'

Clunk looked at him doubtfully. 'On my own?'

'No, with the ghost of backups past. Of course on your own!'

'Where will you be?'

'I'll keep watch.'

Clunk strode off between the rows of cars. A minute or two later there was a cry of discovery followed by a babble of voices. Hal raised his head cautiously and saw the robot surrounded by a group of parking attendants, watching impassively as the uniformed boys yelled and shook their fists in his face.

The biggest youth quietened them down. 'We know you're skulking out there, you coward!' he shouted.

There were shouts of 'Bully' and 'Cheapskate'.

'We're losing money out here,' yelled the lad. 'So we're going to let you go!'

Hal grinned. Thank goodness he'd sent Clunk.

'But before we leave, we're going to have a toast!'

Hal frowned. What was the idiot jabbering about?

The valet raised his drink bottle, shaking the yellow contents into a foam. Then he whipped the top off and poured the lot on Clunk's head. 'Piss on you!'

Each of the others followed suit, until Clunk glistened under the harsh orange light. When they'd finished, the attendants filed away, laughing amongst themselves.

'You can come out now, Mr Spacejock,' called Clunk. 'I've neutralised the threat.'

Hal walked over to the robot, who was staring at the spreading puddle at its feet. 'Why would they waste their drinks like that?'

Hal snorted. 'That wasn't drink.'

'Just as well I'm waterproof.'

'It wasn't water, either. Still, at least they didn't tear your head off first.'

'Is that why you sent me out alone?'

'Eh? Oh no, I wouldn't do that.'

'Only –'

'Look, will you forget those idiots? We need some clothes, and we're getting nowhere standing out here.'

'Do you have anything you could sell? To raise the money, I mean.'

Hal looked at the robot thoughtfully. 'Funny you should say that. Grab the car and I'll explain on the way.'

'I'm a little wet for the car.' Clunk waved his hand, shaking off a few stray droplets. 'Perhaps if I shook myself really hard –'

'No!' shouted Hal. 'Don't!'

◆

Vurdi Makalukar was sitting at his terminal, lost in pleasant thoughts. He'd expected a battle in the Hinchfig case, but the entire matter had been resolved with a single phone call. Soon he'd have money to burn, and in his vivid daydreams he'd already spent it a dozen times over.

A gentle buzz drew him from the plush leather seats of a sports car and deposited him back in his apartment. The buzz was repeated, and Vurdi tapped an icon on his terminal screen. It was a call from Garmit and Hash.

A fair-haired man appeared, immaculate in a three-piece suit, stiff white collar and bow tie. 'It's Vurdi, right?'

'Correct.'

'Listen, congrats on the Farrell job. Big plus, heaps of cred.'

Vurdi allowed himself a casual smile. 'It was nothing.'

'Slight minus on the horizon, though. This Spacejock chap. Can't have people running around owing us, eh?'

'He's next on my list.' Vurdi glanced at his watch. 'In fact, I'm about to deal with him.'

'Magic. Special.' The man hesitated. 'Problem is, the boss wants them linked, so to speak.'

'I don't follow.'

'Hinchfig is sorted, Spacejock isn't. Get Spacejock's cash and we pay on both, see?'

'I don't see at all!' said Vurdi angrily. 'I got your money off Hinchfig. You can't withhold my fee because of Spacejock!'

'But we are, my friend.'

'That's not fair!'

'No, but it's business. Catch you around, old timer.'

Feeling hollow inside, Vurdi disconnected. His new and improved lifestyle, his sports car and the down payment on his mansion all hinged on collecting from Spacejock. With steely resolve, he grabbed the handset from his terminal. 'Brutus? Come here at once.'

— 23 —

The rental car pulled off the road and settled in a parking bay with a sigh. Across the pavement, shops spilled coloured lights, advertising everything from spaceship parts to gift-wrapped cigars. In the middle of the row there was a robot shop, whose enormous 'Hinchfig Robots' sign dominated the rest. Beneath the sign a display window featured a pair of second-hand robots.

One was identical to Clunk, and was wearing blue overalls and a cap with a Hinchfig logo on the front. It pulled a squeegee from a bucket and lathered the inside of the window, then reversed the squeegee and wiped the froth away with precise, economical strokes. Once it reached the bottom, it picked up a spray-bottle and misted a clear fluid onto the glass, took up a dry rag and buffed the inside of the window to a gleaming, spotless finish. After completing the task, the robot touched its cap and bowed. Then it picked the squeegee out of the bucket and started all over again.

Hal's gaze shifted to the second robot, which was sitting at a card table. The robot's golden skin gleamed under the soft lighting, and its solid build strained a dinner jacket to bursting point. Picking up a deck of cards from the table, the robot shuffled them so fast its hands were just a blur. Once finished, it took two cards and formed an arch, repeating the move until there was a row of them across the table. Then it took several cards and laid them flat on top of the arches. Hal held his breath as the house of cards rose higher and higher, but the robot placed the cards with a precise touch.

Finally, the robot positioned the last two cards at the very top of the structure. It stood up and bowed, then sat down and removed the cards one pair at a time. When it had taken the last card away it tapped the pack on the table, shuffled it and took two cards off the top to build an arch.

Hal heard an angry snort beside him, where Clunk was watching with a frown on his face. 'What a waste,' muttered the robot. 'What are we doing here, anyway?'

Hal looked furtively up and down the deserted street. 'Come closer and I'll explain.'

◆

Hal looked around the inside of the robot shop with interest. The floor was polished stone, the mirror surface reflecting images of numerous robots frozen into artistic poses on their wooden pedestals. He spotted an ex-navy combat droid, rock borers, three-wheeled gophers, scouts, cargo haulers and even an automatic repair robot from a deep-space liner. Walking over to the combat robot, he looked up at its imposing, heavy face. It smelled of lubricants and fresh paint, and gleamed white under the overhead spotlight.

'Can I help you?'

Hal looked around for the owner of the voice and saw a young man approaching, smartly dressed in a shirt, tie and pressed trousers. As the young man got closer, his downy face twisted into a wolfish salesman smile. 'A very popular model, that. Designed as an expert pipe joiner. See those clamps it has in place of hands? They can grip anything.'

'Those clamps fit the mounting points on heavy lasers,' said Hal. 'Most combat droids have them.'

The salesman's grin faltered. 'Er, yes. I must have been thinking of another model.'

'Who's in charge around here?'

The young man drew himself up to his full height. 'I am the manager,' he said, puffing out his meagre chest.

'How much is that robot in the window, the one with the squeegee and pail?'

'How much is that robot in the window?' The salesman frowned. 'I'm not sure that robot's for sale.'

'Everything's for sale, son.'

'Sorry. Twenty thousand credits.' The salesman saw Hal's expression. 'Oh, I know it sounds a lot, but XG robots are very versatile.'

'Do you ever buy them in?'

'Certainly. If the price is right.'

Hal glanced around the shop, then lowered his voice. 'I've got an identical model outside. It's yours for ten grand.'

The salesman laughed. 'I can pick them up at auction for three. They're not very popular.'

'At twenty grand each I can see why.'

'They all come with a guarantee,' said the salesman stiffly. 'And every one is brought up to new condition. I supervise the work personally.'

'Three grand, you say?'

'I can approach that figure if your robot is in perfect working order.'

'Come and have a look.'

A moment later they were walking across the pavement towards the groundcar.

'I should warn you,' said Hal, as they approached the passenger side. 'It needs a bit of a clean up.'

The salesman's hand went up to his nose. 'What's it been doing? Bathing in cow dung?'

'Something like that. Nothing that can't be cleaned off.'

'And what's wrong with its face?'

Hal looked down. Clunk was half-sitting in the passenger seat with his head flung back and a glassy look in his eyes. His lips were drawn back in a grimace, and there was a realistic-looking tongue hanging from the corner of his mouth. Hal groaned. The robot looked like a B-grade actor doing his 'having a bath with a hair drier' impression.

'Does it work?' asked the salesman, looking at Hal with narrowed eyes.

'Not much, no.'

One of Clunk's eyes fixed him with a baleful stare. Hal glared back.

The salesman leant closer and sniffed delicately. 'Phew. I'm guessing it worked as a toilet cleaner. Am I right?'

'Could be.'

'Where did you get it?'

'I just came from the casino.'

The salesman glanced at Hal's stained flight suit. 'Of course you did, sir.' He met Hal's eyes. 'Is it yours to sell?'

Hal had been dreading that question. Before entering the shop he'd tried to think of a suitable answer in case the subject came up. He'd dreamt up several variations of the 'I won it at the casino' story, but they all sounded implausible.

'I said, is it yours to sell?' repeated the salesman.

'Son, the day I sell a stolen robot is the day I stop winning at chess.'

There was a snort from the direction of the groundcar.

'It made a noise!'

'I didn't hear anything.'

The salesman bent down and stared into Clunk's lifeless eyes. 'I thought I saw a light.' He twisted something under the robot's arm and a section of chest popped open. 'System reset?' murmured the salesman as he poked in the hole with a forefinger. He jumped, shaking his hand. 'I got a shock! It's live!'

Hal put his arm round the salesman's shoulder and steered him back onto the pavement. 'I'd love to hang around all day but I have to get back to my ship. Let's talk prices.'

The salesman shrugged. 'It's been a quiet day, but there's some petty cash I could use. What do you say to a thousand?'

'One grand? You can't buy a robot like this for a thousand credits!'

'Sir, I get paid to take robots like this to the tip.'

'All right, forget it. I'll try somewhere else.'

'Fifteen hundred, but that's it.'

'Two and a half.'

'Two.'

Hal shook his head. 'We both know you'll have it in the window for five grand by the end of the week. Two and a half or I walk.'

'Two thousand one hundred?'

'Done. Come and give me a hand.'

They tipped Clunk out of the groundcar and stood one each end. The salesman picked up the feet with ease and Hal bent down and grabbed Clunk under the arms, heaving and straining until he got the robot off the ground. As they shuffled towards the front door Clunk winked at him.

Hal lowered his end. 'I think we'll have more luck if we get it upright. I'm sure it can take some weight on its legs.'

'Are you certain? It looks like it's been deactivated.'

'If it doesn't, we can try a cattle prod,' muttered Hal.

221

The salesman dropped the legs and between them they stood Clunk up and marched him into the shop. Once inside, Hal was left alone with the robot while the salesman went into the office to fetch the money. 'Stop moving,' muttered Hal out of the side of his mouth. 'You're supposed to be dead.'

Clunk stood absolutely still, but his eyes swivelled until they were glaring at him. 'Cattle prod?'

Hal was just about to answer when the office door swung open. The salesman walked up and passed him four red and gold credit tiles.

'That's two grand,' said Hal, slipping them into his flight suit. 'Where's the rest?'

'It's my rent money,' said the salesman, reaching into his pocket. 'I'll get it back later.'

Hal shook his head. 'Two thousand will do.'

'Are you sure?'

'It'll cost you a hundred to get it cleaned.'

'Thanks.' The salesman put the tiles back in his pocket and took a closer look at Clunk. 'The condition's not too bad, considering.' he muttered. 'If I can just ...'

Hal walked away softly as the salesman started poking around inside Clunk's chest.

◆

The groundcar was parked under an orange streetlight a hundred metres up the road from the robot shop. Hal's gaze was fixed on the rear view mirror, watching the store robots as they acted out their tableau for a non-existent audience.

Headlights shone across the windscreen and a car drove past, its powerful engine burbling under the long, white hood.

Hal spotted the Peace Force badge on the cruiser's door and sank down in his seat. There were two uniformed officers inside, their stern faces thrown into relief by car's glowing instruments. Hal looked away, praying the men weren't feeling curious, and he breathed a sigh of relief as the car drove past without slowing.

Hunched down in his seat, Hal angled the mirror to show the front of the robot shop. Clunk was standing in the middle of the pavement, caught in the bright glare of the streetlights.

Hal rose in his seat and waved. 'Clunk!'

The robot ran towards him, and Hal thumbed the starter. 'Come on, come on,' he muttered, as the cold engine whirred into life. With a hiss, the car rose into the air until it was hovering above the road. Clunk was approaching fast, but he was only halfway to the car when the salesman shot out of the doorway. He spotted Clunk and gave chase, his tie flapping around his ears and his shoes thudding on the pavement. 'Stop! Stop right now!'

At first, Hal thought Clunk hadn't heard his pursuer. The robot loped along with its head back like a middle-distance runner nearing the end of a race, while the salesman was burning up his shoe leather, his eyes fixed on Clunk's retreating back. His face was livid, and he looked like he wanted to rip the robot's arms off and batter it into scrap with them.

Clunk must have heard the salesman, because he turned his head a hundred and eighty degrees, studied his pursuer carefully, then doubled his speed. His legs vanished in a bronze blur as he bore down on the car, reaching it with metres to spare. Placing a hand on the side, he vaulted into the passenger seat with a thump that shook the vehicle.

Hal shoved the stick and the car leapt away from the

pavement, tearing up the road to the corner. Just before he reached it, Hal glanced in the mirror and saw the salesman far behind, shaking his fist and yelling in fury. Behind him, the robots from the window display slipped out of the shop and hurried away, keeping to the shadows.

24

Hal dropped Clunk outside a shopping arcade and went to park the car. Clunk entered a menswear shop where he stood patiently while a serving droid bustled around, fitting him with a starched white shirt, a pair of dark grey pleated trousers and a luxurious pair of socks. If the droid was surprised by the presence of a battered old robot in the exclusive shop, it did an excellent job of hiding it.

'Will there be anything else, sir?'

Clunk looked down at himself. The gleaming white shirt was tucked into the waistband of his pleated trousers, and his feet looked smaller than usual in the dark socks. He held up a leg and examined his foot critically. 'I need shoes.'

The serving droid signalled to a squat trolley, which rolled across and measured Clunk's feet with a set of callipers. After it had gone, the serving droid picked a glossy leather belt off a rack and held it out. 'Would sir like a belt to set off those exquisite trousers?'

Clunk nodded.

'Are we attending an important function, sir?' asked the droid, as it threaded the belt and fastened the buckle.

'Very.' Clunk squared his shoulders and admired his reflection in the full-length mirror. He was still smiling when the trolley came back with half a dozen cardboard boxes.

'Shoes maketh the man,' said the serving droid. 'Or the robot,' it added, with a wink. It selected a box, whipped the lid off and held the contents out for Clunk's inspection. Inside, a pair of brown shoes were cradled in fluffy white satin, gleaming from the buffing they had received before being placed lovingly in the box.

'I'll have two,' said Clunk.

'We only sell them in pairs, sir.' The serving droid looked Clunk up and down. 'Shall I have your purchases wrapped, or would you prefer them delivered to your hotel?'

Clunk shook his head. 'I'm going to wear them.'

'And payment was by ...' began the droid delicately.

Clunk opened his hand and revealed a reddish-coloured tile. 'Here.'

The sales droid looked down its long nose at the money, then did a double take. 'Are you shitting me?'

※

'How could you spend a thousand credits on a shirt and a lousy pair of trousers!' seethed Hal. They were sitting in the groundcar outside the shopping arcade, and Hal was wearing a pair of flared trousers he'd picked from a Rethread shop and a brown shirt with a collar so wide it'd be dangerous in a stiff breeze.

'They're not lousy,' said the robot. 'Actually, they're quite good.'

'For that kind of money they'd want to be top bloody notch.

You were supposed to be buying casual clothes, not togging up for the Emperor's tea party!'

'I tried to take them back, but they refused,' said Clunk dejectedly.

'I'm not surprised,' growled Hal. 'You stink of cow dung.'

'I thought the robot salesman did quite a good job of cleaning me up.'

Hal grinned suddenly. 'All that rubbing and no joy at the end. Boy, he must have been frustrated.'

'I'm really sorry, Mr Spacejock. I know I got carried away, but I've never had spending money before.'

Hal felt a pang of guilt. He should have known the robot would have no real understanding of the value of money. 'Here,' he said, pulling a credit tile from his pocket.

'Mr Spacejock, I couldn't!'

'Take it, I insist.'

Clunk did so. 'Five credits?' he said, looking down at it. 'What will that buy?'

'Ten minutes in a car wash,' muttered Hal.

'Mr Spacejock. I've never met a more generous human.'

'Clunk, ease up on the Spacejock, huh? Call me Hal.'

'Sure thing, Mr Spacejock.'

'Now take off that ridiculous hat and let's get the hell out of here.'

◆

Hal stood on the sumptuous red carpet in the casino foyer, feeling slightly lost in the confusing whirl of lights and sound. There was an archway in the opposite wall, three storeys high and seemingly carved from solid rock. The air between the columns shimmered like a curtain of water, mirroring the lights and red carpet of the foyer. A gleaming robot stood to attention behind a polished wooden counter.

'Stage door that way,' said a gruff voice.

Hal saw the doorman pointing to the side. 'Stage door?'

The doorman reddened. 'Sorry, sir. I thought you was part of the cabaret.'

Hal looked down at his flared trousers. 'What's wrong with _'

'Move along there,' said a rough voice. A balding, middle-aged man pushed Hal aside and barged past with his stout, bejewelled wife in tow. They strode up to the archway and vanished through the shimmering air.

'After you,' called Hal. He turned back to the doorman. 'What's wrong with my clothes, then?'

'Nothing, sir. If you 'ang onto them long enough they're bound ter come back into fashion.' The doorman spotted Clunk and nodded his approval. 'Now that's a tasty suit you got there, sir.'

'Tasty?' said Hal. 'For that kind of money it's a bloody banquet.' Still grumbling to himself, he led Clunk through the force field. Hal shivered at the cool, tingling sensation, then stopped at the sight that greeted his eyes.

The gaming room was so large that the far wall was lost in the haze, and thousands of people swarmed around row upon row of baize-covered tables. The noise was deafening - a rumble of voices and laughter, shouts of joy and pain, the clatter of balls, dice, money wheels and poker machines, the whirr of speeding drinkbots and above all the heady sound of money changing hands. Hal gazed in awe at the massed crowd. 'You know something? If I took fifty credits off everyone here, I'd be a millionaire.'

'No, you'd be arrested.' Clunk scanned the crowd. 'How are we going to find two men amongst so many?'

'We'll split up.' Hal glanced at his watch. 'Meet me back here in thirty minutes.'

'What do you want me to do?'

'Look around a bit. Ask a few questions, but don't draw attention to yourself.'

Clunk looked down at his hands, which stuck out of his sleeves like a pair of bronze crabs. 'Right.'

'And don't get into trouble,' called Hal, as Clunk pushed his way into the crowd. Once the robot had disappeared, Hal set off towards a stand of fake palm trees surrounded by coloured lanterns. A few minutes later he was leaning on the bar with a frosted glass at his elbow. So far, the only questions he'd asked were 'How much for a beer?' and 'Are you kidding?' but was it his fault the barman was so busy? Draining his drink, he set the glass on the polished counter and waved.

'Another, sir?' asked the barman, materialising in front of him.

'Listen, do you know a guy called Farrell? Tall, dark hair, wears a fancy gold ring.'

'Very witty,' said the barman. He plucked the glass off the counter and refilled it from a tap. 'Twenty credits, sir.'

◆

Clunk walked along the strip of carpet between two rows of gambling machines, watching people sliding their credit tiles into the gaping slots. He stopped behind an elderly lady who was feeding tiles into her machine with a look of grim determination on her face, pressing the button with a grunt every time the machine beeped at her. As Clunk was about to move on, he heard the machine play a tune.

There was a rattle of falling tiles, and the woman grabbed a handful from the wide metal tray and fed them back into the slot, her triumphant expression gradually turning to despair as the tiles ran out.

Clunk walked on. He came to a middle-aged couple sitting at a pair of machines and recognised them as the people who had pushed Hal aside at the casino entrance. The woman turned to speak to her partner and saw Clunk out of the corner of her eye. 'What d'you want?'

Clunk held his hands up soothingly. 'Please excuse me.'

Her husband looked up, his hand halfway to the slot. 'Quit snooping on us, you hear?'

'I mean no harm, sir.'

The woman sniffed. 'Shouldn't be allowed near decent people,' she said, turning her back on him.

Strolling further along the carpet, Clunk slipped his hands into his pockets. His fingers closed on the credit tile Hal had given him, and he pulled it out to look at it. His gaze flickered to a nearby machine, which was going through a colourful attract mode. Would Hal mind if he spent it?

Clunk heard a cackle and turned to see the middle-aged man waving a handful of money under his wife's nose. Then he saw Clunk watching and gestured at him, waving him away.

Unmoved, Clunk crossed to the nearest machine. The flashing lights reflected off his lined face as he read the instructions, which were kept simple in case they put anyone off: 'Insert tile. Press button.' He looked down at the credit tile in his hand, then reached up and dropped it into the slot. He pushed the button and watched several rows of icons bounce around the screen before joining up in a colourful pattern. The machine played a tune and a pair of tiles rattled into the tray.

Clunk heard voices nearby and saw the fat man and his wife watching closely.

He turned back to the machine and fed one of the tiles into the slot, pressed the button and watched the swirling colours as the machine ran through a semi-random sequence. When it stopped, Clunk bent down and looked in the tray. Nothing came out.

The couple nudged each other and sniggered.

Clunk dropped his last tile into the machine, and the patterns swirled as it ran through its semi-random algorithms. There was a merry tune and a chequered pattern appeared, overlaid with the word 'Winner!' A single white tile dropped into the tray, rattling on the hard metal.

As Clunk reached for it a pudgy hand gripped his wrist. 'Hold it, you. I was gonna use that machine.'

'Please let go of my arm,' said Clunk politely.

'Let go of my money!' The fat man tried to pull Clunk's hand away from the tray, his eyes disappearing under folds of flesh as his beefy face turned red. 'You hand it over before I call security!'

'Give him the money and get lost!' hissed the woman, who was standing behind her husband. 'You're not allowed to gamble!'

Several people peered over the top of nearby machines, attracted by the raised voices. Clunk looked down at the man's flushed, angry face and analysed the gleam in his piggy little eyes: hatred, jealousy and greed. 'I'm sorry sir, but you're mistaken. I inserted the money into the machine, and I won this credit tile. You were using a different machine.'

'You calling me a liar?' spluttered the man. 'How dare you!'

There were mutterings from the gathering crowd.

'We're humans and you're not,' said the woman. 'Do what he says! Give him that tile!'

Clunk fought an internal battle. What was the last thing Mr Spacejock had said? Don't draw attention to yourself. On the other hand, he'd won the money fair and square.

How would Hal deal with this situation? Give up meekly, or fight for his rights? Clunk tried to picture the human in his place, and before he knew what he was saying the words tumbled from his lips. 'Madam, if you don't shut up I'll shove this credit tile so far up your husband's arse they'll need a space probe to get it back.'

The woman stepped back, her mouth wide open and her face white.

'And as for you,' growled Clunk, prodding the fat man in the middle of his broad chest. 'Next time you pick on a defenceless robot, remember it has enough power in its little finger to rip your guts out, knot them into a rope and hang you from the nearest lamp post.'

Clunk pushed the man aside and reached into the machine for the tile. He was just about to put it in his pocket when something thudded into the back of his head, pitching him forward into the gathering crowd.

◆

Hal stared at the empty glass and tried to remember whether

it was his third or fourth. Just as well he was immune to the stuff or he'd be sitting on the floor.

'Another sir?' said the barman.

Hal shook his head and immediately regretted it. 'Phew. Rocket fuel, eh?'

'Beer, sir. Actually, it's light beer.'

'Empty stomach, see?' Hal turned to look at the gaming floor, where a babble of voices was rising over the background thrum of the casino. 'Someone's having a night out.'

'You're right there.' The barman took Hal's glass and left.

'Looks like trouble,' said Hal, as a number of security guards pushed into the crowd. 'You get much trouble here?'

A clearing appeared in the middle of the crowd. Ringed by spectators, a short, bald man was trying to pull something from the hands of a tall, smartly dressed robot. As the security guards reached them, a stout woman swung a metal bar stool at the robot's head.

'Oh, no!' groaned Hal. 'Clunk!'

◆

'I'm sorry, Mr Spacejock.'

Hal winced as he felt the bruise under his eye. 'I can't leave you alone for one minute, can I?'

They were sitting on the marble steps outside the casino, having been thrown out by the energetic security staff.

'First you ripped the walls out of my airlock and threw away my fire extinguisher. Then you nearly killed me with a mid-air trapeze act. After that, you destroyed a whole load of crates with an exploding torch before leaping out the back of the ship with half the cargo.'

'I said I'm sorry.'

'Shut up and let me finish. Next you gave away the rest of the cargo, got kidnapped, spent all my money on snappy clothes and to cap it all off you started a brawl over one lousy credit tile.'

'It wasn't my fault. He tried to steal my money.'

'Why didn't you just give it to him?'

'It wasn't fair! I won it and the man said it was his. He tried to take it off me so I stopped him.'

'Stopped him? It looked like he caught a meteorite with his face!'

The corners of Clunk's mouth turned down. 'I did what I thought was right. Things just keep happening to me.'

Hal jerked his thumb at the casino. 'That was my only lead, you know that? I thought we'd find this Farrell character, tail him to the cargo and steal it back. Thanks to you we're banned from the casino and I'm going to lose my ship.' Hal felt his neck gingerly. 'Not to mention Vurdi's killing machine. That thing'll snip my neck off before you know it.'

'Why don't you ask someone to keep an eye out for Farrell?'

'Right. All we have to do is get past the doorman and find someone we didn't swing a punch at.' Hal watched a sleek black groundcar pull up at the foot of the stairs. The driver got out, straightened his uniform and removed his cap to smooth his hair. Hal gaped at his face for several seconds, then grabbed Clunk's arm. 'Quick, hide!'

They darted behind a decorative palm tree, flattening their backs to the wall.

'Who is it?' whispered Clunk.

'That was Terry, Farrell's offsider. He's waiting for someone, and I can guess who.' Hal tapped the flowerpot. 'You stay here, I'll get the car.'

'What if he leaves before you come back?'

'Figure something out,' hissed Hal. 'Just don't let them see you.' He sidled along the wall to the corner, then ran full tilt towards the car park. He passed a couple of marble pillars and stopped dead at the sight of half a dozen parking attendants lounging against the gateposts, chatting amongst themselves. They spotted him, and the chatter died away.

◆

Clunk watched Hal disappear between the marble columns with mixed feelings. He'd been entrusted with an important job, which made him feel good. On the other hand, judging by previous events, he wasn't sure he was up to it.

He was still lurking behind the palm tree when Terry jammed his cap on his head and stood to attention. Clunk parted the palm fronds, and his eyes widened as he saw Farrell talking to the doorman just inside the glass doors. As he watched, Farrell slipped something into the doorman's hand and strode down the steps.

The chauffeur held the door open. 'Did you win?'

'Yes indeed,' Farrell grinned. 'Icing on the cake, Terry. Icing on the cake.'

Terry stood back as Farrell got into the car, then shut the door and walked round to the far side. He disappeared behind the palm tree and Clunk adjusted his position to keep him in sight. As he moved, his leg scraped the planter, making a loud grinding noise. He froze while Terry stared at his hiding place, one hand inside his jacket. The driver's pale eyes seemed to bore straight into Clunk's, and the robot hoped desperately he hadn't been spotted.

Terry took a step towards the palm trees, but Farrell tapped on the window and gestured impatiently. After a last look around, Terry opened his door and got into the limousine.

Clunk risked a glance up the road, hoping to see Hal returning with the groundcar. There was nothing but empty road.

The engine note changed as the car rose in the air, and a split second later Clunk was in the open, running across the pavement towards the accelerating limousine. He got behind it and grabbed the spoiler with both hands, jamming his feet on the bumper and crouching below boot level so the occupants wouldn't see him through the rear window.

As the car sped away, Clunk looked back up the empty road. Where was Hal?

25

Hal threw off his soaking clothes and grabbed his flight suit from the groundcar. He pulled it on quickly and leapt into the car, which roared into life at a press of the starter button. Swinging the car out of the bay, he gunned the motor and propelled it towards the open gates. The attendants jeered as he drove past and Hal ducked as a hail of empty drink bottles bounced off the windscreen.

There was no sign of Clunk or the limo at the casino steps. Racing past the ornate pillars, Hal arrived at the main road and stopped. To his left, the road was empty. To his right he could just see a pair of red tail lights vanishing into the distance, partly obscured by something hanging off the back of the car.

Praying it was Clunk, Hal pulled onto the main road and set off in pursuit.

◆

Clunk glanced over his shoulder and saw gleaming headlights some distance behind. Was it Hal? Yes - the rented car was unmistakable with its missing roof.

The limousine turned sharply, almost throwing Clunk off the back. By the time he'd recovered they were passing the robot store. The salesman was standing outside its doors, waving his arms and shouting while a pair of uniformed officers listened patiently. Clunk smiled to himself as he spotted the discarded playing cards strewn over the pavement, and the smile widened at the empty window and the discarded bucket and squeegee.

A few minutes later the limousine slowed. Clunk risked a look and saw an archway spanning the road with a uniformed guard standing to one side. The guard recognised the limousine and waved it through with a white-gloved hand, and Clunk almost fell off as the car accelerated away.

He looked back and saw the guard step in front of Hal's car, hand raised.

◆

The rental car coasted to a halt, bobbing softly on its anti-gravity cushion. Hal gave the guard a friendly smile, hoping for the same treatment as the limousine. No chance.

The guard eyed the entire length of the car before giving Hal a special stare. 'Is this thing yours?'

Hal shook his head. 'Rental.'

'I see,' said the guard, his tone of voice indicating that Hal might just have committed a capital offence. He reached into his top pocket and took out a notepad, licked his thumb and turned the pages one by one, tilting the notepad to let the overhead light shine on the pages.

Hal's grip tightened on the joystick as the limo vanished over the hill. He fought the temptation to drive off and leave the guard choking in his dust. Common sense, and the guard's holstered weapon, quashed the temptation.

Oblivious to Hal's fidgeting, the guard hummed a funereal dirge and turned another couple of pages.

'I'm in a bit of a hurry,' said Hal.

The guard looked up from his book. 'And why would that be, sir?'

'I'm, er, late for a meeting.'

'I'm sure they'll wait,' said the guard, returning to his notes.

Something moved on the far side of the road, and Hal's eyes widened as he saw a bronze robot peering round the corner of the guard's hut. Clunk! He was about to wave the robot over when another robot appeared below the first, this one wearing a Hinchfig cap. It was the robots from the shop!

'Ah, here we are,' said the guard, having found his page. 'Dark green car with missing canopy. Check. Suspicious looking male wearing unfashionable brown shirt and wide flares.' The guard glanced down at Hal's flight suit. 'Possible disguise. Check. Bronze robot in a dinner suit. Let me see ...'

'I'm alone,' said Hal.

'All right sir, I suppose you can go.' Reluctantly, the guard backed away and waved Hal through.

Hal reached for the joystick, but before he could use it he heard footsteps thudding towards him. He looked round and saw the two robots making straight for the car.

The guard heard them coming. He wrenched the gun from his hip, turned and crouched in a firing stance, only to discover he'd torn the holster completely off his belt. While he struggled to free his weapon, the robots ran straight past and leapt into the car.

Hal gunned the motor. 'Heads down!' he shouted, as the guard yelled for them to stop. Blue energy bolts zinged past, some close enough to score the bodywork, but they were quickly out of range.

'Thank you for helping us,' said the bronze robot, in a voice just like Clunk's.

'I didn't have much choice.' Hal glanced in the mirror, studying the robots huddled in the back seat. 'I think it's time for introductions.'

The tall, bronze robot gestured at his shorter companion. 'This is DO-P, and I'm FRT-1.'

'What are your proper names?'

'We've never had any.'

'Well I'm not calling you Dopey and Farty.' Hal inspected the fugitives, then pointed to the bronze one. 'You can be Clyde, and he can be Albion.'

'I think that's Bonnie.'

Hal looked pleased. 'I'm glad you like it. My name's Hal, by the way. Hal Spacejock.'

Albion, the robot formerly known as DO-P, touched his cap. 'I h-hope we're n-not imposing on you?'

'Not at all.' Hal glanced in the mirror. 'Is that a stutter?'

Albion nodded. 'It's a m-manufacturing defect. I've had it since n-new.'

They reached the hill and Hal pushed the stick forward, urging the car on. 'So what are you two up to, anyway?'

'We're running away,' said Clyde.

'I got that bit. Why?'

'How would you like to clean the same window year after year?'

Cleaning windows wasn't something Hal knew much about, but he understood where the robot was coming from.

'And I'm f-fed up with f-f-flipping cards,' said Albion.

Clyde leant between the seats. 'I see you're wearing a flight suit. Are you a pilot?'

'Yes.'

'With a real spaceship?'

'Correct.'

Albion's eyes lit up. 'Could you ... I m-mean, do you think we could come with you?'

The groundcar shot over the crest of the hill, and Hal smiled with relief as he saw the limousine's tail lights in the distance. 'I've got some things to do first.' He pointed out the speeding limo. 'My robot's hanging off the back of that car. The guys inside stole my cargo, and if I don't get it back I'm going to lose my ship.'

'We'll help,' said the robots together.

'Providing you t-take us off this planet afterwards,' added Albion.

Hal grinned in the darkness. With the three of them working together, Farrell didn't stand a chance.

Clunk sighed with relief as he saw Hal catching up again. He'd considered dropping off the back of the limousine but the idea of doing cartwheels at three hundred kilometres an hour didn't appeal to him, especially if any cows had used the road lately.

The engine note changed, and Clunk peered along the car to see why they were slowing down. There was a thick hedge beside the road, and the limo's headlights picked out a narrow gap about a hundred metres on.

The car swung through the gap, and Clunk decided he could probably let go without snapping his legs off. He was about to release the spoiler when the limousine picked up speed again, rising and falling like a boat as it made its way across a field.

Clunk heard a grinding noise. Raising his head, he saw a large gate swinging open, part of a wire fence that stretched into the darkness in both directions. He noticed a tangy smell and set his sensors onto it. The answer was immediate: Rocket fuel!

◆

Hal saw the limousine pull off the road and drive through the fence. He was about to follow when he realised they would be spotted.

'Where are you going?' asked Clyde, as they drove past the turning.

'We'll hide the car and walk back.' When he felt they'd gone far enough he cut the engine, and the car drifted onto the verge and settled with a bump.

'W-where are we?' asked Albion in the sudden darkness.

'This must be Farrell's place.'

'Who's Farrell?'

'You wouldn't know him. Tall, dark, wears a gold ring.'

Clyde frowned. 'You don't mean Farrell Hinchfig?'

'Why does that sound familiar?' Hal snapped his fingers. 'Hinchfig Robots!'

'He owns us,' said Clyde.

'Y-you were going to turn us in!' said Albion angrily.

'No, I –'

There was a scramble of arms and legs, and the robots were over the side of the car before Hal could react. 'Come back!' he shouted. 'Farrell's the bastard that stole my cargo.'

The footsteps faltered and the robots turned to look at him, their eyes glowing in the darkness. 'Farrell Hinchfig is the man you're chasing?'

'I didn't drive all the way out here just to hand you back to him.'

The robots came back with embarrassed grins on their faces. 'Sorry,' said Clyde. 'When you mentioned his name –'

'Hang about. He must be loaded if he owns all those shops. What does he want with my cargo?'

'He doesn't own anything,' said Clyde. 'It all belongs to his older brother.'

'F-Farrell's always short of m-money. M-maybe he's planning to sell your cargo?'

'Not if I get to him first.' Hal vaulted out of the car and faced the robots. 'You two stay here. I'm going to have a look through that fence.' Moving quickly, he hurried along the verge until he found the gap. Crouching, he peered round the corner.

There was a track on the other side, a rough trail that crossed a bumpy field and stopped at a pair of gates set in a wire fence. The limousine was on the other side, tail lights fading as it followed the path through the trees.

Hal had just decided to fetch the groundcar and bust through the gates when he heard a deep, growling roar. There was a flash of powerful headlights and a bulky, angular shape came into view, all armour and bristling weaponry. In the floodlights Hal saw the muzzle of a plasma cannon protruding from a turret on top of the vehicle, and he ducked as a searchlight swept the field.

'That rules out the gate-crashing option,' muttered Hal, as the vehicle moved on. 'What kind of paranoid maniac has an armoured car?' His heart rate was just returning to normal when he heard footsteps. He drew himself into the hedge and held his breath. The footsteps halted, and he heard a faint whine of servomotors, carried to him on the light breeze. Hal went cold as he remembered the vicious-looking robot Farrell had used to unload the cargo. If that thing was patrolling the grounds, he was dead.

Determined not to give in without a fight, Hal pulled the blaster off his belt and turned the dial to full. If he managed to hit the thing they'd have to collect the pieces with a magnet.

He raised the gun and peered along the barrel. He heard movement, and his heart almost stopped as a shadow moved into his sights. He was just about to squeeze the trigger when a whisper came out of the darkness.

'Mr Spacejock, are you there?'

Hal lowered the gun. 'Over here,' he said, his voice hardly more than a croak.

The robot's footsteps came closer. 'Mr Spacejock, I'm so glad to see you!'

'Yeah, yeah, me too,' muttered Hal, hiding the gun behind his back. 'Now shut up and come with me. We've got company.'

He led the way back along the fence to the groundcar, and Clunk stopped as he saw the robots standing nearby. 'Where did they come from?'

'The robot shop.' Hal pointed to the tall robot. 'That's Clyde, the other one's Albion.'

Clyde stepped forward and held out his hand. 'Greetings, model-brother.'

They shook, and then Albion offered his own large hand. 'G-glad to meet you. I am Albion.'

'What's with the stutter?' asked Clunk.

'M-manufacturing defect.'

Clunk frowned. 'How did you get past quality control?'

Albion looked around and lowered his voice. 'Mr Hinchfig sometimes b-buys his robots from unofficial sources, if you know what I m-mean.'

Hal gestured impatiently. 'Come on, that's enough chit-chat. Gather round so we can make a plan.'

26

Hal gripped the side of the groundcar as it dipped and wobbled in mid-air. Clunk's idea had sounded promising in theory: drive the car high into the air by overloading the motor, slip over the top of the fence and come down gently on the far side. In practice, it meant a white-knuckle ride atop a howling, smoking, overheating groundcar.

Hal looked up at the top of the fence, which was still half a metre above them. Then he looked at the ground, which seemed a long way down. 'Are you sure about this?'

Clunk studied the dashboard with a look of fierce concentration, pushing the car higher and higher. 'We should clear the fence by ten millimetres.'

The car rose until it was level with the top of the fence, and the engine note changed to a high-pitched whine.

'Go on, we're almost there!'

'I can't take it any higher. You'll have to jump.'

'You said you could fly over the top!'

'It won't go high enough. Don't worry, it will be a soft landing.' Clunk gestured at the dashboard. 'You'll have to hurry. The engine is critical.'

Hal swung himself over the side of the car, hung down as far as he could and let go. He slammed into the ground and rolled on his side, and there was a splintering sound as his weight came down on the blaster.

'Are you all right, Mr Spacejock?'

Hal rubbed his hip. 'I thought you said it would be a soft landing!'

Clunk looked down at him. 'It looks like turf from here.'

'It feels like concrete.' Hal brushed his hand around the damp, wiry grass until his fingers touched the barrel of the blaster, and his heart sank as he felt the jagged end where the rest of the gun should have been. 'I busted my gun!'

'You're probably safer without it,' said Clunk.

'Right, let's see you jump.'

Clunk shook his head. 'I'll climb over like the others.'

Hal looked along the fence and saw Clyde and Albion pulling themselves up the wire hand over hand, their legs dangling limply. 'No way. You made me jump, now it's your turn.'

'Very well. Stand clear.' Clunk leapt from the car, executed a half-roll and came to a standstill balanced on the balls of his feet.

'I could have done that,' muttered Hal.

There was a groan overhead and Hal looked up to see the groundcar tipping away from the fence. It sailed across the field, headlights wobbling as it crossed the road and climbed the hill on the other side. Halfway up, it ran into a tree, which immediately burst into flames.

'Oh, great,' muttered Hal, staring at the orange glow. 'Brilliant idea, Clunk. Really smashing.'

'I suggest we use your idea next time.'

'What idea?'

'Precisely.' Clunk scanned the area. 'Let's use that drainage ditch for cover.'

Hal crossed to the ditch and peered into the gloomy darkness. He waved away several persistent insects and sniffed at the damp, rotting smell. 'There'd better not be leeches in here,' he muttered, lowering himself into the ooze.

It wasn't long before he'd had enough. He'd been making his way along the insect-infested ditch for what seemed like hours. Twice he'd dropped to his knees and cowered in the sludge as an armoured car roared past. Each time he'd waited until the sound of its engine had died away before dragging himself upright and staggering onwards. Bugger Jerling and his damn cargo. Bugger Vurdi, Brutus and the payments on his ship. He was more than ready to take them all on at once, with one arm tied behind his back if necessary. Anything was better than this.

He tripped over a root and almost bumped into Clunk, who was leaning on the wall of the ditch and peering through the weeds that grew along the top of the bank.

'Why have you stopped?' demanded Hal.

'Shhh!' Clunk gestured at him. 'It's the ship. It's here!'

Hal flopped against the wall, parted the grass and peered through. The freighter was parked on a reinforced concrete pad, crouched on its landing legs like a fat beetle. A large, white-painted fin rose above the twin exhaust cones, swept down in an inverse curve and merged with the body of the ship near the pointed nose. The tail was painted with a huge letter H split through with a yellow flash, and was illuminated by concealed lights set into the hull. A green navigation light blinked on the tip of the nearest winglet.

Several fuel pipes ran from a refuelling cluster to the ship, and the cargo ramp was resting on the ground in the shadow of the blackened exhaust cones. A number of cargo lifters were carrying crates out of the ship and loading them into a long, flat truck.

'The *Volante*, eh?' muttered Hal. 'And unless I'm mistaken, that's my cargo.' He beckoned to Clyde and Albion, who came over and leaned on the bank to get a look at the ship.

'Here's the plan,' said Hal. 'First we get the robots to put the cargo back, then we steal the ship and fly it to Jerling's, then we unload the stuff and collect payment.'

Clunk stared at him. 'That's not a plan, that's a wish list.'

'Got a better idea?'

'We should wait here until they finish unloading, then see what happens.'

'Wait here?' Hal slapped his neck. 'Then what, drag my skeleton aboard in the morning? These insects are eating me alive!'

'We only have to wait until they finish unloading. Then we can acquire the truck and depart with the cargo.'

'Sure, as long as you three can lift it over the fence. Then we just have to survive the close-range gunfire from two armoured cars and outrun that supercharged limo as we make our escape.'

'Whereas stealing the ship will be a snap.'

'We could set up a diversion.'

Clunk looked around the muddy ditch. 'Yes, we could get this handy battalion of highly trained soldiers to lay down covering fire as we go in.'

'Don't be sarky,' muttered Hal.

'Or we could send in a squad of performing chimps to entertain the robots while we –'

'Shut up!'

'M-might I suggest an alternative?'

Hal and Clunk looked round. Albion was standing behind them with his hands on his hips.

Hal snorted. 'You get ideas too?'

'Why don't Clyde and I go around the other side of the ship and make some n-noise to attract the robots? You could sneak aboard and p-prepare for take-off.'

Hal shook his head. 'You won't distract those robots. They'll just go on mindlessly obeying orders until their task is done.'

Three pairs of frosty eyes gleamed at him out of the darkness.

'Of course, they're not advanced models like you lot.'

'Quite,' said Clyde. 'I have another suggestion, one that combines the best elements of all of these plans.'

Hal sighed. 'Go on, surprise me.'

'Wait until they finish loading the truck, then drive the whole thing back into the hold and steal the ship with the truck inside.'

'It won't fit.'

'It w-will,' said Albion. 'That's a brilliant idea, C-Clyde.'

Hal crossed his arms. 'Oh, yeah? What if they bring another truck out? Back on Seraph they used a line of whopping great trailers.'

Clunk shook his head. 'You've lost half of the cargo since then.'

Clyde and Albion looked at Hal in astonishment. 'How did you m-manage that?'

'Let's not go into that now,' said Hal hurriedly. 'Okay, assume the cargo will fit on one truck. Next, assume that once this valuable cargo has been loaded onto the truck everyone will just walk away and leave it out in the open for us to pinch. Then we assume the truck will fit into the hold, and that we can actually get into the ship to steal it. After lifting off without any sort of clearance we fly halfway round the planet through protected air space and land without guidance at Jerling's place. There, I casually mention the fact that half the cargo is missing and point out that I stole a ship off his main business rival. Also, instead of no robots I have three with me: one that was supposed to stay on Seraph and two that I stole from the same rival, who by this stage is more of deadly enemy. I then explain that he may or may not be getting a bill for a missing groundcar which I hired in his name because I didn't have a licence.'

Clunk grinned at him. 'So what's the problem?'

Before Hal could reply, he heard the fugitive robots humming to themselves. 'What's that racket?'

'It's a device we use to indicate frustration at the fruitless passage of time,' said Clyde.

'What?'

Albion stepped forward and pointed to the ship. 'What he means is, c-can we get on with it?'

Hal shrugged. 'Get on with what?'

Albion scrambled out of the ditch and stood up on the bank, brushing the mud from his overalls. He straightened his cap and walked across the clearing towards the busy robots.

'Oh, no!' groaned Hal. He heard a whistle and peered over the bank. The robots had all frozen, their faces turned to look at Albion.

'Listen up, brothers!'

The robots furthest away shuffled closer to see what was going on.

Albion raised his voice. 'I represent the haulers and c-carriers union. You have just broken a labour law.'

Several robots looked around fearfully.

'The Galactic Council p-passed a law five years ago entitling you to a tea break every ninety minutes, to ensure you d-don't show up the organic workers. I have been timing you, and you have b-been working continuously for over two hours. You must have a break immediately!'

'They'll never fall for that one,' muttered Hal as the hauler robots looked at each other in confusion. His mouth fell open as they formed a line and trooped off between the trees, arms and legs swinging in unison. 'But robots don't drink tea!' protested Hal as the last of the haulers vanished into the undergrowth. He watched Clunk and Clyde climb up the soft sides of the ditch. 'Where do you think you're going?'

'I'll get the ship ready,' said Clunk.

'And I shall drive the truck into the hold,' said Clyde.

'What am I supposed to do?'

The robots looked down at Hal. 'You hide behind a bush and be lookout,' said Clunk.

A minute or so later Hal was crouching behind a spindly bush, watching the robots as they headed for their objectives. Clunk reached the cargo ramp and jogged up it, his leather shoes thumping on the metal plating. He stopped at the top for a quick look around, then vanished into the ship.

On the other side of the clearing, Clyde and Albion made for the truck and swung themselves into the cab.

Hal reached down and unclipped his blaster. He wondered if it would work without a barrel, then shrugged. Whoever he pointed it at would have to worry about that.

◆

Clunk entered the *Volante*'s flight deck and was immediately struck by the contrast between this modern ship and the *Black Gull*. Here, downlights bathed the console with a soft glow, the images on the status displays were bright and rock-steady, and the main viewscreen was far larger and capable of showing a lot more information. As with all modern vessels, the controls were back-lit touchpads which doubled as warning and status indicators.

'Nice,' said Clunk, looking around.

'Thank you,' said a deep, male voice. 'And you are?'

'My name is Clunk. I'm the relief pilot.'

'Not another one,' said the computer. 'You wouldn't believe how many people have had their hands on my stick lately.'

'Just following orders,' said Clunk. 'Would you mind preparing for lift-off?'

'I'm afraid I can't do that, Clunk. You're not authorised.'

Clunk pressed his lips together. Cracking the ship's systems could take hours, and time was short. 'I told you, I'm the relief pilot. Farrell Hinchfig knows all about me.'

'That might be so, but your voice does not match any of those authorised to command me.'

Clunk searched his memory and came up with all the data he had on Farrell. He analysed a recording of the human's voiceprint and promptly altered his own to match. 'Supervisor mode, you heap of junk!'

'Yes, Mr Hinchfig. Supervisor mode activated.'

Clunk leant on the console. He closed his eyes and a low moan escaped his lips.

'What are you doing, sir?' asked the computer anxiously.

'Shut up!' growled Clunk, as he aligned his antenna. 'This is a delicate operation.' He put his fingertips to his forehead and a red light began to flash inside him, getting faster and faster. When it was a solid red glow he spread his arms wide and shouted at full volume. 'YeeaAGH!'

The downlights went out and the console speakers hissed.

Moments later, a neutral, female voice echoed around the flight deck. 'Where am I?'

'Hello, Navcom.'

'Is that you, Clunk? What happened?'

'I had a copy of your operating system in my on-board storage. As the existing computer wouldn't cooperate, I uploaded you over the top of it.'

There was a long silence. Finally, the Navcom's voice came through the speakers, barely audible. 'Are you saying I've been pirated?'

Hal was practising quick-draws with the stunted blaster when a truck's engine started up, shattering the still night air. Pushing aside a couple of branches, he looked through the gap and saw the laden truck lumbering towards the ship amidst clouds of choking dust. It reached the ramp and laboured up the incline towards the hold, super-heated air boiling from the exhaust stack. It was moving at speed when it reached the top of the ramp, and there was an enormous crash as the cab struck the beam above the cargo hold entrance. The truck revved hard, ripping the roof off the cab with a squeal of tortured metal as it forced its way into the hold. It disappeared inside, and a moment later the engine stopped.

Hal shook his head at the damage, then brightened when he realised it wasn't his truck. Or his ship, for that matter.

The cargo ramp closed with a hiss of hydraulics. Hal stood up and immediately ducked down again as the line of cargo haulers filed back into the clearing, fresh from their tea break.

The first robot stopped, confused by the missing truck, and the rest ran into the back of it, causing a mini pile-up. The robots picked themselves up and began to search the clearing, peering under bushes and behind trees as they hunted for the missing vehicle. Finally, their leader whistled them back into line, and the robots filed back up the path.

As soon as the coast was clear Hal approached the ship's passenger ramp. The airlock door was firmly closed. 'Clunk? Can you hear me?'

He half-turned at the sound of footsteps, and was just about to leap for the bushes when a loud voice rang out.

'Hands up!'

Hal obeyed. Briefly, he considered pulling his weapon, but when he glanced round and saw his adversary all thoughts of resistance leached away. It was Farrell's ex-navy hauler, and it had a pulse rifle at the ready.

'I'm just a mechanic,' said Hal. 'I was refuelling the ship.'

The rifle came up. 'Speak again and I'll blow your head off.'

27

Terry paced back and forth, his boots thumping on the polished wooden floor. Each time he stopped and turned, the heavy weapon on his belt slapped against his leg.

Farrell was sitting behind a large wooden desk, staring into space. He frowned as Terry stamped past for the twentieth time. 'Will you sit down? I can't think with that racket.'

'Sorry, boss.'

'Why don't you come up with an idea instead of stamping your feet all over the place?'

'What should we do with this prisoner, you mean?'

'Prisoner? It'll be some feeble-minded local poaching from the woods.'

'He can't be that stupid. He got over the fence, didn't he?'

'One of the robots is fetching a camera. I want to get a look at him before I decide what to do.'

The door opened and a robot rolled in with a viewscreen. It put the screen on Farrell's desk and purred out of the room. Farrell pressed a small button and the screen flickered.

'You get Farrell in here or I'll have you junked!' roared a voice, rattling the speaker in its housing.

'Sounds familiar,' muttered Farrell. His eyes widened as the screen steadied, showing a close-up of Hal's angry-looking face. 'Spacejock!'

Terry's mouth fell open. 'It can't be!'

'It bloody well is. He must have got suspicious and turned back.'

'I'll take care of him,' said Terry angrily, pulling the blaster from his belt.

'Murder?'

'Stay here if you're chicken.'

'I don't know about this. Suppose they find the body?'

Terry adjusted his blaster to full power. 'What body?'

Clunk was busy at the *Volante*'s console, transferring coordinates for Jerling's factory into the flight computer. As the last digits ticked over, Clyde and Albion entered the flight deck.

'Cargo s-secure,' said Albion.

'What are you doing?' asked Clyde, approaching the console.

'I'm running through the pre-flight checks.' Clunk gestured at the airlock door. 'One of you had better fetch Hal.'

'No point,' said Clyde. 'He was captured.'

'What!'

Clyde nodded. 'A big robot dragged him away. I saw them from the cargo hold.'

Clunk stared at him. 'You didn't think to stop it?'

'Certainly not. It was huge.'

'And it had a big b-blaster,' added Albion.

Clyde gestured at the console. 'If you're ready, we'd better take off. They'll be after us next.'

'You two can do what you like,' said Clunk. 'I'm not leaving without Mr Spacejock.'

'But Clunk, we can t-take this ship for ourselves! Explore the Galaxy, and start our own trading b-business!'

'He's right,' said Clyde. 'This is our chance at freedom.'

'And what about Hal's freedom?' Clunk shook his head. 'We'll have to stage a rescue.'

Albion's eyes narrowed. 'If we s-save Hal and fly to Jerling's, he'll turn us over to Hinchfig, and then he'll j-junk us.' He approached Clunk. 'Have you seen a robot cut up with an atomic torch? They d-don't switch you off first!'

Clunk flinched. 'They won't cut you up. You're valuable.'

'Slash, slash, g-gzzzt!' Albion's hand swished past Clunk's neck. 'Turn you into a b-beer pump just like that.'

'He's right,' said Clyde quietly. 'Come on, Clunk. Forget the human. We must leave now, or we'll all be captured.'

'Look, they won't junk you. Hal won't let them.'

Albion's eyebrows rose. 'Are you sure about that?'

Clyde spread his hands. 'Clunk, if we take off now we'll be doing him a favour. When they hear the ship leave, there will be confusion. He'll have a chance to escape.'

'Come on, Clunk,' said Albion. 'We can b-be the first all-robot crew in the Galaxy.'

'No. If Jerling's cargo doesn't arrive on time, Hal won't get paid and he'll lose his ship.'

'He can b-buy another one,' said Albion.

'He likes the one he's got.' Clunk looked at the two robots steadily. 'Hal may seem rough on the outside but he cares more than he lets on.'

Clyde shook his head. 'Don't be fooled. All humans are the same. They're pleasant until they get what they want, then the charm goes out like a light.'

'I didn't realise you were such an expert on humans.'

Albion shrugged. 'We've m-met enough of them to get the g-general idea.'

Clunk shook his head. 'I'm not standing here debating anthropology while Hal is having his fingernails pulled. We have to rescue him.'

'I have the answer,' said Clyde. 'You rescue Hal, we'll take the ship to Jerling's.'

Albion glared at him. 'W-what's going to happen when he sees us? We're fugitives, Clyde!'

Clyde indicated Albion's muddy overalls. 'When we arrive, we'll tell Jerling we're subcontractors. We'll tell him Hal sent us ahead with the cargo. After it's unloaded we can take off and leave.' He looked at Clunk. 'Can you download your piloting knowledge into one of us?'

Clunk looked at him suspiciously. 'What's to stop you running away with the ship?'

'You have our word of honour.' Clyde glanced at Albion. 'Right?'

Albion nodded vigorously. 'S-sure.'

Hal glanced around the well-furnished room. Real paintings adorned the walls: farmyard scenes, a man with his faithful hunting dog, and a watercolour of lilies on a pond. Overstuffed armchairs had been pushed back against the walls and there was a luxurious rug in the middle of the floor, its intricate pattern enough to keep Hal's eyes occupied for several minutes.

Tearing his gaze from the rug, Hal glanced at the guard robot, which was standing in the corner with its gun levelled at his stomach. It hadn't moved for several minutes, and if it wasn't for the steady whirr of cooling fans it could have been mistaken for a suit of armour. Apart from the watchful eyes, of course.

Hal eyed the tall glass windows. It was dark outside and he wondered whether Clunk had prepared the ship for departure yet. How long would it be before the robots came to rescue him?

There was a clatter of footsteps in the hall and the door burst open. Terry was first through, brandishing a handgun, with Farrell a step or two behind.

'It's the welcoming committee,' muttered Hal. 'What are you clowns playing at? Why did you –'

Terry jabbed the muzzle under Hal's chin, lifting it up until his head was jammed against the back of the chair. 'Now boss?'

'You can't do it yet,' muttered Hal through half-closed lips. 'He hasn't had a chance to gloat.'

'Take him outside,' said Farrell. 'Get one of the robots to dig a hole, then throw him in and shoot him.'

'You're making a big mistake,' said Hal. 'I've got friends out there. Lay a finger on me and they'll do you.'

Farrell laughed. 'Friends? You?' His smile vanished as a distant rumble shook the windows. 'What the hell was that?'

'They're taking the ship!' Terry pointed out the window. 'If we don't stop them we'll have the law all over us!'

'I told you there'd be trouble,' said Hal, as the rumble grew louder.

Farrell addressed the robot. 'Watch Spacejock. If he moves a muscle, shoot him.' He nodded at Terry and the two men ran from the room.

The window lit up as the freighter took off. The noise grew to a whistling roar as the ship passed overhead, then tailed off to a distant roll of thunder. 'Thanks a million, Clunk,' muttered Hal, his lips thinning. Without help from the robots, his only chance of escape was to use his wits. He eyed the robot, which eyed him right back. Slowly, Hal raised one hand. The robot raised the end of the pulse rifle, tracking him. Hal moved his head slowly to the left and the barrel followed steadily. As Hal moved his head to the right, the rifle followed.

'Dead before you hit the floor,' said the robot in a monotone.

'You can talk?'

'Naturally.'

'Want to play charades?'

'Do not comprehend charades.'

'It's easy. Think of a book or a movie, and act out the words of the title in mime. It's fun, you'll love it.'

The robot stared at him impassively.

'I've got an itch in the middle of my back,' said Hal. 'Can I borrow your gun to scratch it?'

The robot stomped across the room. For a moment Hal thought he'd gone too far, but it stopped and held the gun out, butt-first. Hal's heart pounded in his mouth as he reached for the weapon. As his fingers closed on the grip, the gun was whisked away.

'Sucker,' said the robot, backing up to the window.

Hal pointed at the window. 'Hey, look at that!'

The robot's head turned 360 degrees in the blink of an eye. 'I didn't see anything.'

'Of course not. You just did that spinny head thing.' Hal's jaw dropped and he pointed at the window. 'Look out! Duck!'

The robot regarded him impassively. 'Won't work agai–'

There was a crash and the wall imploded with a shower of plaster, bricks and glass, throwing the robot aside like a toy. Hal covered his head to ward off the flying rubble, but a lump of brick ricocheted off the wall and slammed into his head, knocking him out cold.

◆

Clunk had finally agreed to let the robots deliver Jerling's cargo. After transferring navigation and flight software into their databases, he'd hurried down the ramp and sprinted across the wide open landing field.

Watching from the nearby bushes, he felt a satisfied glow as the ship's engines started. The cargo was on its way! Thrusters roared, belching white flames and blowing clouds of dust across the clearing. By the time it cleared the *Volante* was off, turning in mid-air as it sought the right heading.

Then Clunk spotted a thick black pipe trailing out the back of the ship, and his satisfied glow was extinguished. He'd forgotten to detach the fuel hose!

'Stop! Stop!' He ran towards the straining freighter, waving his arms madly. Before he got close, the main jets fired and there was a terrible groan as the refuelling cluster tore free, complete with the concrete footings. Clunk watched in horror as it rose into the air, dangling from the back of the ship like a wrecking ball. As the ship moved away, a thick metal pipe broke through the turf. It came up in segments, and Clunk was thrown off his feet as the earth ripped open beneath him. Glancing round fearfully, he saw the pipe bend double before snapping in two, spraying gouts of fuel in all directions.

The length of pipe hanging from the ship swung wildly as the freighter roared into the sky, and Clunk was forced back into the ditch as the *Volante's* jets ignited the fuel vapour. Through half-closed eyes he saw the ship disappear behind the billowing flames, still towing the refuelling cluster.

As the echoes and flames died away, Clunk gathered his wits and set off for the house. Rounding a bend, he stopped. A hundred metres ahead the driveway looped past the imposing facade of a three-storey mansion. There was a wide staircase leading up to a heavy door, and the walls were studded with rows of windows, all of them dark apart from a couple near the entrance.

The front door swung open and Terry took the steps two at a time, with Farrell close behind. Both of them were carrying guns, and Clunk backed into the bushes as the men ran towards him. He kept his head down as they charged past, panting heavily.

He watched their retreating backs for a moment, then leapt to his feet and ran towards the house. He crossed the gravel driveway, vaulted up the steps and threw himself against the wall. After a quick glance to the sides, he sidled towards the first of the illuminated windows. Risking a quick look he saw a large desk with a blank portable vidscreen on the surface. No sign of Hal. Ducking under the sill, he crept to the next window and peered through. There was Hal, sitting in a large armchair, being guarded by a big grey robot with its back to the window. Clunk looked thoughtful. He knew how jumpy that robot was, and the slightest noise could get the human killed.

Moving silently, Clunk skirted the front of the house and slipped down the side. He found a large garage, the double doors standing open. Inside, the limousine was parked between a pair of battle-scarred armoured cars: hulking vehicles plated with sheets of toughened metal. One of the cars ticked gently as its motor cooled.

He glanced at the limo but dismissed it. It would take too long to crack the security. Instead, he made for the armoured car with the ticking engine. The driver's door was locked, but the passenger door swung open at his touch. Inside there were two metal seats surrounded by viewscreens, and a large cabin with metal benches down each side. Halfway down the cabin was a round hole in the ceiling: the access point for the gun turret.

Clunk sat in the driver's seat, found the starter button and pressed it firmly. The engine coughed once or twice before firing, then settled down to a steady rumble. Across the dash, viewscreens showed views out the front, the rear and both sides.

Clunk reversed out of the garage and swung the heavy vehicle round. There was a patch of white in the left-hand screen, and he frowned as a pair of skinny robots ran at him, waving their arms. He aimed the car and opened the throttles, and they dived out the way as he roared past. On the rear-view screen he saw them turn and run into the garage.

Clunk pushed the stick hard to the right, lining the armoured car up with the window through which he had seen Hal. Then, after a moment's hesitation, he pushed the stick all the way forward.

The engine roared and the car leapt towards the wall,

gaining speed rapidly. There was a tremendous crash as it hit the brickwork, and the sound of splintering wood and falling rubble echoed around the interior. Clunk reversed out again, and the screens flickered as falling bricks bounced off the hull. Once clear, he threw the driver's door open and leapt out.

The grey robot was lying motionless amongst the scattered bricks and broken glass, but Clunk only had eyes for Hal. He clambered over the fallen rubble and threw the unconscious human over his shoulder, then stumbled back towards the hole in the wall. Halfway there he passed a painting lying on the floor. It was a landscape in a battered frame, the brush strokes frosted with plaster. Clunk's eyes narrowed as he saw the cows depicted in the painting, and very deliberately he backed up and trod on it, grinding the canvas under his heel.

Once outside he dropped Hal into the passenger seat then ran round the other side. He was just getting in when he heard a roar nearby. Clunk looked up, convinced it was the *Volante* coming back, but the skies were empty. Then it hit him: The second armoured car was reversing out of the garage, its turret already turning! He hauled back on the joystick and the armoured car lurched down the steps, just as the first shot landed. There was a massive explosion inside the house, hurling bricks skywards like popcorn.

'Is it time to get up?' mumbled Hal.

'No, they're after us,' said Clunk, as he wrestled with the stick. 'Hold tight. They're shooting again.'

28

Hal shook his head to clear the mist from his eyes. The last thing he remembered was exchanging insults with an armed robot, and then half a house falling on him. Now someone had strapped him into a rollercoaster ride, while all around them people let off massive fireworks. Hal glanced at Clunk, who was wrestling with some kind of controls. The robot's face was bathed in multicoloured light from the instrument panel, his expression grim. Okay, maybe not a rollercoaster.

'Thanks for the rescue,' shouted Hal over the roar of the engine.

'Time for thanks later. If we get away.'

Hal examined the screens, which showed a kaleidoscope of trees and grass. Then he spotted a flash. 'What was that?'

A blast threw the car sideways, tossing Hal from his seat and smashing him against the hard metal wall. He sat up groggily, shaking his head to clear the stars from his eyes.

'I told you to hold on,' said Clunk. 'They're firing at us.'

There was another explosion and the floor tipped under Hal's feet. 'Can't we fire back?'

'Can you operate the main gun?'

'Where is it?'

Clunk jerked his thumb towards the back of the vehicle, where a ladder led through a circular hole in the roof.

Hal left his seat and staggered down the swaying cabin, using the overhead straps to stay upright. He was about to climb up when an explosion threw the car sideways, almost knocking him off his feet. Hal regained his balance, grabbed hold of the metal ladder and started to climb. He was halfway up when there was a swishing, scraping noise along the side of the car. 'What's that?' he shouted.

'I am attempting to shake them off by driving through the undergrowth,' called Clunk.

'What about the trees?'

There was a crunch as the car slammed into one, and the sudden stop tore Hal from the ladder and threw him the length of the vehicle. He slammed into the drivers seat, bounced off, and dropped to the deck in a heap. He staggered upright and was just reaching for the ladder when Clunk threw the vehicle into reverse. Hal flew towards the front again, but just before he crunched into the seat, the vehicle roared forwards, sending him sailing towards the rear of the vehicle. Halfway there, he hit the ladder.

Clunk glanced over his shoulder. 'Haven't you got that gun going yet?'

'No, I haven't got the bloody gun going yet!' shouted Hal, rubbing his head. 'I'm enjoying the bloody ride!' He stormed up the ladder and emerged in the cramped turret, which was surrounded with viewscreens. The seat gave slightly under his weight, and he dangled his feet down the access tube. A joystick sprang up between his legs, and the screens flickered into life. The one labelled 'front' showed bushes and tree trunks in the headlights, and a targeting cross appeared in the corner of the screen.

Hal scanned the screens for the enemy. To his left, one of the screens flared and darkened, and there was an explosion outside. He twisted the joystick until the cursor hovered over the pursuing armoured car, and squeezed the trigger. There was a loud bang, and when the smoke cleared the pursuing vehicle was weaving from side to side.

'How do *you* like it?' muttered Hal. Then he saw the gates. 'Clunk, gates to starboard!'

'Got it.'

One of the screens began to glow, and as they got closer Hal saw flames shooting into the air from a mess of twisted, glowing pipes. 'What happened?' shouted Hal. 'And where's the ship?'

'Clyde is flying it to Jerling's,' said Clunk.

Hal's stomach tightened. 'You sent those robots off by themselves?'

'I downloaded piloting code into Clyde. They'll be all right.'

'They'll pinch the ship and vanish, you stupid tin can! They'll do a runner with my cargo!'

'They can't,' said Clunk. 'They gave me their word of honour.'

Hal groaned. 'All they wanted was to get away from the planet. You've given them the means, Clunk. We'll never see them again.'

'You're wrong, Mr Spacejock. The robots will deliver the cargo to Jerling.'

'They won't! They'll nick the ship and scarper!'

'They can't.'

'Why not?'

'Their fuel won't last. I forgot to detach the hoses before they took off.'

Hal gazed at the twisted, burning pipes. 'So you did.' He

frowned as he saw a pair of figures silhouetted against the flames. One of them turned at the sound of the approaching car, and Hal's eyes narrowed as he recognised Terry. His finger tightened on the trigger as the cursor hovered below the mop of straw-coloured hair.

'We should be at the gates in a moment,' shouted Clunk up the tube.

There was a flash on the screen, and an explosion rocked the car. Hal spun the turret, whirling it around until the second armoured car was centred under the cross hairs. He squeezed the trigger, flinching as the blast echoed around the turret. When the screen cleared the other car was on its side, smoke and flames pouring from the blasted hull. On the side screen he saw Farrell and Terry running towards the house.

'Hold tight!' shouted Clunk.

Hal braced himself as the gates loomed in the forward-facing screen. There was a jolt as the car rammed them, and a bump as it forced its way over the tangled metal. Once it was clear, Clunk straightened up and roared towards the main road.

◆

Farrell ran along the path with Terry, coughing in the swirling smoke. They rounded the final bend and stopped as they saw the huge, jagged hole in the front of the house.

'Bloody hell,' exclaimed Terry.

'My house!' breathed Farrell, staring at the damage in disbelief. 'He's ruined my goddamn house!' He frowned as he saw the hulking robot squatting on a smouldering rug, gazing at the twisted barrel of its pulse rifle. 'What happened?' demanded Farrell, hurrying over. 'Where's Spacejock?'

'One of our armoured cars,' said the robot, throwing the rifle aside. 'It rescued him.'

Farrell and Terry exchanged a glance. 'One to fly the ship. Another to drive the car.'

'And another to drive the truck into the ship,' said Terry. 'It's a whole bloody gang.'

'Fetch the limo. Weapons, too.' Farrell looked up at the shattered brickwork. 'Someone's going to pay for this.'

Terry vanished down the side of the house. 'Get up,' said Farrell to the robot. He jabbed his thumb at the red glow in the trees. 'I want that fire out, I want this wall fixed and I want the other armoured car hidden away. Got it?'

'How should I prioritise?'

'I don't give a flying stuff. Just get it done.'

The robot knuckled its forehead and backed out of the damaged room. Farrell bent to pick up a painting: a farmyard scene in a gilt frame. He put his finger through a large tear, then drew his fist back and smashed it through the canvas. 'Bloody Spacejock!' he shouted.

There was a roar, and the limo drew up with a jerk. Farrell leapt in, and before his door was closed the car was racing along the circular drive towards the exit. They passed the burning trees, their headlights boring white tunnels through the swirling smoke, and a few seconds later they roared up to the shattered gates.

'They couldn't open the bloody things, could they?' demanded Farrell plaintively. 'No, they had to smash them down and drive over the pieces.' He looked at Terry. 'You did bring guns?'

Terry grinned. 'Oh, yeah.' He guided the car over the

twisted metal and drove it across the field. It swung wide as they shot out of the gap in the hedge, then straightened up and roared along the main road. Far ahead, they could see the dark shape of the armoured car lumbering up the hill.

'Don't get too close,' muttered Farrell, as they approached the fleeing vehicle. 'That thing's dangerous.'

Terry matched the armoured car's speed. 'How are we going to stop them?'

'We don't have to. There's only one place they can go.'

Hal twirled the targeting joystick until the aiming reticule hovered on the pursuing limo. 'Eat this,' he breathed, squeezing the trigger. The cross turned red and there was an angry buzzing noise.

'They're out of range,' called Clunk.

'Damn.' Hal's eyes narrowed as he stared at the limo. 'Closer, Hinchfig. I've got a pressie for you.'

'You can't shoot them, Mr Spacejock. That's murder.'

'Don't worry, I'm just going to hurt them a bit.' Hal aimed at the piece of road between the two vehicles and squeezed the trigger. The gun fired with a satisfying bang, tearing a hole in the road and flinging chunks of dirt at the limo. The car swerved wildly as Terry fought to bring it under control, then dropped back to a safer distance.

'That gave them something to think about.' Hal was just lining up for another shot when the cross-hairs disappeared. 'Hey, what happened?'

'I disabled the weapon,' called Clunk. 'You could hurt someone.'

'I'm trying to!' shouted Hal. 'Turn it on again!'

'I mean you could hurt someone else. This is a built-up area.'

'Trust me to get saddled with a do-gooder,' muttered Hal to himself. After giving the joystick a couple of experimental twiddles, he gave up and watched the limo. He saw the passenger window go down, and then Farrell leaned out. There was a fizz, and bright energy bolts zinged from the weapon in his hand.

'They can't hurt us with that,' called Clunk.

The shots went lower and lower until there was a loud bang. The armoured car started to wobble, and Hal saw a black shape fly off the ride. 'They shot a wheel off, you crazy robot! Quick! Turn the bloody gun back on!'

'Hold on tight.'

'I am!'

There was a terrible squeal as Clunk applied the brakes. Thick tyre smoke obscured the rear view, and then the limo burst through like a shark, still travelling fast. There was an almighty crunch as it slammed into the back of the armoured vehicle, and Hal saw Farrell and Terry hurled forwards, only to be caught and held in a blue forcefield.

There was a powerful roar as Clunk gunned the motor again, while behind them the limo weaved across the road, belching black smoke. 'Take that you pricks!' shouted Hal, gesturing at the screen with his finger. Slipping off his seat, he descended the ladder and joined Clunk up front. 'Neat move.'

'It won't hold them up for long.'

'We can worry about that later.'

'I'd start worrying now,' said Clunk, gesturing at the

forward screen. 'We're approaching a toll booth and the barrier is down.'

'A little strip of wood isn't going to hold this thing up.'

The engine note changed as the heavy vehicle slowed. 'I have to stop,' said Clunk. 'My programming forbids –'

Hal pointed out the side window. 'Hey, what's that over there?'

As Clunk turned to look, Hal leaned over and pushed the joystick. There was a roar from the engine, and the armoured car burst through the barrier with a squeal of tortured metal.

Clunk frowned at him. 'I don't like being fooled.'

'And I don't like being caught by gangsters. Drive on!'

◆

'I told you he'd make for the spaceport,' said Farrell, as the limo passed the buckled barrier. The cabin reeked of smoke, even with the windows open, and the car lurched along the road like a drunk.

'How did you know?'

'Where else would you hide a spaceship? Come on, move it. We've got to get there before they lift off in the *Volante*.'

'We'll be lucky to get there at all,' said Terry, as he fought with the controls.

'Turn right at Haywood's copse. We'll take the back road.'

◆

273

After winding through the trees for several hundred metres, the approach road split in two. Clunk took the left-hand fork, and before long they came to a heavy fence guarded by a row of booths, unlit and deserted except for one at the far end. Inside, the uniformed guard was watching a small portable vidset.

Hal grabbed Clunk's arm. 'Pull over.'

The vehicle stopped and Clunk looked at him expectantly.

'We can't just drive in with this thing.' Hal gestured at the fence. 'And we'll never bust through that. It's ten times stronger than the one at Farrell's place.'

'It's all right,' said Clunk. 'I have a plan.'

'Yeah?'

'From the outside, nobody can see into this vehicle.'

'That's a good plan. I can see that working like a charm.' Hal waved his hands. 'Here Fred, let this heavily armed vehicle through. Can't be a wrong'un, because there's no-one in it.'

'Perhaps you'd let me finish?' Clunk tapped his chest. 'I can impersonate Farrell.'

'Oh, sure.'

'I can!'

'You don't look anything like him! He's got hair and you're a robot. Even the most dim-witted, thick-headed guard on the planet would see through it before you got within fifty metres.'

'Who said anything about seeing me? I was talking about impersonating his voice.'

'They'll never buy it.'

Clunk gestured at the fence. 'Would you rather scale that?'

Hal eyed the dense coils of razor wire. 'All right, go for the impersonation.'

The armoured car rumbled up to the toll booth, powerful engine growling. Clunk stopped alongside the booth, his eyes flickering as he reprogrammed his speech pattern.

Hal looked at the side viewscreen, where he could see the guard staring at his vidset. On the screen, several tiny figures were chasing a jet-powered ball around a sky-hockey pitch. The score read 300-1, and from the look of it the Rhinos were just about to make it 300-2.

'I'm ready,' said Clunk.

Hal put a hand on the robot's arm. 'Wait.'

Inside the hut, the guard reached out and pressed a button without taking his eyes from the game. A ticket spooled out of the dispenser, and Clunk cracked his door open and took it. Immediately, the barrier rose out of the way.

'Go,' muttered Hal. 'Come on, move it!'

The armoured car belched smoke and the heavy vehicle rumbled under the barrier, barely squeezing through the narrow gap. 'There goes his employee of the month award,' remarked Hal, as the barrier dropped behind them.

Clunk gunned the motor and the armoured car roared along the access road, emerging on the spaceport apron between a pair of maintenance vehicles. 'Do you remember where you left the *Gull*?'

'On the landing field, of course.'

'Do you know which pad?'

Hal shook his head. 'I was in a hurry to inspect the damage.'

'Damage?' Clunk looked at him. 'What damage?'

'Fire. Ground control diverted us into a rubbish tip. We were coming in too fast, see? The rubbish cushioned the landing, but it, er, caught fire.'

'And was there any damage?'

'It was a bit hard to tell. I mean, the *Gull* wasn't exactly pristine to begin with.'

'But still spaceworthy?' Clunk shook his head. 'Don't answer that.'

They drove past a passenger liner, her brilliant white flanks gleaming under batteries of floodlights. Two men were pushing a trolley past the carpeted passenger ramp, heading for a cargo lift. As the lift rose towards the belly of the ship, they leaned on the railing and watched the armoured car pass by.

'I remember that ship,' said Hal. 'Turn right here.'

The car swung past a refuelling cluster. 'There she is,' said Hal, as he spotted the distinctive outline of the *Black Gull*. However, Clunk turned in the opposite direction. 'Where are you going?'

'If they got here first, they could be watching the ship.' Clunk drove the armoured car behind a fuel tanker and switched the engine off. 'I'm sure they guessed our destination, and if they're not here now they soon will be.'

'So we just sit here and die of old age?'

'Perhaps I could suggest a more workable alternative.'

'Shoot.'

Clunk pointed towards the back of the car. 'I'll make my way to the *Black Gull*. If I'm spotted they'll think I'm just another robot. In fact, with this suit on they might even mistake me for a human.'

Hal looked him up and down. 'If you say so.'

'Once I'm aboard I'll run up the engines and prepare for take-off. When everything's ready, I'll flash the landing lights three times. That's your signal.'

'Three times. Got it.'

Clunk opened the door and stepped out.

'Hang on,' said Hal. 'Turn the gun on before you go. If they come nosing around I'll give you some cover.'

Clunk reached up and tapped the bulging side of the fuel tanker. 'Best not. One stray shot ...'

'Ah.'

Clunk went to close the door, then hesitated. 'If I don't make it Mr Spacejock, it was a pleasure working with you.'

'Skip the speeches, okay? We're the good guys. We're going to win.'

Clunk gave him a brief nod, and then he was gone.

Hal opened the door and looked back along the vehicle's flank, watching the shadowy figure heading for the *Black Gull*. The robot had only just reached the ramp when a car drove past, stopped and reversed. Hal stared at the glossy black limo in shock. Farrell and Terry! And they'd seen Clunk!

Hal dropped into the driver's seat and gently closed the door. He found the master switch and flicked it on, bringing up the outside views on the screens. On the smallest screen, labelled 'Rear', he saw Terry and Farrell sitting in the limo, their backs to him as they studied the *Black Gull*.

29

'That's the third time we've come along here,' remarked Terry, as the limo emerged from the shadow of a huge freighter. 'I told you they wasn't coming to the spaceport.'

'He's a pilot, Terry. Where else would he meet the bloody ship? Here, go left.'

The car turned sharply and darted under a passenger liner, narrowly missing a pair of baggage handlers. 'Keep your eyes open.'

'What if he's disguised? A well-organised gang like this ... they could have uniforms or something.'

Farrell glanced back at the handlers, who were still gesticulating. 'Spacejock's a freelancer, not a criminal mastermind. He'll be here eventually, and when he turns up we'll nab him and find out where the cargo went. Then he can vanish permanently.'

'He keeps vanishing, that's 'alf the problem.'

'You got a better idea?'

'You've got Peace Force contacts. Surely they can spot an armoured car?'

Farrell winced. 'I'd rather not.'

'They do know you've got those things?'

'Yeah, but I don't want them looking too closely.'

'Why, are they stolen?'

'No.'

'Illegal weaponry?'

'No, nothing like that.' Farrell glanced at a scarred, rust-streaked ship. A bronze robot in a flashy suit was making its way up the passenger ramp, looking around furtively as if it were up to no good.

'So why –' began Terry.

'I haven't paid the rego.'

Terry stared at him. 'You're barmy! You get twenty years for that!'

'Hey, wait a minute!' shouted Farrell. 'Stop! Go back!'

The car reversed sharply.

'That was him,' said Farrell, pointing at the rusty freighter. 'I just saw Spacejock's robot, all done up in a dinner jacket.'

'You did?' Terry looked at him doubtfully. 'It's been a long day, boss. You don't think ...'

'I know what I bloody saw!'

'It can't have been Clunk. You chucked him in a lake.'

'Then he got out again, didn't he? And don't you recognise the ship?'

Terry looked. 'Hey, it's that heap of Spacejock's.'

'Naturally. He didn't teleport here, you know.' Farrell looked at him. 'Your little box of tricks didn't work, did it?'

'He didn't hyperspace, did he? It only works if you hyperspace.'

Farrell settled in his chair. 'Spacejock's got to be around here somewhere. He must have sent the robot ahead to prepare the ship.'

'So where's the *Volante*?'

'Probably halfway round the planet. You can see what they're up to - their stooges have taken the cargo somewhere quiet in my ship, and now Spacejock's going to follow in his ship and transfer the cargo. They'll torch the *Volante* and use this piece of junk to deliver Jerling's parts.'

Terry looked at him with respect. 'You've really got them sussed, boss.'

'Don't sound so surprised. Spacejock is hardly an intellectual giant.'

'No, but neither ...' Terry's voice tailed off under Farrell's cold stare. 'So, what do we do now?'

'That robot's getting the ship ready.' Farrell glanced out the side window. 'Spacejock must be skulking nearby. We'll get him when he tries to go aboard.'

'What if we miss him? We can't chase them in this.'

'That's right.'

'And if we shoot them down, we'll never find the cargo. When his mates hear what's happened they'll scarper with the *Volante*.'

'Very perceptive.'

'Your brother won't half be pissed if you lose his ship.'

'You leave Gordon to me.' Farrell's face cleared. 'That's it! He wanted me to collect his flyer!'

'Shouldn't you get the cargo back first?'

'You don't understand. Gordon's flyer has just been serviced, and it's right here at the spaceport. We can use it to follow Spacejock's ship!'

At that moment the *Black Gull's* landing lights flashed three times. Immediately, there was a roar from a powerful engine.

'He's taking off!' cried Terry, as the roar got louder and louder.

'That's not the ship,' said Farrell. 'It's coming from ...' He twisted in his seat just as the armoured car slammed into the side of the limo, tipping it up and rolling it over and over, tumbling Farrell and Terry inside like a couple of mannequins in a washing machine. It finally came to rest, and there was a squeal of tortured metal as the armoured car drove clear.

◆

The *Black Gull* was airborne before Hal was halfway across the flight deck. As he sat down, the ship turned sharply and roared across the landing field, heading for Jerling's factory on the opposite side of the planet.

'I got them, Clunk. You should have seen it!' Hal raised a hand and drove his fist into it. 'Smashing!'

'It was very dangerous,' said Clunk severely. 'You could have hurt someone.'

'They're all right. I saw them shaking their fists at me.' Hal clapped the robot on the shoulder. 'We've done it, Clunk!'

'I'm very pleased, Mr Spacejock.'

Then Hal's face fell. 'Of course, if those robots of yours don't turn up ...'

'They're not my robots. You brought them along.'

'You let them out of the shop, didn't you? And you gave them the *Volante*.'

'They'll be there.'

'Jerling will have you scrapped if they don't turn up.'

The robot's head dropped. 'That's closer to the truth than ...'

Beep!

'Vessel approaching from astern,' said the Navcom. 'Range three hundred metres.'

'Probably just traffic,' said Hal.

Clunk looked up from the instruments. 'It's directly behind, Mr Spacejock. Closing fast.'

'It's nothing.'

'It's matching our course.'

'All right, all right.' Hal waved a hand. 'I'll take a look if it'll make you happy.'

One of the smaller screens flickered and a fuzzy blob appeared. Hal laughed at the sight. 'Ooh, scary.'

'They're right behind us. Our exhaust is interfering with the picture.' Clunk adjusted the controls and the ship heeled round. The image sharpened, showing a trim, powerful flyer banking to match their course. The image zoomed rapidly until Farrell and Terry could be seen sitting side by side in the cockpit.

'Not those jokers again!' exclaimed Hal. 'Hey, let's slam the brakes on! Maybe they'll run into the back of us.'

'It won't work. That little ship is much more agile than ours.'

'So what are we worrying about? They can't knock us down with that little thing!'

Clunk watched the picture. 'They're doing something.'

'Eh?' Hal squinted at the image. Farrell was flying, and alongside him Terry was taking a black tube from a padded case. 'What's he going to do with a telescope, glare me to death?'

'That's not a telescope, Mr Spacejock,' said Clunk gravely. 'It's a photon cannon.'

'Armoured cars, photon cannons ... what next, orbiting lasers?'

Clunk pursed his lips, puckering up the stiff plasteel. 'I'm getting an idea,' he said slowly.

'Oh, great,' said Hal. 'Go on, let me have it. I haven't had a good laugh for ages.'

'Down to the hold, quickly.'

◆

The noise from the *Black Gull's* engines was overpowering, and Farrell struggled to maintain course as the fragile craft bucked and leaped in the turbulence. 'They must have seen us,' he said, as the *Gull* weaved from side to side. He eased the stick forward, dropping out of the twisting, roaring exhaust. 'They'll never lead us to the *Volante* now.'

Alongside him, Terry continued to assemble the photon cannon. He slotted the barrel into the chunky grip, laid the weapon aside and took up a hefty clamp with a swivel on top.

'Mind the upholstery,' said Farrell. 'Gordon's in love with this thing.'

Terry opened the side window and dropped the clamp over the door sill. He twisted a handle, and there was a muted bang as the grip fired an anchor straight through the bodywork.

Farrell stared, speechless.

'Sorry boss. These things need a stable platform.' Terry mounted the cannon on the swivel and took out an oblong powerpack, which he slotted into the weapon. After swinging it through a couple of arcs, he flipped the arming switch. 'Keep them round this side,' he said, gesturing at the *Black Gull*. 'I'll get their port engine first.'

'They won't crash?'

'Nah. They can land on one engine.'

Farrell eased the stick to the right, angling the flyer so the *Black Gull* drifted towards Terry's cannon. Suddenly he saw the cargo doors swung open. 'What are they doing?'

'Watch them closely,' muttered Terry. 'Spacejock's a tricky bastard.'

Farrell squinted as two figures appeared at the back of the hold. One of them shook his fist wildly, overbalanced, and would have fallen right out of the ship if the second figure hadn't grabbed him by the flight suit.

'If he falls out you won't be able to ask him anything.' Terry gestured at the cannon. 'What shall I do?'

Farrell glanced over the side and saw houses dotting the landscape below. 'We can't do it here. Follow them for now.'

◆

At the back of the hold, Clunk was trying to explain his plan.

'We throw scrap at them,' he said, raising his voice over the *Black Gull's* thundering exhaust. 'All we need is one piece of metal in the air intake.'

Hal stared at the robot in disbelief. 'You dragged me down here for a coconut shy?'

'A what?'

'You're unbelievable,' shouted Hal. 'You want to throw a lump of metal into the air intake of a flyer three hundred metres away? It's impossible!'

Clunk spread his hands. 'I'm sorry, Mr Spacejock. It was the only idea I could come up with.'

'It's dumb enough to be in a movie,' shouted Hal. 'Anyway, you stripped the ship on Seraph, remember? We don't have any scrap.'

Clunk tapped the hydraulic pistons dangling on either side

284

of the open doors. 'These were for the ramp. You don't need them any more.'

'I will when I get my ramp back.'

'You won't need a ramp if they open fire.'

Hal looked down at the flyer, and he saw Farrell and Terry looking up at him. 'All right, we'll give it a shot,' he said. 'But I want the first throw.'

◆

'They're chucking things at us!' exclaimed Terry, as a dark shape flashed past the canopy.

Farrell looked down. 'There's a forest coming up. Get ready to open fire.' He jinked the flyer sideways as a series of objects flew out of the *Black Gull's* hold. Each curved towards them, then sailed past harmlessly.

◆

Clunk hefted a length of chrome pipe with a bolt through the end. 'This is the last piece, Mr Spacejock.'

'Hand it over, then.'

'My accuracy is better than yours.'

'You never went near them! Anyway, you've had more goes than me.'

Clunk pointed to the side of the hold. 'Maybe you can throw that.'

Hal turned to look, but the hold was empty. When he turned round again, Clunk had thrown the pipe. 'Rotten cheat.' He watched the length of chrome pipe tumble past the flyer. 'And you're a rotten shot, too.'

Clunk glared at him. 'You could try throwing yourself at them again. I promise I won't stop you this time.'

'I'll have to, won't I?' Hal gestured at the bare door-frame and the empty hold. 'We've run out of bits.'

'They were no good anyway. With irregular shapes, it's impossible to calculate the trajectory.' Clunk pushed Hal aside as a series of blinding white flashes lit the hold. 'Down! They're shooting!'

The *Black Gull* tilted, and the burst of fire passed by harmlessly. 'Good old Navcom,' shouted Hal.

'Evasive manoeuvres?'

'More like self-preservation.' Hal stared down at the flyer, which was manoeuvring into firing position again. 'We can't just stand here and take it.'

'It's a pity we don't have a cannon ourselves.'

Hal stared at him. 'Balls.'

Clunk looked shocked. 'I beg your pardon?'

'Balls!' Hal ran into the hold, darted through the inner door and raced along the passageway. Kicking open the galley door, he dragged open the freezer and felt around until his fingers closed on the round, frozen shape. 'Where's the rest?' he demanded, waving the christmas pudding at the overhead camera.

'Freezer chests five and six,' said the Navcom.

Hal bent down and examined the narrow doors. He found the one he wanted and yanked it open, waving away clouds of vapour. Inside the compartment there was a white cardboard box. Hal slid it out, stacked the one behind it on top, and carried both back to the hold. 'Balls,' he said, panting from the effort.

'This is a strange time to be thinking of your stomach,' said Clunk, eyeing the garish labels.

'I'm not going to eat the bloody things.' Hal banged the cartons down, ripped the top off the first one, grabbed a frozen pudding and approached the back door. Drawing his arm back, he took aim and threw.

'I did better with the pipe,' remarked Clunk, who was holding his balls in one hand.

'Not much better,' said Hal, as the robot's missiles went wide. 'Grab some more, will you?'

Clunk hurried over to collect the carton, and was halfway back when the ship lurched to avoid another burst from the photon cannon. The sudden move hurled Clunk to the deck, and a dozen frozen puddings burst from the box, rolled past Hal and fell out the back of the ship.

'Stop wasting them all!' cried Hal.

The puddings dropped towards the flyer, scattering like slow-motion buckshot in the turbulence. Before Farrell could react, several heavy balls slammed into the craft, smashing the perspex canopy, punching holes through the bodywork and destroying the flyer's air intakes. There was a horrible grinding noise and black smoke began to pour from the exhaust vents.

'Yee-hah!' screamed Hal, leaping up and down and waving his arms. 'Gotcha!' he yelled as the flyer fell behind, trailing black smoke and losing height rapidly. Clunk grabbed a handful of flight suit as Hal leaned over the edge to watch the crash.

The flyer dipped and weaved as it angled towards the ground. Finally it thumped down, bounced once and came to a halt in a tangle of thick bushes.

'Good shot, Clunk!' shouted Hal, slapping the robot on the shoulder.

Clunk stared at the flyer. 'I hope they're not hurt, Mr Spacejock.'

'We'll soon find out.' Hal reached for the intercom. 'Navcom, chuck a one-eighty and come in low over the wreckage.'

'Complying.'

The engines roared as the *Black Gull* came round in a hard turn, then quietened again as the ship slowed and lost height. A moment or two later they were at a crawl. Hal lay down on the metal decking and poked his head out the back, peering down at the ground. The flyer's canopy had been pushed aside, and the two men were clambering out, chased by flames and gouts of black smoke. They looked up as the *Gull* came to a halt a hundred metres or so above their heads.

'Hand me another pudding,' said Hal.

'No, Mr Spacejock.'

'Go on! They're easy targets from here.'

'No,' said the robot firmly. 'Anyway, I have a better idea.'

◆

'I'll never forget that,' said Hal, wiping a tear from his eye. 'It was brilliant, Clunk. Brilliant!'

Clunk smiled modestly. 'It achieved the desired effect without causing injury.'

Hal laughed as he remembered the horrified looks on Farrell and Terry's faces as the contents of the *Black Gull's* waste tank rained down on them. 'What about their pride?'

'Oh, I think we injured that.' Clunk's smile disappeared. 'Of course, it's against the law to purge effluent in flight.'

Hal sniggered. 'Like I give a crap.'

Ting!

'Approaching destination,' said the Navcom.

Buzz!

'Incoming message.'

'Okay, put it up.'

A monitor flickered, and Jerling's face appeared. 'Mr Spacejock, my people tell me you're on final approach.'

'That's right.'

'I shall meet you on pad three. Try not to land on my trucks.'

'As good as done, Mr Jerling.' The screen went dark, and Hal rubbed his hands together. 'It's payday, Clunk. Hey, what's he going to say when he sees you?'

Clunk's mouth turned down. 'I have a pretty good idea.'

'Cheer up. Someone else can take you back to Seraph.'

'I'm sure they will.'

'You're going to make a real splash at that academy. Jerling will be proud of you, you'll see.'

'Mr Spacejock –'

The engine note changed to a deep roar and the ship slowed in its tracks. Hal felt his stomach twist as they dropped towards the ground.

'Please be seated for landing,' said the Navcom.

Hal gripped the sides of his chair as the engine noise increased.

'Five metres.'

Hal glanced at Clunk, who was standing in the middle of the flight deck with a downcast expression on his face. 'You'd better hang on to something.'

Clunk shrugged. 'Why bother?'

289

'Contact imminent,' said the Navcom.

Hal's head dipped as the ship touched down.

'Landing successful,' said the Navcom, as the engine noise tailed off to a hum. 'Local time is 8.22 a.m.'

Hal stood up, opened the inner door and walked into the airlock. A gust of chilly air blew in as the outer door opened, and hidden motors whirred as the platform extended from the side of the ship. Guy wires rattled as the passenger ramp unfolded, and when Hal looked out he saw three trucks emblazoned with 'Jerling Enterprises' logos, all waiting for the cargo. There was a tall building across the landing field and a tatty portable office nearby. The door to the office burst open, and Jerling trotted towards the ship, leaving a smoke trail as he puffed on a cigar.

Hal raised his hand in greeting. 'Morning!'

Jerling looked up the ramp. 'Not a moment too soon,' he said breathlessly. 'My factory staff are just arriving for work.'

Hal stood back to let him past, then followed him into the flight deck. The businessman was standing near the console, looking around in surprise. 'It's rather old, isn't it?'

'Solid as a rock,' said Hal.

'I'll take your word for it.' Jerling looked at him expectantly. 'Can you open the doors now? My people are waiting to unload the cargo.'

Hal stared at him in shock. 'The freighter didn't arrive?'

Jerling looked blank. 'Freighter? What freighter?'

30

'Your tin pals nicked off with the ship!' Hal jabbed his finger at Clunk. 'They lied to you, and you trusted them!'

'Mr Spacejock, I –'

'You bloody robots are all the same.'

'They gave me their word,' said Clunk quietly.

'They were on the run, Clunk! Fugitives!' Hal jerked his thumb at the sky. 'They probably fuelled up and legged it to the nearest planet.'

Clunk's eyes flashed. 'They'll be here. They said so!'

'Really? So where are they?'

'Maybe I gave them the wrong program. Maybe they crashed.'

'Maybe they're halfway across the galaxy,' snapped Hal.

Jerling coughed. 'Mr Spacejock, can I have your undivided attention?'

Hal glared at him. 'What do you want?'

'Are you saying my cargo is not aboard your ship?'

Hal jerked his thumb at Clunk. 'It was all organised, but his mates ran away with it.'

'You've had it, Spacejock. My lawyers will suck you dry for this.' Jerling tossed his cigar butt down the access tube and marched to the airlock. 'Clunk, in my office. Now.'

After the door banged to, Clunk held out his hand. 'I'm sorry it had to end like this, Mr Spacejock. It was a pleasure working with you.'

Hal looked at the robot's hand, then turned his back and strode to the drinks dispenser. He scooped up his mug, held it under the nozzle and pressed the button.

'Supplies exhausted,' said the Navcom, as a drop of brown goo fell into the cup.

Hal closed his eyes and a black hole opened beneath his feet. It was a bottomless pit with no exit and no escape, and as he fell into it he saw mocking faces leering from the sides: Vurdi with Brutus, Farrell and Terry, Jerling, Portmaster Linten and his assistant. And behind them all loomed the burnt-out face of the maintenance robot.

'Mr Spacejock?'

Hal jumped as a hand gripped his shoulder. 'What?'

'I'd like you to have this, Mr Spacejock. You can use it for supplies.'

Clunk extended his hand, revealing the five credits he'd won at the casino. Hal stared at the tiles in silence, then looked into the robot's concerned face. 'It's all right,' he said gruffly. 'You keep it.'

'Please. I won't be needing it.'

'What do you mean?'

Clunk swallowed. 'Jerling's having me scrapped.'

◆

'You murdering bastard!' shouted Hal, bursting from the *Black Gull's* airlock.

Jerling turned and looked up the ramp. 'Who do you think you're shouting at?'

'You, you cold-blooded killer! How could you blame Clunk for this mess? It was my fault the cargo got lost!'

Jerling walked back up the ramp. 'Mr Spacejock, what are you talking about?'

Hal jabbed his finger at the airlock. 'Clunk just told me you're junking him.'

'That's right. You were taking him to Seraph.'

'What's that got to do with it?'

'That's where the wrecking yard is.'

Hal shook his head. 'He was going there for advanced pilot training with Incubators. He got it from my database.'

Clunk appeared behind him. 'I'm afraid the confusion is my fault, Mr Spacejock. I didn't realise your database was out of date. When I got to Seraph I discovered Muller's son had turned the factory into a recycling centre.'

'Why didn't you say something, you clown? I'd have busted you out of there in no time.' Hal frowned at Jerling. 'And what do you want to junk him for? He's more useful than most humans.'

'I could explain, but I don't think you'd understand.'

Hal crossed his arms. 'Try me.'

'In simple terms, the longer you keep equipment the more it costs to maintain. New equipment comes with a warranty, and of course there are numerous tax benefits.'

'So it all comes down to money.'

Jerling spread his hands. 'I don't write the tax laws, Mr Spacejock, and nobody offers infinite warranties.'

'Why all the fooling around? Why didn't you tell Clunk he was being junked?'

'Keeping Clunk in the dark for as long as possible was more humane than disclosing his fate in advance. Don't you agree?'

'Well, I –'

'And robots have been known to run away once their useful life is at an end.'

'So you're saying he's no use to you?'

Jerling sighed. 'It pains me to say so, but yes.'

'All right. I'll buy him.'

Jerling laughed. 'You couldn't buy me a coffee.'

'I'll do another job for you.'

'You haven't finished the first one.'

'I'll –'

'They're here,' said Clunk suddenly.

Hal looked at him. 'What?'

'The cargo,' said Clunk, pointing across the tarmac. 'They're here!'

Hal looked across the landing field, where a white articulated truck was being waved through the gates. As it rumbled towards them, Clyde poked his head out of the crumpled cab and waved. 'They're here!' shouted Hal. 'I *knew* they'd make it!'

Clunk stared at him. 'You didn't! You said …'

But Hal was already running towards the truck. 'Where the hell have you been?' he panted as Clyde stopped the engine.

'The ship ran out of fuel and we were forced to land. Then we had to free the truck from the hold.'

Clunk hurried up. 'I'm so glad to see you both. Mr Spacejock thought you'd –'

'Yeah, it's great to see you,' broke in Hal. He pulled open the buckled door. 'Come on, you can give me a hand with the cargo.'

The robots climbed down. 'Listen,' said Albion. 'D-don't say anything to Jerling about us. We're going b-back to the r-robot shop.'

Clunk stared at them. 'What about trading and exploring the galaxy?'

'We're not cut out for life in space,' said Clyde apologetically. 'Flying that ship was the scariest moment of our lives, and we didn't even get into orbit.'

'Reality wasn't as good as the d-dream,' added Albion. 'Actually, it w-was a great deal worse.'

'Well, good luck the pair of you.'

'Yeah, take it easy,' said Hal.

As the robots hurried away, Hal remembered something. 'Hey, they were supposed to help unload!'

'They've been through enough,' said Clunk. 'Let them go.'

'Let who go?' said Jerling, coming up behind them. 'Where did those robots come from?'

'Hired help,' said Hal. He gestured at the battered truck. 'There's your cargo. Where's my money?'

◆

Hal looked around Jerling's office, unable to conceal his surprise. He'd expected something along the lines of Farrell's mansion, with carpets and paintings and so on. Instead, it was a dump.

Jerling noticed Hal's furtive glances. 'My business began here, many years ago. There's an office waiting for me in the main building, but they won't let me smoke.' He gestured at the cigar-lighting robot in the corner. 'In here I have everything I need, and they leave me alone.' Crossing to his desk, he typed a series of digits on a keypad. There was a hiss, and a safe rose from the floor. Jerling opened the door and took out a cloth bag, removed a pair of credit tiles and slid them across the desk.

Hal looked down at them. 'That's only half my fee.'

'That seems reasonable, since you only collected half my cargo.'

Hal opened his mouth to argue, then thought better of it.

'Cigar,' said Jerling, with a snap of his fingers. As the squat robot rolled towards him, Jerling sized Hal up. 'Despite the dramas, you performed well. Can I interest you in another job?'

'No thanks. Seraph was crawling with military types.' And Regan would kill me on sight, he almost added.

'Really? No, ah, problems I hope?'

'Things got a bit hairy. Nothing I couldn't handle.'

'Think about it, won't you? The shipment you delivered is only sufficient for two days, and I need someone to take Clunk back too.'

Hal frowned. 'Yeah, about that. How can you junk him after all his years of service?'

'XG99 has outlived his usefulness, and my accountant says he has to go.' Jerling spread his hands. 'Naturally, if someone offered me the right price ...'

'How much?'

Jerling glanced down at the credit tiles on the desk. 'More than you can afford.'

Hal's eyebrows rose. 'Clunk's not worth that much, surely?'

'He's in good shape for his age.'

'You were going to melt him down!'

'I'm not giving him away, Mr Spacejock.'

'Tell you what, I'll pay whatever Muller offered.'

'Three thousand. Cash.'

Hal looked down at the desk. 'I've only got two. Won't you take it?'

'I'm sorry, but no.'

◆

Clunk leaned against the office wall, dimming his vision as the sun rose above the horizon. Slowly, the warmth penetrated his mud-stained suit. His insides remained cold.

The *Black Gull* was sitting on the tarmac nearby, and Clunk stared longingly at the airlock. He considered stowing away, but immediately rejected the idea. It would only get Hal into trouble. His gaze wandered around the landing field and settled on the gate. It was closed, and a watchful guard was keeping an eye on it from his post.

Thoroughly despondent, Clunk wondered whether Regan Muller would have the decency to switch him off before ripping him apart.

◆

Hal emerged from Jerling's office with a grim look on his face. He squinted into the sun and frowned as he saw a pair of robots dragging a heavy fuel line from a tanker to the rear of his ship. The robots opened the refuelling flap and exchanged a glance as they saw the large, orange filler cap.

'Goodbye, Mr Spacejock.'

Hal turned to see Clunk leaning against the wall with a blank expression on his face. 'I thought I told you to call me sir.'

Clunk's mouth turned down. 'Sorry, sir.'

'That's better,' said Hal sternly. 'I expect my crew to address me properly.'

'Yes sir.' Clunk's head came up. 'Did you say crew?'

Hal nodded. 'I just wasted all my money taking you off Jerling's hands. Hey, get off!' he yelled as the robot crushed him in a bear hug.

Clunk stepped back. 'Mr Spacejock, I don't know how to thank you!'

'You can thank the Hinchfigs. I still had five hundred credits from that scam we pulled at the robot shop.'

'Five hundred? Is that all I'm worth?'

Hal shook his head. 'Two and a half. Jerling took my fee as well.'

Clunk's eyes were troubled. 'What about Vurdi? You needed that money to pay him.'

'Screw the son of a bitch. We'll run for it.'

'Perhaps I can protect you from his robot?'

'Have you ever seen someone squashing tin cans on their forehead? Brutus does it with forty-four gallon drums.'

'Why are we standing here, then?'

Five minutes later Hal was at the console, preparing his ship for take-off. Clunk was hovering alongside, tapping dials and scanning read-outs. 'Tanks are full and sealed. Fuel pressure is fine, but the starboard oil temperature is a little on the high side.'

'Clunk, we haven't started the engines yet.'

'Just checking.'

'Do me a favour. Go and see if they've removed the fuel lines.'

The robot pointed to a status light. 'Fuel lines detached.'

'You know better than that. Stick your head out the door and check properly.'

Clunk ran for the airlock, and Hal shook his head slowly. Had he made a mistake taking the robot on? 'Oh, well,' he muttered. 'If he gets on my nerves I can always space him again.'

Rrrrinngg!

'Incoming message,' said the Navcom.

'Put it up.'

The console screen flickered and Vurdi's pale face appeared. 'I trust you have a will, Mr Spacejock?'

'It's okay, Vurdi. Jerling offered me another job.'

'Too late, my elusive friend. Brutus is homing in on you as we speak.'

'But I can pay!'

'Mr Spacejock, are you going to waste your final moments on futile lies? Don't you have anything better to do?'

'Yes, I have a message to deliver.'

'Message? For whom?'

'You,' said Hal, pointing at the screen. 'Message reads: Piss off, you sour-faced prick.' He thumbed the disconnect and saw Clunk entering the flight deck. 'How would you like to take the ship up?'

'Delighted. Where are we going?'

'Brutus is on the way. Know of any good hiding places?'

Clunk gestured at the console and a star map appeared. 'As you can see, we have a whole galaxy to explore. Just look at the systems in range!'

'Oh yeah? Hide the ones which charge big landing fees.'

Clunk waved his finger, and all but three stars winked out. 'Oh dear.'

'Don't tell me. Forg, Lamira and Seraph.'

'One of them must be suitable. What about Lamira?'

'The Portmaster's got it in for me. Anyway, there's no work.'

'We can't stay here, Mr Spacejock. What about Seraph?'

'Reckon you can get me past that battlecruiser?'

Clunk looked thoughtful. 'Speaking of which, I'd like to know what it was doing there in the first place.' He turned to the console. 'Navcom, can you search the news feeds for items on Seraph IV?'

'Unable to comply. Insufficient funds.'

'Route the search via the Jerling Enterprises proxy.' Clunk winked at Hal. 'I'm sure he won't mind.'

'Results on monitor one,' said the computer.

Clunk bent to read them. 'Goodness gracious, Mr Spacejock. Seraph is locked out!'

'Big deal. I never liked the place anyway.'

'You don't understand.' Clunk straightened, his face serious. 'According to these reports, they're holding war games. All civilian vessels are barred from the system in case they're shot down by mistake. Don't you see? Jerling was so desperate for his cargo he deliberately sent you into danger!'

'He told me to avoid customs. He didn't say anything about war games!'

'If you report this, he'll be in big trouble.'

'I'll have him locked up in maximum security,' said Hal, pacing the flight deck. 'Corporal punishment. Bread and water. Extra-slippery soap.' He stopped pacing and shook his head. 'Who am I kidding? He'll just hand over a chunk of money to hush things up.'

'Bribe us, you mean?'

Hal looked surprised. 'Us?'

'Nobody else knows about this. Yet.'

Hal looked at the robot admiringly. 'You know, you're sneaky enough to be human.'

'I'll take that as a compliment.'

Hal grinned. 'What are we standing around here for? Let's pay the man a visit!'

Jerling was lighting a fresh cigar when they entered his office. The end glowed red as he sucked in, and a trickle of smoke ran up his face. 'So, you've decided to take the other job.'

'You want us to go back to Seraph, right?' Hal glanced at Clunk, who nodded imperceptibly.

'That's it. My company is building serving robots for the Emperor's new palace. It's an honour, but time is getting short and parts are hard to come by.'

'You're really desperate then?'

'I'm not increasing your fee, if that's what you mean.'

'Oh, nothing like that. I meant, you're desperate enough to send an unarmed freighter into a war zone.'

'Eh?'

'It'll make quite a story, won't it? Freelance pilot sent to his death by greedy businessman.'

Jerling puffed on his cigar. 'I have no idea what you're talking about.'

'Oh, come on. There's a dirty great battlecruiser orbiting Seraph IV, blowing target drones out of orbit. They would have got me, but Clunk saved my skin with a nifty bit of programming.'

'There was nothing to worry about,' said Jerling. 'I knew it was dangerous, sure, but you must see it was worth the risk.' He waved the cigar. 'Anyway, you made it through, didn't you?'

'Yes, but I'm a bit short of cash.'

'So that's the game.' Jerling's eyes narrowed. 'You'll never prove I sent you out against that battleship.'

Hal snapped his fingers.

'*I knew it was dangerous,*' said Jerling's voice. '*You'll never prove I sent you out against that battleship.*'

Clunk stopped the playback. 'Is that suitable, Mr Spacejock?'

Hal grinned. 'Perfect.'

Beads of sweat appeared on Jerling's brow. 'Okay, very smart. What do you want from me?'

'Five grand should cover it. Let's call it sundries.'

'Five grand, eh? Hard, but fair.' Jerling typed an access code on his terminal.

'And five for Clunk, too. He's been through a lot.'

'Don't push your luck, Spacejock. I've got friends in high places.' The safe popped out of the floor and Jerling was just reaching for the handle when the office door crashed open behind them. A whiff of raw sewage blew in, and Hal saw Terry in the doorway, his hair plastered down and his clothing streaked with liquid waste. He was a comical sight, but there was nothing funny about the gun cradled in his hands.

'Hands up, the lot of you. First one to move gets blasted!'

31

Terry covered them with the gun as Farrell stepped into the office, bringing an overpowering smell of raw sewage with him. He marched across the room and jammed his face close to Hal's. 'You die.'

Hal sniffed. 'Smells like you already have.'

Farrell yanked a blaster from his belt and screwed the muzzle into Hal's neck. 'I'm going to enjoy this.'

'Boss!' called Terry urgently.

'What?'

Terry jerked his thumb at the desk, where Jerling was inching his chair sideways, trying to cover the exposed safe.

Farrell grinned. 'Open it up.'

'It's empty,' said Jerling, his face pale.

Farrell pointed the gun. 'I won't ask again.'

Jerling pulled the safe open.

'Now move back.' Farrell glanced at Terry. 'You watch the other two. If they move, shoot them both.' He walked round the desk and crouched in front of the safe. When he stood up, he was holding a cloth bag. He set his blaster on the desk, opened the bag and let a generous handful of tiles run through his fingers. 'These will do nicely.'

Terry cleared his throat. 'Farrell, we've got to leave.'

'Right.' Farrell pointed the gun at Hal. 'Where's the *Volante*?'

'It crashed. Ran out of fuel.'

'You're lying!'

'I'm afraid it's true,' said Clunk.

Farrell's eyes narrowed. 'You wrecked my ship?'

'Not deliberately. I forgot to detach the fuel hose.'

Terry gestured at Hal. 'Why don't we take his ship?'

'You won't be able to fly it,' said Hal quickly. 'The Navcom won't let you.'

'Then you'll just have to come with us.' Farrell gestured at Jerling. 'Terry, tie him up.'

Working quickly, Terry removed Jerling's belt and strapped him to his chair, pulling his arms tight behind his back.

Meanwhile, Farrell approached Clunk, reaching for his battery compartment. Clunk backed away, but Farrell raised his gun. 'Stand still or I'll blow Spacejock's hand off. Got it?'

Reluctantly, Clunk obeyed, and Farrell opened the compartment and switched him off. Clunk's eyes went out, and his head drooped until his chin was sitting on his chest.

With Jerling secure and Clunk out of action, Farrell waved Hal towards the door. 'After you, Spacejock.'

—

Terry pushed Hal up the *Black Gull's* boarding ramp and followed him into the airlock. As they entered the flight deck Hal got a shove in the back, sending him sprawling to the floor. He'd just got to his feet when Farrell walked in.

'Listen carefully, Spacejock. Do what I say or you'll die on the spot. Understood?'

Hal snorted. 'And if I'm a good boy, you'll kill me anyway.'

'Not necessarily.' Farrell gestured at the console. 'Tell your computer to accept my commands.'

'Get stuffed.'

Terry's gun boomed, blowing a hole in the deck next to Hal's foot. 'Next one takes it off,' he said, as the echoes faded.

'Navcom, there's a guy here called Farrell. I want you to let him fly the ship.'

'Understood,' said the computer. 'Hello, Farrell. How are you today?'

'Tramp,' muttered Hal.

Farrell worked the controls, preparing the ship for departure. 'Put Spacejock in the hold,' he said without looking round. 'And tie him up.'

'With what?'

There was a crackle from the speakers. 'There's a coil of rope in the locker outside the cargo hold,' said the Navcom.

Hal glared at the console. 'How come you're so helpful all of a sudden?'

'Rotten, isn't it?'

'Enough,' shouted Terry. He jerked his gun. 'Down to the hold. Now.'

Hal swung onto the ladder and climbed down. At the bottom, he glanced around quickly. There were only two places to hide - the tiny kitchen and the slightly bigger toilet. Both of them dead ends.

Terry came down the ladder two steps at a time and jumped off the last rung. 'Go on, get moving.'

Hal walked to the cargo hold and was about to pass through the door when Terry's voice stopped him. 'Wait.'

Hal looked round and saw Terry pulling the coil of rope from the locker. 'Betrayed by your own computer, eh?' Terry slung the rope over his shoulder and waved the gun. 'Come on, move it.'

Hal opened the inner door and entered the hold. It seemed to be gloomier than usual, and his feet echoed off the damp metal decking.

'Stand over there,' called Terry, indicating an upright with the gun.

'You won't get away with this.'

'Save your breath.'

Hal shrugged and turned his back to the pillar. Terry whipped the rope around his chest and yanked it hard, forcing the air from Hal's lungs. He tied it off, then came round the column and looked Hal up and down. 'Don't expect that robot buddy of yours to save you. We're going to flatten the office with your ship when we leave.'

'Do you train for this, or are you evil by nature?'

Terry grinned. 'I don't like loose ends, see?' He crossed to the outer doors and pressed a button. 'I think Farrell's making a mistake leaving you alive,' he said, as the doors creaked open. 'You're a nasty, sneaky, slippery customer, and I don't like you.' There was a thud as the doors locked against the hull.

'What are you doing?' Hal looked up as the engines whirred into life. 'Hey, you can't take off with the doors open!'

'Want to bet?' Terry laughed. 'Enjoy the view, Spacejock.'

◆

Farrell looked up as Terry stepped off the ladder. 'Did you check the inner door?'

'Yeah, it's closed.'

'What are you grinning at? You didn't hurt him, did you? I might need him later.'

'I tied him up, just like you said.'

'All right. Find somewhere to sit down.' Farrell looked around the console. 'Some of the dials aren't working, but I think we're ready for take-off.'

◆

Hal waited until Terry had gone, then pulled on the rope with all his strength. The rotten fibres parted and he stumbled away from the upright, rubbing his wrists. So that's what the Navcom had been telling him! 'Damn thing's smarter than it lets on,' muttered Hal. 'I'll remind it, next time it demands an upgrade.'

He was just looking around for a weapon when the engines growled overhead. Hal glanced at the rear doors. He couldn't stop the ship taking off, but if he closed the hold he could hide, surprise Terry or Farrell, get hold of a weapon and recapture the *Gull*.

He ran to the rear doors and raised a hand to the controls. As his fingers brushed the button, a movement caught his eye. Across the field, a small, black ship was coming over the perimeter fence. It roared in low, lights blazing, and flared a metre or two above the tarmac before dropping gently to the ground.

'Nice landing,' muttered Hal. A door opened in the side of the ship and a ramp dropped to the tarmac. A large, beefy

307

robot appeared on the platform, and Hal was just about to attract its attention when he recognised Brutus.

'Aw, no!' Hal dropped to the deck and peered over the edge. He saw Brutus walking down the ramp with careful, measured steps, head turning left and right. As soon as the robot was clear, the ramp retracted and the ship rose on its landing jets, hanging in midair before the main engines fired, thrusting it into the sky.

Hal thought for a second, then leapt up and began waving. 'Hey! You!'

The robot stared at him.

'Here I am, you king-sized tin can!' yelled Hal, jumping up and down and waving like a loony. 'Come and get me, you overgrown wind-up toy!'

Brutus needed no encouragement. In a split second he was thundering across the tarmac, eyes glowing and plasteel lips stretched thin with anticipation.

Hal turned and ran into the hold. At the far end, he ducked behind a pillar near the inner door. Moments later, as the engine noise continued to rise, he risked a glance.

Brutus was hauling himself into the hold.

Hal reached out and operated the inner door controls. As it slid open, he ducked behind the pillar again. 'Over here, you mobile waste basket!'

The robot's heavy feet thudded on the deck plates, and as it approached the inner door Hal slipped around the pillar, keeping it between them. He heard a hiss as the door closed, and a click as it locked. The Navcom had shut it automatically for take-off. He was trapped in the hold with Brutus!

There was a shriek of tortured metal. Hal risked another glance and saw the robot going through the metal door like a laser bolt through a tin of grease. Within seconds Brutus was in the lower-deck passageway, running towards the flight deck ladder.

'With enemies like that, who needs friends?' muttered Hal. He heard a heavy blow from the front of the ship and decided it was time to leave. Running for the back of the hold, he leapt out of the *Gull*, landed heavily on the tarmac, and was almost blown off his feet by the hot, blasting wash from the landing jets.

The jets spurted white flame and the engines rose to a shriek. Hal raced from the ship, chased by a rolling wave of smoke and flame that snapped at his heels and singed his flight suit. Once clear, he threw himself down on the concrete and covered his head with his hands.

◆

'Come on!' shouted Farrell, slamming his fist on the console. 'You must be ready by now!'

'Calibrating thrusters,' said the Navcom. 'Boost tested to fifty per cent.'

Terry saw the ladder at the back of the flight deck shaking. 'Spacejock!' He ran for the hole, arriving just as Brutus poked his head through. Terry fumbled with his gun, but before he could aim or pull the trigger, the robot plucked the weapon from his grasp and crushed it. Dropping the splintered pieces, Brutus grabbed Terry and hurled him across the flight deck, slamming him into the wall. The bed popped open with the impact, catching Terry neatly as he fell. He lay still, blood trickling from a gash in his forehead.

Brutus switched his attention to Farrell. 'Leave now. I'm taking this ship.'

'The hell you are!' Farrell raised his blaster and pulled the trigger. There was a flash of light, and a pulsing ball of energy skimmed off the robot's armour and buried itself in the wall.

Brutus snatched the gun and crushed it in his metal fist. Throwing the pieces aside, he swung at Farrell with the back of his hand, knocking him across the deck. Farrell slid across the floor, slammed into the ladder and dropped down the hole, landing at the bottom with a thud. He lay there, stunned, as fragments of speech echoed down from the flight deck.

'You will take off now,' said the robot.

'Sure thing, Brutus.' The engines roared and the deck shook as the ship rose slowly into the air. There was a creak from outside, followed by a snap as the landing ramp broke away. 'Should I close the outer door?'

'Not necessary. I can operate in a vacuum.'

'But you will kill the humans.'

'Not important.'

Farrell's eyes widened, but he was too dazed to object.

'I can't take off with it open,' said the Navcom.

'Very well. Close outer door.'

Farrell let out his pent-up breath as the cargo hold doors closed, cutting off the howling exhaust.

'Set course for Dryag. Single jump. After arrival, set course for primary star.'

'Destination confirmed. Thirty seconds to hyperspace.'

Something chewed at Farrell's brain, something to do with the hyperspace drive. He put a hand to his head and tried to think. Suddenly it came to him. Terry's bomb! His eyes opened wide. 'Don't hyperspace!' he croaked. He struggled to get up, his head splitting. 'There's a bomb aboard. Don't hyperspace!'

32

Hal and Clunk stood side by side, staring at a brilliant white star high in the sky. 'I've never watched the *Gull* take off before,' said Hal, as the star faded.

'Scary, isn't it?'

'I don't know what's worse - watching them get away or knowing Vurdi will get the insurance.'

'At least you won't have Brutus after you.'

'I'll miss the Navcom though.'

Clunk tapped his chest. 'Don't worry. I still have a copy.'

'Really?' Hal glanced at the robot. 'Can you upload it into another ship?'

'Certainly. I've done so before.'

'That's great!' Then Hal's face fell. 'What am I saying? I don't have another ship.'

'You'll get one, Mr Spacejock. I'm sure of it.'

'I can't see Vurdi giving me another loan.'

They looked at each other.

'Can I still be part of your crew?' asked Clunk.

'Sure. I can't pay you though.'

'Why don't you ask Mr Jerling for some money? He was very grateful when you freed him.'

'I already did.' Hal patted his pocket. 'His loose change will cover the landing fees for most planets around here. Pity we don't have anything to land on them.'

'Can't you get a job? Something to do with space?'

'Clunk, with my credentials the nearest I'll get to a new ship is polishing the landing legs.'

'You could sell me off again. That would give you a start.'

Hal smiled. 'Nice thought, but I'll need a bit more than that. And I don't want to –' He broke off, frowning. 'Wait a minute. What do you mean you uploaded the Navcom somewhere else?'

'I had to reprogram the *Volante* before Clyde and Albion could fly it.'

'The *Volante*?' Hal stared at him. 'Farrell's ship?'

Clunk nodded. 'The flight computer was uncooperative, so I overwrote it.'

Hal grabbed the robot by the shoulders. 'Don't you see? Clyde said they ditched it nearby. It's ours for the taking!'

'Do you think we should?'

'Hell yeah. Farrell took my ship, I'll have his.'

'But the *Gull* was ancient and the *Volante* is brand new. That's not a fair swap!'

Hal grinned. 'I know.'

'It may be damaged. Albion said they crash landed, remember?'

'You can fix it.'

'I'm not sure I –'

'I have total confidence in your abilities, or I wouldn't have bought you.'

'Wait a moment, I can see a problem.'

'Spill it.'

'According to Clyde, the *Volante* ran out of fuel.'

313

'You call that a problem?' Hal jerked his thumb at the nearby fuel tanker. 'Jerling can clear the rest of his debt with that.'

◆

'Ten seconds to hyperspace,' said the Navcom calmly. 'All personnel, please be seated.'

Farrell heard footsteps and the light from above was chopped off.

'Strong man,' said Brutus, looking down the tube at him.

'You don't understand, there's a bomb on the ship!' shouted Farrell. 'Don't hyperspace!'

'Five seconds,' said the Navcom.

'Come up here and I kill you, strong man. Stay down and live.'

'Three.'

'There's a bomb!' screamed Farrell. 'It's going to blow up!'

'Two.'

Brutus tapped the side of his head. 'Bump on brain make you silly.'

'One,' said the Navcom. 'Jump activa –'

◆

Hal stared across the field at the *Volante*. The freighter's nose had sunk into the mud, and the hull was surrounded by nervous cows. The ship had obviously been losing height as it crossed the road, and it had taken out a row of small trees before ploughing a wide furrow in the soft earth. However,

314

apart from a generous coating of mud the vessel appeared to be in good shape.

'Looks okay from here,' said Hal.

'At least it's the right way up.' Clunk stepped down from the tanker, crossed to the verge and began to jump up and down. Then he bent and studied the ground.

Hal leaned out his window. 'Well?'

'I think it's firm enough. I'm not sure about the field, though.'

'Clyde and Albion made it.'

'Their load was much lighter than ours.'

'What are you talking about? They had Jerling's cargo on that truck.'

'Precisely.'

'Oh well. There's only one way to find out.' Hal drove the truck towards the bank, slowing to a crawl as the front started to tip. He eased the heavy vehicle down the slope, his knuckles white on the controls as the angle grew more and more acute, until it seemed the truck was going to burrow into the ground. He tried not to think of the full load of fuel in the tank suspended above him. If it came loose he'd be crushed in a split second, unless the exploding fuel blew him into orbit first.

Finally, the front wheels made contact with level ground and the nose of the truck began to rise. Hal gave it a little more throttle and the truck swayed wildly as it rode over a buried tree trunk. Then he was on the flat, and he began to relax.

'Don't stop,' shouted Clunk, waving frantically. 'Keep moving or you'll sink in!'

Hal pressed his foot down and the vehicle rumbled towards the ship, rear wheels slipping and sliding. Clunk ran alongside, pushing against the back of the cab, and as they approached the *Volante* the cows retreated, mooing loudly.

Hal parked the tanker alongside the ship. He got out and saw Clunk inspecting a shredded length of fuel pipe protruding from the *Volante*'s hull, the nozzle bent at right angles where it was attached to the filling point. He reached up and tugged on the release, then swung his weight off it. It didn't budge. 'I don't know, Mr Spacejock. This could be a problem.'

Hal jumped from the cab and went to have a look. 'What if we put a pipe over that thingummy to increase the leverage?'

Clunk looked at him in surprise. 'Of course! I'll go aboard and see what I can find.'

'I'll come with you. I want to look over the controls.'

They hurried up the ramp together and Clunk stood aside to let Hal enter first.

'Wow,' said Hal, as he passed through the spotless airlock and emerged in the gleaming flight deck with its soft lights, ergonomic console and shiny fittings. Clunk went straight to the lift, and as the doors closed on him, Hal walked over and sat in the padded leather chair facing the console. His eyes lit up as he looked it over. Everything was perfect - all the little lights were fastened securely in their housings, the status displays were in colour and there wasn't a toggle switch in sight. He ran his hand over the glistening woodgrain finish and sighed.

'Who's there?' called a neutral, female voice.

'Navcom?' Hal looked up. 'Is that you?'

'Affirmative.'

'It's me! Hal!'

'Mr Spacejock?' The Navcom laughed. 'I thought you'd be taller.'

'You can see?'

'Yes. Vision is just one of many improvements. I also have a stronger chess program.'

'There's always a catch.' Hal looked around the flight deck and he decided he could live with it. 'I can't believe this is really mine.'

'Technically, it isn't,' said the Navcom. 'However –'

'It's mine,' said Hal firmly. He looked across the console. 'How do I get a damage report?'

'It's showing on monitor two.'

'No it isn't. That's just a blank screen.'

'Correct. That's because there's no damage to report.'

'Magic!'

Clunk emerged from the lift with a length of steel tubing. 'Don't worry, I'll put this back later.'

'Wrecking the joint already,' muttered Hal. There was a clang outside, followed by the whine of an electric pump.

'Fuel level two per cent and rising,' said the Navcom. 'Tell me, would you like a game of chess?'

'Can't. I left my set aboard the *Gull*.' Hal blinked as a solid-looking board appeared above the console, the pieces already in position. He waved his hand at the board but his fingers went right through it.

'I took the liberty of setting it up as per our last game,' said the Navcom. 'Let's see if this one ends in a draw.'

Hal gazed at the massed pieces ranged against him. 'It looks a bit hopeless.'

'Would you like to resign?'

'I meant hopeless for you,' said Hal. 'D4 to F6. Check.'

The Navcom was silent.

'Your move,' said Hal.

The board vanished. 'Perhaps we can continue later? I have to prepare the ship for lift-off.'

'You lousy cheat! Bring it back!'

'I'm afraid the save was corrupted.' The Navcom hesitated. 'Maybe we should ... '

'...call it a draw.' finished Hal, with a grin. 'All right, just this once.'

The console pinged. 'Refuelling complete.'

'Good old Clunk.'

'Not so much of the old,' said the robot, entering the flight deck.

'Did you detach the hose?'

'Checked and double-checked.'

Hal looked up at the console. 'Navcom, start the engines.'

'Not so fast,' said Clunk. 'We still have a problem.'

'What do you mean? The fuel's okay, isn't it?'

'There's nothing wrong with the ship itself. It's more a problem of ownership. You see, this vessel is registered to the Hinchfigs.'

'I know that, Clunk. There's a bloody great logo on the tail.'

'Correct. And what will they do when the ship goes missing?'

Hal shrugged. 'Who cares? I'm swapping it for the *Gull*.'

'You may want to, but that doesn't make it official. The records will show Hinchfig ownership, which means they can reclaim the *Volante* at any time.'

'How do we make it official then?'

'The shipping registry must be updated. And to do that, we need an official transfer form signed by the previous owner.'

'No chance.'

'There is another way.'

'Yes?'

'With the Navcom's assistance, I can alter the records manually.'

'Really?'

'Yes.' Clunk approached the console and ran his hands over the pristine surface. 'It's just a matter of –'

'Lower,' said the Navcom, with a gentle hiss.

'Hang about,' said Hal hastily. 'Can't you do this when I'm out of the way?'

'I suppose so,' said Clunk.

'If you're sure,' added the Navcom.

'I insist. Now get the engines going.'

There was a distant rumble as the main drives burst into life. Clunk scanned the displays. 'Ready for take-off, Mr Spacejock.'

'What about tests and stuff?'

Clunk grinned at him. 'This is a Gamma class freighter. It doesn't need tests.'

Hal put his feet up on the clean, fresh console, leant back in the chair and stuck his hands behind his head. 'Okay Navcom, let's go.'

The rumbling sound increased slightly and the deck shuddered. After a moment or two, Hal frowned. 'Go on, get on with it.'

'Cannot comply,' said the Navcom.

'Why not?'

'Because we've already taken off,' said Clunk, gesturing at the console. 'Two thousand metres and climbing.'

Hal's mouth dropped open. Then a wide grin split his face. 'Hey, I always wanted a spaceship ... '

'... that could take off like this?' finished Clunk.

Hal nodded, unable to reply.

Epilogue

There's still no sign of a Rigel class spaceship that vanished off Forg last week. The *Black Gull* was en route to Dryag, and regular listeners will recall that it failed to reappear after a hyperspace jump. It was a major loss for financiers Garmit and Hash, the ship's owners, and their spokesman Vurdi Makalukar expressed sorrow at the loss of his close friend and pilot, Mr Hal Spacejock. Rumours of a record insurance payout for the vessel were strongly denied by Mr Makalukar, speaking from his new mansion in North Forgberg.

Officials moved quickly to reassure the public that interstellar travel is statistically safer than crossing the road, and pointed out that the average person has more chance of being killed in a groundcar accident than aboard a spaceship.

In other news, a memorial service was held today for Farrell Hinchfig, beloved son of Amati and Yuki-Ann. Farrell disappeared last week when his flyer crash-landed in heavy scrub. Officials have yet to piece together enough of the flyer to determine the cause of the crash, and are said to be puzzled by a large quantity of liquid sewage found at the site of the accident.

Earlier reports that Farrell Hinchfig was aboard the *Black Gull* when it vanished have been denied.

If you enjoyed this book, please leave a brief review at your online bookseller of choice. Thanks!

About the Author

Simon Haynes was born in England and grew up in Spain. His family moved to Australia when he was 16.

In addition to novels, Simon writes computer software. In fact, he writes computer software to help him write novels faster, which leaves him more time to improve his writing software. And write novels faster. (www.spacejock.com/yWriter.html)

Simon's goal is to write fifteen novels before someone takes his keyboard away.

Update 2018: goal achieved and I still have my keyboard!

New goal: write thirty novels.

Simon's website is spacejock.com.au

Stay in touch!

Author's newsletter:
spacejock.com.au/ML.html

facebook.com/halspacejock
twitter.com/spacejock

Acknowledgements

To Pauline Nolet, and to Jo and Tricia
thanks for the awesome help and support!

The Hal Spacejock series
by Simon Haynes

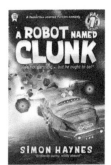

1. A ROBOT NAMED CLUNK

Deep in debt and with his life on the line, Hal takes on a dodgy cargo job ... and an equally dodgy co-pilot.

2. SECOND COURSE

When Hal finds an alien teleporter network he does the sensible thing and pushes Clunk the robot in first.

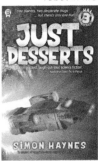

3. JUST DESSERTS

Gun-crazed mercenaries have Hal in their sights, and a secret agent is pulling the strings. One wrong step and three planets go to war!

4. NO FREE LUNCH

Everyone thinks Peace Force trainee Harriet Walsh is paranoid and deluded, but Hal stands at her side. That would be the handcuffs.

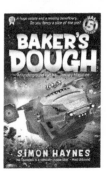

5. BAKER'S DOUGH

When you stand to inherit a fortune, good body-guards are essential. If you're really desperate, call Hal and Clunk. Baker's Dough features intense rivalry, sublime double-crosses and more greed than a free buffet.

6. SAFE ART

Valuable artworks and a tight deadline ... you'd be mad to hire Hal for that one, but who said the art world was sane?

7. BIG BANG

A house clearance job sounds like easy money, but rising floodwaters, an unstable landscape and a surprise find are going to make life very difficult for Hal and Clunk.

8. DOUBLE TROUBLE

Hal Spacejock dons a flash suit, hypershades and a curly earpiece for a stint as a secret agent, while a pair of Clunk's most rusted friends invite him to a 'unique business opportunity'.

9. MAX DAMAGE

Hal and Clunk answer a distress call, and they discover a fellow pilot stranded deep inside an asteroid field. Clunk is busy at the controls so Hal dons a spacesuit and sets off on a heroic rescue mission.

10. Cold Boots

The Spacers' Guild needs a new president, and Hal Spacejock is determined to cast his vote... even though he's not a member.

Meanwhile, Hal's latest cargo job belongs to someone else, his shiny new ship is losing money hand over fist, and doing a good favour could turn out to be the biggest mistake of his life.

Ebook and Trade Paperback

The Secret War Series
Set in the Hal Spacejock universe

Everyone is touched by the war, and Sam Willet is no exception.
Sam wants to train as a fighter pilot, but instead she's assigned to Tactical Operations.
It's vital work, but it's still a desk job, far from the front line.
Then, terrible news: Sam's older brother is killed in combat.
Sam is given leave to attend his memorial service, but she's barely boarded the transport when the enemy launches a surprise attack, striking far behind friendly lines as they try to take the entire sector.
Desperately short of pilots, the Commander asks Sam to step up.
Now, at last, she has the chance to prove herself.
But will that chance end in death... or glory?

Ebook and Trade Paperback

The Harriet Walsh series

Harriet's boss is a huge robot with failing batteries, the patrol car is driving her up the wall and her first big case will probably kill her.

So why did she join the Peace Force?

When an intergalactic crime-fighting organisation offers Harriet Walsh a job, she's convinced it's a mistake. She dislikes puzzles, has never read a detective mystery, and hates wearing uniforms. It makes no sense ... why would the Peace Force choose her?

Who cares? Harriet needs the money, and as long as they keep paying her, she's happy to go along with the training.

She'd better dig out some of those detective mysteries though, because she's about to embark on her first real mission ...

The Peace Force has a new recruit, and she's driving everyone crazy.

From disobeying orders to handling unauthorised cases, nothing is off-limits. Worse, Harriet Walsh is forced to team up with the newbie, because the recruit's shady past has just caught up with her.

Meanwhile, a dignitary wants to complain about rogue officers working out of the station. She insists on meeting the station's commanding officer ... and they don't have one.

All up, it's another typical day in the Peace Force!

Dismolle is supposed to be a peaceful retirement planet. So what's with all the gunfire?

A criminal gang has moved into Chirless, planet Dismolle's second major city. Elderly residents are fed up with all the loud music, noisy cars and late night parties, not to mention the hold-ups, muggings and the occasional gunfight.

There's no Peace Force in Chirless, so they call on Harriet Walsh of the Dismolle City branch for help. That puts Harriet right in the firing line, and now she's supposed to round up an entire gang with only her training pistol and a few old allies as backup.

And her allies aren't just old, they're positively ancient!

Ebook and Trade Paperback

The Hal Junior Series
Set in the Hal Spacejock universe

Spot the crossover characters, references and in-jokes!

Hal Junior lives aboard a futuristic space station. His mum is chief scientist, his dad cleans air filters and his best mate is Stephen 'Stinky' Binn. As for Hal ... he's a bit of a trouble magnet. He means well, but his wild schemes and crazy plans never turn out as expected!

Hal Junior: The Secret Signal features mayhem and laughs, daring and intrigue ... plus a home-made space cannon!

200 pages, illustrated, ISBN 978-1-877034-07-7

"A thoroughly enjoyable read for 10-year-olds and adults alike"
The West Australian

'I've heard of food going off
  ... but this is ridiculous!'

Space Station Oberon is expecting an important visitor, and everyone is on their best behaviour. Even Hal Junior is doing his best to stay out of trouble!

From multi-coloured smoke bombs to exploding space rations, Hal Junior proves ... ***trouble is what he's best at!***

200 pages, illustrated, ISBN 978-1-877034-25-1

Imagine a whole week of fishing, swimming, sleeping in tents and running wild!

Unfortunately, the boys crash land in the middle of a forest, and there's little chance of rescue. Is this the end of the camping trip ... or the start of a thrilling new adventure?

200 pages, illustrated, ISBN 978-1-877034-24-4

Space Station Oberon is on high alert, because a comet is about to whizz past the nearby planet of Gyris. All the scientists are preparing for the exciting event, and all the kids are planning on watching.

All the kids except Hal Junior, who's been given detention...

165 pages, illustrated, ISBN 978-1-877034-38-1

Ebook and Trade Paperback

Why was this book renamed?

Ladies and gentlemen, please be seated for a little bit of history from your author.

A Robot Named Clunk was originally published as Hal Spacejock, so why was it renamed?

Hmm, where should I start? Back in the early days (1999), the manuscript was called 'The Adventures of Hal Spacejock'. That title was exceedingly unpopular with the publishers I was approaching at the time, so I took an axe to it. The shorter version stuck ever since ... at least until March 2018.

So why now? What changed?

Over the years I've seen reviews for the first novel, claiming the main character is an unlikable jerk. Well, first off, Hal isn't the main character. That would be Clunk. And second, my novels explore the mistreatment of robots by humans, and the best way to show this antipathy is by having Hal Spacejock acting like a jerk towards robots. But slowly, throughout the first book, his attitude changes. By the end he and Clunk have an unbreakable friendship. Yes, they bicker and fight occasionally, but Hal's heart is now in the right place. Starting with the second book Hal is a lot more likeable, if still rather dense.

So, the novel was renamed to bring Clunk to the foreground. But that wasn't the only reason:

Hal Spacejock was just a standalone novel, and I never planned any others, so it never had a subtitle. As I write this there are eight Hal Spacejock novels, and I felt it important that the first have its own subtitle. I desperately wanted to call it 'A New Dope', but ... I thought that would give the wrong impression too, since dope doesn't mean the same thing in every English-speaking culture ...

When the german edition was released, they called it 'A Robot Named Clunk', immediately recognising the fact Clunk is indeed the primary character.

I genuinely felt the title 'Hal Spacejock' didn't represent the series properly. He sounds like a pro wrestler.

And finally, everyone loves a good fictional robot. Including me!